OVERHEARD

EDITED BY

JONATHAN TAYLOR

SALT

CROMER

PUBLISHED BY SALT PUBLISHING
12 Norwich Road, Cromer NR27 0AX United Kingdom

First published by Salt Publishing, 2012

Printed in Great Britain by Clays Ltd, St Ives plc

Typeset in Paperback 9.5/14.5

ISBN 978 1 97773 26 6 paperback

1 3 5 7 9 8 6 4 2

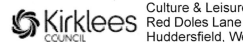
twin daughters, Miranda and Rosalind. He has a website:
www.jonathanptaylor.co.uk

For My Mother

'Did there not cross your mind some thought of the *physical power of words*? ... This wild star – it is now three centuries since with clasped hands, and with streaming eyes, at the feet of my beloved – I spoke it – with a few passionate sentences – into birth.'

EDGAR ALLAN POE, 'The Power of Words'

CONTENTS

SHOUTING STORIES

SINGING STORIES

INTRODUCTION

□ □ □ □ □

"He do the Police in different voices."
—CHARLES DICKENS, *Our Mutual Friend*

When I was older than I should have been for this kind of thing, my mother read *The Lord of the Rings* out loud to me, a couple of pages a night for – well, not quite a thousand and one nights, but not far off either. At an age when I should probably have been playing computer games, or something called 'football' on the street, I was instead sitting on the arm of my mother's chair, listening to her 'doing the elves in different voices,' to paraphrase Dickens. And, of course, I loved it – hence the dedication in this book, twenty-five years (give or take) later. More immediately, I loved it so much that, just a few years post-*Lord of the Rings*, I started doing the same, occasionally reading stories or sections of novels out loud to my father, who by that time had dementia. Given the nature of his condition, we never got very far, because he couldn't remember what had happened chapter to chapter (and eventually page to page); so *The*

Lord of the Rings was out, but short stories – and particularly short-short stories – were still just about manageable, or rather memorable.

These experiences were certainly memorable for me, and left me with an abiding sense of the 'orality' and, indeed, 'aurality' of narrative fiction. Fiction, I believe, is meant to be spoken and heard as well as read – and not just children's fiction. Many of us have vivid memories of being read to as children – and good children's stories are acutely aware of their own orality and, indeed, performativity, as evinced by Michelene Wandor's two interlinked stories in this collection. For me, though, such orality and performativity spill over boundaries of genre and age. As far as genre is concerned, my most memorable experience of being read aloud to involved a work of fantasy, not a genre immediately associated with oral storytelling; and I felt it important to demonstrate, in the following collection, how diverse are the possibilities for reading aloud in many different genres, some more readily associated than others with an oral culture. That is why, alongside the children's stories and a ghost story (by Deborah Tyler-Bennett), both of which are obviously genres with strong oral storytelling traditions, there are also, for example, speculative fiction stories (by Adam Roberts, Robert Shearman and Joel Lane), a romantic comedy (by Adele Parks) and works of historical fiction (by Jane Holland and Kathleen Bell). There is also a great deal in this collection that is specifically 'adult' in subject matter (for example, the stories by Alexandros Plasatis, Hanif Kureishi, David Belbin and Ian McEwan), which reflects my own belief and experience that adults enjoy being read aloud to as much as children.

As I say, for me, reading aloud spilt into adolescence and eventually adulthood, and has stayed with me ever since: as a slow reader, who came late to reading by myself, I still find myself moving my lips whilst reading, and sometimes voicing dialogue under my breath, much to the bewilderment and discomfort of fellow passengers on buses and trains. In this context, reading out loud becomes associated with conventional signs of madness; but then, silent reading, which involves hearing voices in one's own head, might similarly be classified as a form of lunacy.

This book is for those who want to embrace such lunacy – the suspect, anarchic lunacy that is oral storytelling. It is for those people who want to hear voices in their heads. It is for people who want to talk to themselves, whisper seductively to themselves, have arguments with themselves. It is for people who want to put on, or try out different voices, identities, histories. This putting on, or trying out can be in the reader's own head, or out loud to others. The stories in this collection might equally be read out loud to others, or 'performed' on the reader's mental stage, heard in the reader's mind's-ear. The stories' voices should hopefully be as clear (and 'audible') to an individual reader as they are when performed aloud to an audience – and by 'audience' I mean everything from an audience of a thousand in an auditorium, to a lone listener sitting on the arm of a mother's chair.

Nineteenth-century novelists were, of course, often very good at this kind of doubleness, whereby a story might work both out loud to an audience and 'in loud' (to coin a phrase) to oneself. As is well known, Charles Dickens's novels were just as often read out loud within families and households as they were read alone; and Dickens himself became a famous performer of his own work, doing all the characters in different voices. He was a master – both on the page and out loud – at characterising voices, and capturing their individual quirks, tics, inflections.

It might and has been argued that this 'vocality' of fiction faded after Dickens's death and the gradual demise, in the later nineteenth century, of the serialised novel – so that a great deal of twentieth-century fiction was not written with the spoken voice in mind to quite the same extent. Of course, this is deeply questionable as a literary-historical generalisation; but whether partly true or not, there is little doubt that, in the UK at least, recent years have seen a kind of revitalisation, or burgeoning of a performance scene where prose is read out loud. From the 1990s onwards, the idea of reading fiction aloud has become increasingly commonplace in all sorts of different contexts, including festivals, conferences, public readings, lectures, book launches and open-mic events; and recent years have even witnessed the development of various organisations across the UK dedicated to stories in performance (as in, to give just a few examples amongst many, Hello Hubmarine in Derby, Short Fuse Fiction in Leicester and Brighton, Rattle Tales in Brighton, Electric Tales in Edinburgh, Are You Sitting Comfortably?, The Book Stops Here, Storytails and All Ears in London, Liars' League in London, Leeds and New York, and Literary Death Match in venues worldwide). At the same time, 'traditional' oral storytelling has continued its hugely-popular revival in the UK, aided by the foundation of the Society for Storytelling in 1993 (which includes a useful list of local and regional storytelling organisations on its website). Likewise, audiobooks remain popular, as do the short stories broadcast on BBC national and local radio stations; but these well-established outlets have been supplemented in recent times with the boom in independent radio stations and web-based media (for example, the arts-based Resonance FM in London, Radio Wildfire in Birmingham, Short Story Radio on the net, as well as YouTube and thousands of other websites).

All of the stories included in this collection have been performed in one or more of these different contexts. In these contexts, fiction is re-infused, it seems to me, with the spirit of Dickens; in these contexts, fiction is once again both a written and an oral art, as it was in the nineteenth century – as, indeed, it has been since the earliest times. From Homeric poets to village storytellers to nineteenth-century serialisations, storytelling clearly has a very powerful oral tradition, running alongside – and originally preceding – its written history. Good fiction writers often draw on this oral tradition: some of Salman Rushdie's *oeuvre* is a case in point, as is, in this collection, Catherine Rogers's piece, 'The Derby Poet.' The piece is a contemporary reconception of a traditional oral tale, which exists in various forms across different cultures and histories. Rogers is an experienced oral storyteller, and her piece bears the imprint of this experience: it is simply told (in the best sense), it is linear, with a definite beginning, middle and end, and it ends with a kind of moral.

If Rogers's story is the closest in this collection to the oral tradition, many of the pieces bear traces of this tradition, and share characteristics with traditional oral tales: many of the pieces are, in a broad sense, linear and self-contained, with obvious beginnings, middles and endings (however ambivalent); many are chronologically told; many of them encompass only one or two main characters and one relationship; many of them are simply (again, in the best and most beautiful sense) told, with direct, concise and straightforward language; many include recurring images, phrases or refrains, which help listeners orientate themselves within the narratives; many include very little introspection and inwardness on the one hand, and outward description on the other; and many of the stories have definite, if not necessarily moralistic, endings. Clearly, these characteristics are not exclusive to stories for reading aloud – no particular characteristics one might name are – but they arguably make a story more suitable for oral performance. Obviously, there is no definite boundary between a story which only works on the page, and one which works in performance; but perhaps, in a broad sense, the latter kind of story often has more in common with the traditions of oral storytelling than the former.

One of the principal characteristics of stories from this tradition – a characteristic which is linked to their linearity and self-containedness – is surely brevity. As has often been remarked, traditional oral tales are usually concise and fast-moving. All of the stories in this collection are the same. To put it simply, they are all short: there are few stories in this collection which are longer than 2,500 words, and none which would take longer than about twenty minutes to read aloud. Some, including those by Tania Hershman, Denise Hayes, Kate Pullinger, Emma J. Lannie, Judith Allnatt, Simon Perril and myself, are very short indeed, and fall into the category of flash fiction, or short-short stories (to use a less loaded term). It almost goes without saying that short, self-contained stories are going to be particularly suited to being read aloud, or performance. When Dickens was performing his work in the 1860s, he could have expected almost all of his audience to have some prior awareness of characters and the wider, novelistic contexts from which his chosen episodes arose; but writers nowadays cannot count on such prior awareness on the part of audiences, so novelists, in particular, often have to spend time contextualising their chosen excerpts in readings. Short story writers generally do not have this problem, and the stories in this collection can be performed or read aloud with no preparation at all: they provide their own frame, their own context, in a small space, or short span of time.

So, on a simple level, their shortness and self-containedness is what makes these stories suitable for reading aloud or performance. A lot has been said about the way in which, in the UK at least, short stories have, on average, arguably become shorter over the last few decades, particularly given the recent exponential growth of flash fiction, or short-short stories. No doubt some of the growth of short-shorts is due to the way in which prose fiction has sometimes been marginalised in the smaller UK literary magazines, which, for financial and editorial reasons, have traditionally concentrated on poetry, with space for one or two short-short stories almost as an afterthought. Without many small-scale magazines giving space to longer short stories, writers, and especially emerging writers, have tended to concentrate on short-shorts. At the same time, short-shorts also suit the performance circuit more than longer stories, for obvious reasons: at public events, neither open-mic slots nor even featured artist slots provide time enough for longer short stories; and in single-artist performances, audiences tend to get restless if the writer reads for too long at a time without a break. In all of these different contexts, the short-short story clearly works well, providing a self-contained and satisfying experience for an audience. Indeed, there is a definite relationship, even correlation, between the growth of flash fiction and the simultaneous development of increasing numbers of performance outlets for fiction writers: faced with these new live forums for disseminating their work to an audience, fiction writers have (consciously or unconsciously) tailored their stories accordingly. In that sense, modern fiction writers are again reminiscent of traditional village storytellers: both tailor the form and content of their work to suit their audiences.

Some of the stories included in this collection also bear traces of the oral storytelling tradition in another sense, in that they include storytellers within them. Just as the central character of Rogers's story is a poet-storyteller, so storytellers turn up all over the place in this collection – as in, for example, the sexual athlete in Alexandros Plasatis's story, the grandmother in Deborah Tyler-Bennett's story, the air stewardess in Robert Shearman's story, the medium in Karen Stevens's story, the actress in Louis De Bernières's story. The people in these stories demonstrate the power and omnipresence of different kinds of oral storytellers in our world. In bedrooms, within families, on planes and phones, from the afterlife, we seem surrounded by thousands of different voices, all telling or trying to tell us stories about themselves or ourselves.

And the point – as Dickens realised – is that these story-telling voices are all different, all unique. As I say, Dickens's characters – many of whom are themselves storytellers – are all given distinctive (and convincing) voices. Most, if not all, of the stories in this collection are Dickensian in that respect – that is, they seek to capture distinctive voices. This, I think, is one of the principal characteristics of prose fiction which works out loud as well as on the page (and no doubt it is also one of the principal characteristics of good prose fiction in general): the ability to capture individual voices, and stage the dramatic clash between conflicting voices. PJ Carnehan's story might be read as a kind of allegory in this sense, since it is actually a story about a voice. Here, voice and story are fused and become one; and many of the other stories in the collection come close to such a fusion.

In their performative fusion of voice and narrative, some of these stories also come close to the monologue form, to the point that, in a number of cases, the first-person narrator's voice is absolutely central to the story – *is* the story, in a sense. The pieces by Hanif Kureishi, Kate Pullinger, Katy Darby, Jane Holland, Claire Baldwin and Robert Shearman all exemplify Alan Bennett's well-known analogy (in the 'Introduction' to *Talking Heads*) between the monologue and short story forms. By extension, some of the third-person narratives in this collection might be seen as duologues, or even mini-dramas: the stories by Panos Karnezis, Aimee Wilkinson, Adele Parks, David Belbin, Salman Rushdie, Tania Hershman and many others fall into this category; Lee Rourke's story is part script (or, to be more specific, transcript); Ian McEwan's story is a comedy-drama about the making of (what might loosely be termed) a drama.

In their dramatisation of conflicting voices, some of these stories come close to another parallel genre: radio drama. It is no coincidence that BBC Radio 4, the radio station most well-known for its radio drama, is also well-known for its short stories: radio drama is, in an obvious sense, oral storytelling where the different voices are literally, rather than metaphorically, different voices. That is the one and only point of divergence between the two genres, the addition of sound effects or music nothwithstanding. Indeed, sound effects and music are often as important to stories as they are to radio drama. Many of the stories here employ sound effects, including those by Alexandros Plasatis, Will Buckingham and Deborah Tyler-Bennett; many more have an explicit or implicit musical soundtrack which accompanies parts of them, or is even integral to the plotline, including those by Ian McEwan, Michelene Wandor, Blake Morrison, and myself. Such emphasis on music and sound, of course, is one of the key elements which makes a story suited to reading aloud or performance. Just as the best radio dramas often self-consciously use sound as a structural and narrative device (hence the prevalence of radio dramas about musicians, for example), so stories intended for oral performance are often structured around auditory, rather than purely visual, images. In this regard, Jo Baker's story is a fascinating case in point, because it is explicitly about the relationship between visual and auditory images: the narrator is newly blind, so the story describes his transition from a reliance on visual to auditory (and, indeed, tactile) imagery. In this way, the story makes an ideal introduction to the collection, at least for a non-visually-impaired reader, since it takes him or her on the same journey as the narrator – that is, from a primarily visual world to the strange world inhabited by most of the ensuing stories, where auditory imagery comes to the fore.

This is not just a matter of subject-matter, storyline or narrative structure: inevitably, auditory imagery on a structural level also infuses the style and language of a story on a micro-linguistic level. To put this another way: if many of the stories here include auditory or musical aspects in their subject-matter, many of them also are infused with a language which is itself 'musical,' in the broadest sense. Many of the stories in this collection use musical effects and techniques as part of their very language: Claire Baldwin's story includes pseudo-musical refrains and repeated phrases; Adam Roberts's science fiction story uses rhyming couplets; Vanessa Gebbie's story is stylistically reminiscent of a kind of musical pointilism; Tania Hershman's piece is like a miniature set of variations on a theme; Simon Perril's piece is a kind of 'prose poem' (though he himself might disavow that particular term), whereby the beautiful musicality of the language becomes almost more important than conscious or logical 'sense.'

As a kind of prose poem, Simon Perril's piece makes explicit what is more or less implied by all of the stories here – namely, the overlap between stories suited to reading aloud and poetry. To a lesser or greater extent, the musicality of the prose in these stories shades into a kind of poetry – to use the term in its widest sense, a kind of 'performance

11

poetry.' And there is an important connection to be made between stories suited to reading aloud – to performance of some kind – and performance poetry. The development in recent years of many new contexts in which prose is performed is, in part, a belated off-shoot of the performance poetry scene, which dates back to the 1980s and beyond. Spoken word events, which are the home of performance poetry, have increasingly included space for flash fiction writers who want to share in the excitement of a direct connection with a live audience. By sharing spaces and contexts, fiction writers and performance poets have come to learn from each other, and there is (I think) considerable mutual influence between them in various quarters. This mutual influence remains largely unexamined, as does the effect of a developing performance scene on short fiction as a whole. By contrast, the significance of performance poetry as a phenomenon has long been recognised, and there is a significant body of published literature, both by individual practitioners and in anthologies, which aims to capture the energy and music of performance poetry on the page. There is, though, no comparable literature for stories in performance, and this collection seeks to redress that omission; it seeks to demonstrate the power, music and sheer range of possibilities in this respect – to show, if nothing else, how musical language is not just the preserve of performance poetry, or poetry in general.

It is the performative musicality of their language which makes these stories sound attractive out loud, even when members of the audience are not necessarily following every word, or the intricacies of plot. We all know how difficult it is to follow any story (or, for that matter, poem) the first time we hear it, especially from within a large audience, or in the less formal spaces, such as pubs or cafés, where stories are sometimes performed; but what most, if not all, of the writers in this collection understand is that there is a deeper, less conscious pleasure associated with hearing stories (and poems) out loud – and that is the kind of pleasure afforded by music, in this case the music of stylishly-written prose. The best radio dramatists have long since understood that the musical pleasure of listening to stories for voices can transcend the more rational pleasures afforded by following plotlines or characters' interactions: no-one, on hearing Dylan Thomas's *Under Milk Wood* for the first time, could possibly expect to follow all the interwoven narratives. The visceral pleasure here is not (or not just) provided by the individual storylines, but rather in their interwovenness – in the interplay of voices, the musical counterpoint and, of course, the melodiousness of the language itself. The words and their meanings come to matter less than the overall musical effect. On a smaller scale, the same applies to stories read aloud, where the musical kind of pleasure afforded to a listener or an audience is sometimes more important than the conscious meaning, logical sense or plotline.

Such musical pleasure is partly pre-verbal, and, if one were a psychoanalyst, it might be tempting to see in it a faint echo of the child's pleasure in the mother's voice: in the womb, the child obviously has a physical and pre-verbal connection with the mother's voice; and much later, in a very different sense, young children often take great pleasure in hearing stories (from, for example, their mothers) without necessarily understanding them. Understanding comes later, and is necessarily a secondary and weaker pleasure to the musical one of a lulling voice, or voices.

Consciously or unconsciously, stories suited to reading aloud play on the musical pleasures of a lulling voice, or voices – and, as such, might be seen as flashbacks to earlier states, and ultimately the vocal connection between mother and child; hence, perhaps, why so many of the stories here (including those by Judith Allnatt, Felicity Skelton, Sara Mae-Tuson, Gemma Seltzer, Kate Pullinger, Ailsa Cox and Katy Darby) are either about childhood, or relationships which originated in early childhood. In a sense, these stories are attempts to reconstruct or re-vocalise the pleasures of a lost, infantile and pre-verbal music – just as the book as a whole is an attempt to recapture something of my (slightly later) experience of sitting on the arm of my mother's chair, hearing elves in different voices.

A NOTE ON ORDERING

An anthology like this needs to be open to two different kinds of readers: those who want to read the collection end to end, and those who want to dip into individual stories. Obviously, the stories need to work on their own individual terms, but there also needs to be some kind of overall coherence or narrative structure to the collection, however vague, so that it provides a satisfying reading experience as a whole. Moreover, the collection needs to demonstrate the diversity of possible approaches, without appearing fragmentary or disjointed. These are the kinds of (partly conflicting) imperatives I have borne in mind when editing, selecting and ordering the material included here.

As well as giving the book some kind of overall narrative coherence, I have also split up the collection into sections, which form smaller narratives on their own – that is, 'Whispering Stories,' 'Telling Stories,' 'Crying Stories,' 'Laughing Stories,' 'Shouting Stories,' and 'Singing Stories.' Within these sections are grouped stories which overlap, maybe in their tone, style, structure, subject-matter, imagery, voices, emotions, characters, relationships, or landscapes – stories which, in various ways, whisper, talk, cry, laugh, shout or sing (all out loud) to one another. The names of these various sections should not be taken literally: good stories are not often emotionally monolithic, so a 'crying' story might also include humour, a 'laughing' story tragedy. Likewise, what happens emotionally centre stage in a story may be very different to what happens in the background, and a story's style, structure or tone may convey very different emotions to its ostensible subject-matter. In these ways, all of the stories included here overflow with different, conflicting and competing voices to which – I hope – it is a delight to listen.

REFERENCES AND FURTHER READING

Some books:

Alan Bennett, *Talking Heads* (London: BBC, 2007).

Will Buckingham, *Finding Our Sea Legs: Ethics, Experience and the Ocean of Stories* (Kingston upon Thames: Kingston University Press, 2009).

Charles Dickens, *Our Mutual Friend*, ed. Stephen Gill (Harmondsworth: Penguin, 1985).

Walter J. Ong, *Orality and Literacy* (Abingdon: Routledge, 1988).

Salman Rushdie, *Haroun and the Sea of Stories* (Harmondsworth: Penguin, 1993).

Ruth Sawyer, *The Way of the Storyteller* (Harmondsworth: Penguin, 1976).

Deborah Tyler-Bennett (ed.), *Speaking Words: Writing for Reading Aloud* (Crystal Clear Creators (CCC) Publishing, 2005).

Some websites:

BBC Radio 4, www.bbc.co.uk/radio4

Crystal Clear Creators, www.crystalclearcreators.org.uk

Federation for European Storytelling, www.fest-network.eu

Liars' League, http://liarsleague.typepad.com

Literary Death Match, www.literarydeathmatch.com

Radio Wildfire, www.radiowildfire.com

Rattle Tales, www.rattletales.org

Resonance 104.4FM, www.resonancefm.com

Short Story Radio, www.shortstoryradio.com

Society for Storytelling, www.sfs.org.uk

Storytails, www.storytails.org

Thresholds, International Short Story Forum, http://blogs.chi.ac.uk/shortstoryforum

Write Out Loud, www.writeoutloud.net

WHISPERING
STORIES

JO BAKER

BLUE SIGN, 75 MILES

□ □ □ □ □

He sat down at the next table, bringing in a cloud of cold air from the street. He scraped his chair around, dug in his pockets, then stood up again to take off his coat. She carried the coffee over. He offered to pay, but she wouldn't hear of it.

"Are you okay?" Her voice was low. "I mean, clearly you're not okay."

"I'm really sorry."

She sat down and shuffled her seat forward, into my patch of sight. The vision was muted, seen through pond water, but oh my God, the colours. Coppery hair and a slate-blue coat, or suit or dress, I couldn't tell what she was wearing, but the *colours*: they were perfectly complementary and lovely. I hadn't realised how starved I'd been.

"I did ask," she said.

"But you don't expect, you know, the truth."

If she noticed me staring, I couldn't tell, and I didn't much care anyway. Bloke my age, in my state: she could make allowances. Anyway, she had the guy's troubles to distract her.

It's a reflex, like sneezing; the urge to share the misery. His wife had left her mobile lying out. He shouldn't have looked. There were texts from a male colleague; suspiciously friendly, nothing conclusive. He'd been carrying the worry around with him for days. Then he'd bumped into this acquaintance in the street and she'd asked him how he was.

"We just haven't had time for each other. Not lately. You saw her at the Christmas party," he said, "how did she seem then?"

"I don't know. I don't know her really. Gorgeous dress."

"It suits her, red."

I just tuned out, disappeared into the hiss of the espresso machine, the clatter of china and the layered babble of conversation. The air is densely populated there; you don't have to hear anybody. My attention was all on the colours; they seeped into what was left of my sight, like watercolours on wet paper.

You taught me the route patiently, arm in arm, counting steps, drawing my attention to kerbs and corners, helping me get a hang of the stick.

Uneasy on my feet, still sore, I learned garden walls rough under fingertips, the green upholstery of privet hedges, the cool silk of glass shopfronts. I felt the rumble of a bus at the bus-stop, and the wave-like surge and fade of passing cars. The coffee shop seemed dark from outside, but inside it glowed with halogen spots; they streaked my sight like street lamps, like driving at night in the rain.

"Take a seat, sir?" She was just a Polish accent and black smudges in white skin, but the contrast was strong, the symmetry good. "I'll bring your coffee over for you."

A couple of months ago and I'd have caught her eye, tried to make her laugh, seen if it might go somewhere. Couple of months ago and it might have. Now, though, I was the object of her kindness. I just gave her my two-pound coin and shuffled away to find a table. Freud said that all neuroses to do with the eyes are really to do with the balls: fear of being blinded is really a deeper-seated fear of castration. Bollocks, I used to think. An eye was just an eye, and fear of being blinded was just fear of being blinded. I'm not so certain about that any more.

When I drew out a chair, a man at the next table shuffled in to make room.

"You all right there?"

"Yes," I said. Then, "Thanks."

He turned away. I sat down. The conversation batted back and forth behind me like a friendly game of badminton. The Polish girl arrived with my coffee, and was pleasant, and I was rude, and she went.

I lined up cup and napkins on the tabletop. The contrast of white china on dark wood is helpful. Nearby a boyish voice spoke – enthusiastic, one-sided, presumably into a mobile phone – and through it all Spanish guitar and the hiss of steam and the clink of crockery. I lifted my cup, and drank, and set it down again and pressed a napkin to my

lips, and sank into my pit, thinking of the terrible kind-
nesses of young women, and of you, your warm-milk tones,
your hand steady under my arm. Your fury all pushed down
now, all packed away, now that there are these more pressing issues, the practicalities of me to deal with.

"Ha!"

The laugh made me jump, slop coffee.

"So where is she now?"

"Ballet. She loves it. She gets to dress up and be a butterfly –"

"And you get a bit of a break?"

"Half an hour to myself on a Saturday morning. With
Andy away, it's a godsend."

It was Saturday: I hadn't known. The world rippled and
settled differently. Gemma might visit. Might be visiting at
that moment, taking her chance, with me out of the house.

"And all you get is me griping."

"No, seeing you, it –" she hesitated "– grown-up
company, outside of work, I don't get much of it. It does
me good."

"Good."

"Yes, well. Thanks."

He laughed. "It's no trouble."

A pause. I imagined smiles, eye contact. The urge to
touch.

"Oh Christ! Is that the time?"

A fluster and scramble and she was past me, heading for
the door, calling out goodbye. It was her. A trail of copper
hair and soft blue clothes. Those colours.

He sat on. He drank his coffee as if it was an afterthought. I heard the synthetic click and tap of an iPhone,

heard him breathe. He wasn't happy. But I envied him. The possibilities.

You said it was good to establish routine, to develop my independence. I could see you, in your busy, moving, turning way, always three things on the go, a smile on your face that was never exactly directed at, but was almost certainly about, me.

It was, of course, and you knew it, the independence of a goat tethered out on the green. The turf nibbled to the roots; the same narrow circuit, day after day. Everything at home – sofa, paintwork; even you, especially you: your face, your body – it was all so familiar. The sofa is green, the paintwork white, and you are beautiful. I knew that; I'd known it for years. But now, unbidden, I would see it. My palm resting on the worn patch on the arm of the sofa, I'd glimpse the square weave of the sage fabric. I'd brush past the doorjamb, and out of some filing cabinet at the back of my brain there it'd be – the chipped paint, a fingernail of dark wood beneath the strata of white. You'd slip your arm under my arm, and I'd see the blue in the inner fold of your elbow. The mole on your wrist, like a speckle on a pancake.

The Polish girl would ask, "The usual?" and I'd thank her and hand over my two-pound coin, and tell her to put the change – negligible as it was – in the tips jar. Two-pound coins I have found to be a blessing. Distinctive, easy in the hand, still capable of buying an Americano.

For a fortnight, I kept thinking they would be in, and would fumble from table to table, hoping to catch their voices. I imagined their need, that increasing ache for each other, wondered if they were doing anything about it yet, or were still teetering deliciously, guiltily on the brink. At the door's swing I'd crane around, following footsteps, hoping for a copper streak, a glimpse of underwater blue. Maybe they were meeting somewhere else. Maybe coffee shops were out of the question now. Maybe now they were in the twilight world of parked cars and hotel rooms. If so, they'd have to avoid each other in daylight and in public: the physical consciousness of each other burns. You can see it a mile off.

The details: daylight on skin, a tracery of veins, a faint fuzz of hair on a cheek; that's what I envied them. The last thing I ever saw with any clarity was a motorway sign. I was heading for that conference on Titian and a girl I barely knew, but for the prospect of whom, naked, I had dismissed the pulse and pressure in my eyes as fatigue, a virus; no time to deal with it right now. Monday, I'd ring the doctor, if it hadn't resolved itself by then. I pulled onto the motorway. I saw the blue sign, 75 *miles*. Then beyond the street lamps' glow, there was nothing. And for a moment I was staring blank, baffled, lost. Then rattling over the hard shoulder. Slammed into the bank, standing on the brake, a scurry of saplings, the roar and throb of blood.

I stumbled through mud. I sat down in the smell of oil and burnt rubber and crushed grass.

The only time I had ever been so scared in all my life was on the labour ward, when the baby's heartbeat stuttered and failed, and you foundered, your grip slipping from the world. The midwife's hurried whispers with the registrar, and the brisk shift to the operating theatre.

Those moments when everything is clear. When what matters most is sharp as broken glass.

Then one time I caught the trail of her hair, like a sparkler-burn, and I reached for a chair-back and sat in nearby. She was speaking, and it was so soft and insistent that for a moment I thought I'd stumbled upon a turning point – a confession of distress, or guilt, or even love – but then there was a clatter, and I knew the sound, a rainbow of felt-tips hitting the deck, and scattering.

"O-oh." A child's voice: the daughter.

"Oh dear."

Chairs scraped. They fumbled for the pens, hands and knees.

"Excuse me, sorry –"

And then she was there, close, leaning in, her hair so near I could have, if I had dared, touched it. Sunk my fingers into it. The scent of her too, of vanilla and burnt sugar.

"That's okay." My hands shook. I folded my arms. "Did you get them?"

"Yeah, thanks."

And she was gone, out of sight.

"There we go," she said. "Let's be more careful now, please, shall we?"

I saw mother and daughter, heads bent, the neat shading of a grown-up hand, a child's wilder work. I sketched it in from Gemma's childhood, of course. The two of you colouring fairies and ballerinas at the kitchen table. Your hand smooth still, hers tiny, blotched with colour. Just a glimpse

I'd caught round the edge of the door, heading back to my study. Never any time.

I waited for the man to join them. They would keep the talk light. The child would carry on with her colouring, and would give uneasy, sidelong looks, unsure of mummy's new friend.

I thought, this could have been you; years ago, when Gemma was little. Me away at some conference, and you left alone with the child again. It'd never occurred to me before, that I might have made you lonely.

Ten minutes later, the woman packed up their things and zipped the girl into her coat and they went. A little fraught, perhaps, the way she chivvied the child along, but no sense of disappointment, of having been left waiting. No-one had been missed.

You went back to work, which was inevitable, but I was surprised how much it affected me. I was supposed to be getting back to work myself; I was supposed to be getting used to the new computer, but I couldn't. However smart it might've been, however user-friendly, it stood no chance of actually making me *see*. And I couldn't see how I could ever really return to work like mine, if I couldn't see.

Books terrified me. Their vague spines, the grey fuzz inside. I'd have to learn to read again, with fingertips; but these books, a lifetime's books, they would always be opaque.

I was troubled by the notion of you out there in the world.

I remembered sand-dunes, the deep blue sky, you peeling off your dress, laughing, turning, sun on your skin.

I missed Gemma. She only visited at weekends, when you'd be home; even then she'd follow you out of the room. I didn't know where to start with her.

I tried radio – various stations: 3, 4 and 6; I played music and audio books, but that just seemed to clutter up the house, disorientate me, make me lose count of steps. I'd find myself lost, confronted by blank wall where I'd expected a doorway, a bookshelf where I'd thought the mantlepiece would be: I couldn't let myself drift for even a minute. I switched off the tunes, the cheerful chat. And days were blank and white and interminable.

The two of them, though. They had something.

In the coffee shop, heaving myself out of the sofa, I dropped my cane. Someone ducked through my line of sight.

"Here you go, mate."

A touch on the back of the hand, to orientate me to the stick. It was him. Was she there too?

"Thank you."

"I've seen you here before," he said.

"It's handy. I know my way around."

I fumbled my coat on. I wanted to stay now, but it was too obvious that I'd been about to leave.

"See you then," he said.

"Yeah. See you." The words like burrs. He turned back to her; I turned towards the wet light of the doorway and the empty day.

"There's just never any time." She sounded different. "It's just one thing and then another –"

"We can make time." His voice was pitched low, urgent.

"Can we though?"

"I think we have to."

I passed them, looking out for her, but caught unexpected colours: this woman was claret-warm, her hair bog-oak black, and they leaned so close that they blurred together, and I knew it was his wife.

Outside, cars heaved and surged. My fingertips brushed glass, privet, brick; everything else seemed unstable, shifting, apart from these tangible things. Things that you have made me notice.

In the hallway, you're a blur of pale hair, and that long-loved green shirt. Your wrist is delicate and warm. I'm stunned by you. That you persist, that you can still be touched, when I myself have been there and gone and back again and so much absent. I want to ask, is it too late, or is there still time for me to make time for you? Can we make time together? Can we grow pockets of it, pots, fill rooms, let it pool out into the street? And I want to tell you, that there is blue in the crook of your elbow; that there's a mole on your wrist as dark as chocolate. I know. I remember. I did see.

EMMA J LANNIE

ONE TWO

□ □ □ □ □

The boy called Bear is riding his bicycle up and down my street. Clattering, screeching. He is fast, and the wind gets in his hair and makes him a blur. I know it's him, even when he's moving too quickly for me to see his features. It's the shape of him I recognise. The squaring of his shoulders and the way he holds his head. And because he moves so fast, I am able to make things slower.

One.

Two.

I see my world in time-lapse. The way he turns to look up at my window, and how his eyes are the most perfect mix of green and blue and grey. And his stupid mouth wants me. He curves his lips when he thinks this, and in slow motion I see it.

I walk outside and stand by the gate. Of their own

accord, my hands tangle themselves behind my back. The boy called Bear kisses me. The world doesn't stop, but something shifts, maybe a mountain range far away, in the middle of an unnamed sea.

He has his hands on my face and we've agreed to this. This is happening because we talked about letting it happen. We are strangers enough to not be shy.

The boy called Bear has a voice that makes me shiver, when he uses it just right. He doesn't do this often, but when he does, it cuts across all my unknowing and makes me only want to lean into him, press myself against him. And sometimes I let go and do that. And he's warm and kind of still. And the kisses that come are long and we don't stop to breathe, we just keep on, one, two, and his hands move up underneath my jumper and I don't push them away.

And I don't even know his middle name. Or his favourite colour. But what I do know is how his mouth tastes at one, two a.m. in the rain. How the salt of his skin is caught on his lips. How kissing with him in my doorway, with everyone else all asleep, makes me thirsty, makes me want things to never stop.

The boy called Bear wants me to go up to his room with him. We take the stairs. One, two, at a time. When we get there, I slow the world down again, and as we're walking across to his bed, I get to think about every single movement. I watch the way he dips his head and bites his lip, and the way his lungs fill as he takes deep breath after deep breath. The tiny hairs on the back of his neck stand up the closer I get. I reach out my hand to touch between his shoulder blades, and it takes me an age to get there.

There is a pause, and we are the punctuation. The bed, and all that will happen on it, is an ellipsis.

As time speeds back up, I remember things about my body. How it has felt like this before, felt these things before, but how it is never the same. But there's always the heartbeat. That one-two, one-two repeating over and over in the background of everything. And sometimes it's as slow as when time stops altogether. But right now, in this very moment, my heart hammers away insistent, holds my whole body between the beats.

DAVID BELBIN

GAMES IN BED

□ □ □ □ □

Like most men, in Jane's limited experience, Tom had trouble staying awake after sex. This created a particular problem. Even the briefest daytime doze brought on one of his migraines and Tom had to be on air every evening. He couldn't perform when he had a headache.

Cutting out the sex wasn't an option. Jane often worked away at weekends, but most weeks there was a day when her schedule allowed her to finish at lunchtime. Afternoons in bed helped to keep their marriage strong.

It was Jane who came up with the idea of playing games to prevent Tom from falling asleep. Nothing too demanding. A silly quiz or word game.

"If you had to sleep with one soap opera character, which would it be?" was one of hers.

"Best five TV programmes set during the Second World War" was his. Tom liked games where you put things in order of importance. And lists. They took turns to come up with movies whose titles began with 'l'. Or every city they'd visited. Tom invented a version of *Call My Bluff* where he'd list three rock groups and Jane would have to say which one he'd made up: was it The Mynah Birds, The Electric Chair or The Incredible Submarine Band?

As they got older, silliness sometimes eluded them. Occasionally, bitchiness crept in. One afternoon, for example, Jane suggested that each detail those of their friends they most disliked. That year, they reduced the size of their Christmas card list by seven.

Tom worked as a late-night talk-show host on local radio. It was a job he loved, apart from the low pay. Some of their afternoon games provided material for talk-ins on his show, but others were too close to the knuckle for comfort.

"Let's say," she suggested, this afternoon, "that, God forbid, you had a fatal accident. Which of our friends do you think I'd end up with?"

This was a question that Tom had considered more than once, but the other way round. He'd been sensible enough to keep it to himself.

"You're stirring the pot, aren't you?"

"I'm interested to know who you think I'd suit."

One of their rules was that either could turn down a game, and suggest an alternative. In his sleepy, post-sex miasma, Tom revised, rather than rejected the question, making it apply to them both.

"How about *suppose one of us died, which of our friends do you think we'd end up with, presuming that they were single too?"*

"Agreed," Jane said. "Top three, in ascending order."

Tom thought about his choice. He was prone, in idle moments, to think about women he'd like to sleep with, and the circumstances that might bring such an event about. Dwelling on the necessity of Jane's death to this scenario spoilt the fantasy. But now that she'd suggested the hypothesis, he felt free to speculate. Time to clarify the rules.

"We're not talking about which of our friends we find attractive. Or who we might have a casual thing with if we were both single. We're talking about who we might end up with if, theoretically, the other one of us were dead. Let's say there's been some vast plague, loads of people have died so a lot of our friends would be single too."

"Then everybody would be too traumatised to think about sex."

"A suitable period of mourning has passed. It's time to move on. Anyway, I'm not talking about sex," he said, although he was. "Relationships are more about companionship than they are about sex."

"They still need sex to get them going," Jane pointed out. "Mind you, if one of us were to die, the other would be much more likely to marry someone who didn't know us as a couple. More of a fresh start."

"Do you want to play this game or not?"

"Want. Are we doing two lists, a top three for ourselves and one for each other?"

"Just for each other. I don't want to hear who you lust after."

"Game on. I need time to think. I'm going to the bathroom."

Tom tried to work out which of their male friends most admired his bride. Jane had retained her looks, but was not a trophy wife, like Lisa Spencer, nor an exercise freak, like the bootilicious Tracey Haynes, who presented the early show that followed his. These were women whose husbands had to keep an eye on their friends. Sexual desire was so specific, so diverse. Tom knew which of his pals liked to check her out. Didn't mean they'd marry her if he dropped dead.

Jane was gone a long time. Tom came up with four candidates. He would amend the order in between turns.

When Jane returned from the bathroom, she had put on a T-shirt that she sometimes slept in, although it was not cold. Knickers too. Tom sensed that, by invoking death, they had crossed a line. She launched into her turn.

"In reverse order, three to one, the women we already know who you're most likely to be shacked up with a year or two after my tragic, early death. At number three, presuming that she and Simon divorced or he was dead too, I pick Katey Maund."

"Katey? You can't think that I fancy Katey!"

"You must fancy her a little. I've seen you watch her breast feed. You're very good with her and Simon's kids. She's told me she admires you. That's the largest part of attraction, isn't it? Finding someone who likes us for what we are. Your turn."

Tom thought Jane's approach was flawed. Of course a man glanced at a woman when she was feeding her baby. It was the only time – accidents and affairs aside – you were allowed to see the whole breast. Jane, he decided, was deliberately blowing the early rounds. So would he.

"I could see you with Keith Porter."

"I couldn't see me with anyone called *Keith*," she said. "Did you pick Keith because he's single, or because you know that he likes me? It can't be because I like him. I don't."

"You laugh at his jokes. He's good company."

"I've talked to a couple of his exes. Both said that, apart from a low kind of charm, the one thing he has going for him is a bigger than average cock. Is that why you chose him?"

"How would I know that?" Tom said, testily.

"I suppose I might screw him if I were hard up, just for the experience. But marry him? Come on."

"Whatever," he said. "Your turn."

"I could see you with Julia," Jane observed. She turned away and began to file her nails, leaning over the bedside waste paper bin. She did not see the sudden flush that ran across his face.

For Julia had been his one slip. The affair took place before Julia met Dan but six years after Tom married Jane. The first giddy rush of their marriage was long over. Tom was twenty-eight. A man's sexual peak. A time when hormones could still make you take stupid risks. His cock had told him he'd get away with it, no worries. His cock was right.

In those days, he hardly saw Jane. Sales conferences most weekends. Julia was a BBC trainee. She knew Tom was married. She could see he was lonely. As was she, new in town and working the graveyard shift. With him.

One weekend, several weeks into the affair, the two of them bumped into Dan, who had been best man at Tom's wedding. Pretended they were working. Dan asked for Julia's phone number. A decade later, the couple had three children. Those furtive fucks in her flat were ancient history, a secret from both Dan and Jane. Or maybe Dan knew what had happened, but was too tactful to say.

"I like Julia a lot, but she's Dan's wife. I can't think of her that way."

"Who invented this game? Anyway, if your best friend's dead, and I'm dead, doesn't it behove you to take on his wife and kids?"

"*Behove*. That's a very biblical word."

"And the appropriate one. Your turn to do me. And don't say Dan. You know I don't fancy him."

"You haven't come up with a serious candidate for me yet. Maybe we should choose our own."

"No, you were right before," Jane said. "That's too dangerous. I don't want to know who you fantasise about fucking when I'm dead."

"Who says I . . ."

"I know what men are like. Women can be into someone without wanting to ravish them. Men can't."

"That's a gross simplification."

"If it's a simplification, you're admitting I've hit on a truth," Jane said. "Who did you choose for me?"

"It's not so much choosing as predicting."

"The weather forecast then. Which man will rain on me?"

"I thought . . . Samuel."

"He doesn't count as a friend," Jane said. "He's my ex-boss."

"You get on well with him."

"Doesn't mean I'd marry him," Jane said. She wondered how much Tom knew about her and Sam, as she used to call him. During Sam's divorce, they'd had him round for dinner a couple of times. Jane liked Sam. He might be her boss, but he treated her as an equal. She fancied him, too, and was having a wobble about Tom at the time, though she disguised it pretty well. Biological clock stuff. Motherhood was starting to seem attractive, despite their having agreed not to have kids.

At the end of a long working Saturday, Sam had put on this pained, *I'm such a loser* act, and made a pass. They had a drunken snog. When he wanted to go further, she said no, but of course they went further at the next conference. Sam made her feel bad about not going all the way. She tossed him off to shut him up. Or maybe she dreamt that bit. So much drink was involved. She never let him talk her into his room after that.

Sam soon married again. When he got a new job, she was promoted to his old one. They still saw each other professionally, and, occasionally, remembered to flirt, but no heat remained, no risk.

"OK," Jane said. "I accept that Samuel is a bit more convincing than Keith. Time for our number ones."

"I propose a twist," Tom said. "I want to know what you think I think. I write down who I chose for you and who I think you chose for me. You do the same."

Jane made a humming noise while she weighed up the potential danger. Then she found them both a piece of paper. Jane knew who Tom would end up with *if* they were both available *and* he had the confidence to go for her. Kelly was married to a lawyer, ten years her senior. She listened to Tom's show, which was more than Jane ever did.

Guessing who Tom would pick for her was more difficult. The only one of Tom's friends that Jane could imagine herself with was Mac, his producer. They had easy, freewheeling phone conversations when she had to call the studio, and always found time to talk at parties. Mac was married to a childhood sweetheart whom he had outgrown. Now and then, when they were alone together, he managed to find a way to imply that he would like to shag Jane silly. But Tom had no idea of this.

Honesty games were for the young, Jane decided. Easy to play *truth or dare* when you could still dare anything and barely be touched by it, when confessing secret desires and acting upon them could be exalted into a principle. Older, you were hemmed in by the past. The thought of starting up with someone else scared her silly. At work, she'd read actuarial statistics that said a woman her age was likely to have another forty-five years to live. Forty of those would be with Tom, who she would outlive by five years. They were only a third of the way through their life together. That thought was enough to make her want to start again with someone else. Anyone else.

"Have you filled yours in yet?" he asked, gently, as though sensing her turmoil. The times he could read her mind surprised Jane more than those when he misread her completely. Suppose, by writing 'Kelly' she prompted him to start an affair with her, an affair that – by the childish tit and tat they had never quite outgrown – she half owed him?

Tom wrote down two names. They exchanged slips of paper, carefully folded. Jane imagined the situation she had forced him to imagine, a black and white movie scene where she succumbed to a photogenic illness. On her death bed, she asked Kelly, recently widowed, to look after Tom. Her tearful friend agreed.

Neither of them unfolded their slips at first. Jane thought about how much she loved Tom, who was still in a job he should have been promoted out of a decade ago. Tom, who didn't complain when she worked away every other weekend. There had been a time when she rather hoped that he was having an affair. It would have eased her guilt. But if he had, she'd not been around enough to notice the clues. Now they were an old married couple and he had written down the name of the person he thought she ought to end up with after his death.

The mature, grown-up thing to do would be to crumple up the slip of paper, throw it in the bin. But she had never been grown up or mature, and neither had he. If they threw the papers in the bin, each would only get it out later and look at the other's answer. In fact, Tom had already opened hers. He was reading it with a thin, wry smile.

She opened his. He had correctly guessed what she would say, and vice versa.

"You think I'd have a chance with Kelly, do you? Most glamorous woman we know. Or are you just flattering me?"

"No more than you flatter yourself," Jane said, grinning. "But she's not having you."

"What if she already has?" he teased.

"What if I've already had Mac?"

"Have you? Is that why you wrote his name, to test me?"

"Wouldn't you like to know? Is that why you wrote Mac's name too? Has he said something about liking me?"

"He always has his eye on you. You must think I'm blind!"

"Not blind, just stupid." Jane threw herself at Tom and tickled his armpits. He tried to push her off and she began to laugh. They hadn't had a mock fight like this in years. One thing soon led to another. Later, they would need to find a new game to keep themselves awake.

DENISE HAYES

TUNNEL HEARING

□ □ □ □ □

I'm woken by the silken plop of a rat slipping into the inky water of the canal. It's hard to sleep long or deep these winter nights.

Further down the tunnel Dudley Lil is muttering and mumbling in her gin-fuelled nightmares, and up above me a trapped pigeon thrashes its wings in soft panic against the damp roof.

The earth's cold seeps into my bones like slow poison.

Years ago barge-workers lay on their backs like me and stared into the darkness. In tunnels more tight than mine with not an inch to spare for a towpath they walked the walls to move their narrowboats forward. What strength they had! Treading the brickwork and pushing their past behind them.

The Town Hall clock strikes twelve and in the distance down by the basin I can hear the screams of some drunken slut. The bells of St. Ambrose were also chiming midnight when I stood by my garden gate for the last time. On the twelfth stroke I looked up at the black abyss of my bedroom window and for a moment considered going back to lie beside her.

My beautiful, treacherous wife.

Then I legged it.

DEBORAH TYLER-BENNETT

MISS MOUNT

□ □ □ □ □

I've always considered those closest enjoy the act of scaring us. A bit like the story Grannie Sledmere used to fish out on festive occasions, the one she swore true. When a child, I used to wait for her to tell it, though the telling meant a night out-staring roseate bedroom wallpaper, making malign faces of the pink and olive.

Not that I'd tell you about Grannie Sledmere, or wallpaper at 20, Lockdeane Terrace. You have me down as better bred, testament to elocution lessons with Mr Briggs that Ma and Grannie pooled resources for, and the grammar school place attained with a much fussed-over scholarship. You and I have worked together for months now, sharing a few adventures, but not my past, or yours, come to think of it, and not my fears over the man in the corridor.

Funny, I can still make out Grannie's beech-leaf-backed hands folding as she rose to the tale's occasion, lined lips wrapping around first words: "I had six brothers, now only four's left, as you know. Our Will died when e were a babby, scarletina. Then there wore Billy. Sunniest soul y'd ever clap eyes on. Died when e were nineteen, down't pit. Like lots of lads. Pit prop fell on him, then some o't ceiling. Mam said it didn't even get into the papers. Shameful, those days! Colliery at Swethy Bank it wore. All on 'em went but Jem, as become a stockinger."

Here, she'd look around for impact. "Course, I knew Billy'd die, soon as that mustosh grew." By rights, certain doom after growing a moustache should have had comic potential, but not if you knew what followed: "I were't eldest, and Billy were't youngest, and from when he were three, I knew he'd die as a young man."

Never doubting her, though not believing that sort of thing, I wondered why she made something so close an entertainment. Still, perhaps she passed her need to tell on as, if you only knew it, I'm about to do similar.

"When he were about three, Mam were out selling Fry's Bars to the Electric Theatre queue. Don't ask where she got em. I were lookin after him. Gave him his bath by't fire, and as I dried him, we played 'Peep-bo.' I'd cover his face wi a towel, and pull it away, and he'd pull a face. 'Peep-bo' (tongue stickin out), then he'd cover me and I'd do similar. 'Peep-bo' (I'd cross my eyes until I looked like old lass Winters down't road). Oh, he loved it, doing it times if you'd let him.

"'Peep-bo. I see you,' and then . . ."

"Then?"

"One time he hid, I pulled the towel, and it weren't him I wore lookin at. All I saw were a young man wi a bruised, dead face. Thin mustosh, parted hair, a great red mark above one eye. How I saw him full size, I'll niver know. No sooner seen than gone – our Billy back and gostering. Well, at the time, I didn't let on to a soul.

"As our Billy grew, I watched him become that young man. Oh, sometimes I'd forget, but then he grew that mustosh. Times I wept in the pantry for him when everyone were off somewhere. That day they brought him back and laid him out, I niver needed to look to see that great red mark above his eye, the rest on him, perfect."

Grannie's story, long past. Now, as I sit in your drab, regulation painted office you smile, and hand me a drink of what passes for tea, in its soap-green cup. I remove a bag of butter-less gingerbread from my pocket and pass it to you, saying I made too much for one. Your grey eyes twinkle, and those usually strict features weave around a grin. The moss-coloured much-worn cardigan, under that tweed suit's in need of darning, your hair and moustache are more flecked with grey than at our first meeting, I'm sure of it.

You can't know my tale's a breath away – like Grannie at a family gathering, I wait my moment. Will this be it? This? This? Will I scare you with something new, or do you already know it?

As it is, the man who ghosts this building's already between us, surely as if actually there, and making me realise that, even given present circumstance, there's reason your office appears over-barricaded.

"You wouldn't know it butter-less."

Lies, shared contraband.

"Yes. It sometimes tastes better without."

As I close the door you've begun to hum 'Run Rabbit.' I smile. Grannie loved a song.

That small corridor between your office and his haunt shrinks. *Clack. Clack.* My heels against parquet. *Clack. Stump. Clack.* That gap in flooring laid down at least five decades ago. *Clack.* So I won't hear his breath. *Clack.* Nearly across the corridor to the further door, leading to the People's Hall with its vaulted roof and rudimentary red glass windows. As I enter, the *Clack* grows augmented, and the peeling cross above the next door glowers in its ox-blood ire.

Your allocated office on one side, corridor away from the vaulted hall, mine on the opposite, further corridor away. What lies in those corridors and between's unspoken, like someone's fear of walking home in the dark. We mustn't complain. Space's at a premium now, and we're lucky to be here, ours hardly being essential war work.

"Of course," the Minister's man beamed, "we appreciate commissioning of new art outside the capital is desirable, that's why you exist. We've found you offices in the old People's Chambers with storage space in the People's Hall. Funny, before the previous war it was intended for a lecture venue catering for all types of groups, but some good intentions never do bear lasting fruit. Shame, as records show that by 1915, there were all sorts of public events happening here. Then, before you knew it, the place was as good as derelict as the town centre seemed to shift. You're its new lease of life, you might say, ironic really."

We were to store commissioned artworks from all over the country in the hall, until picked up for touring exhibition. "What if there's a raid?" you'd asked, only to be told some sacrifices were inevitable.

Now, first canvases are stacked, only front pictures being unwrapped and visible. "Our little treat," you'd said, "we can't have all those glorious works and not display them, at least for ourselves." Some names I recognised, Piper . . . Ayrton . . . Sutherland . . . Others remain less certain of. Still, something of England seems suspended in each canvas: a land girl drives a tractor over impossibly emerald fields; a church I think I once visited reduced to jarring black and ochre brush-strokes.

"Folk'll pay for that during wartime, whitever next!" Grannie would've chuckled. Our man, though, she'd have recognized his presence, just as I do.

On occasion, lingering over canvases, I feel studied. Knowing I'll turn and face no-one makes me more determined to savour them unhindered. Sometimes, I think there's a pause of someone about to say something, at others, encountering sharp breath against my neck, as if I'm the intruder.

"How's it going, Miss Mount?" the Minister's assistant breezed on her inaugural visit. Plump and purposeful, she looked like the woman whose conversation's overheard by Hitler and Goering on the poster, and I wanted to take her to the hall and leave her – an experiment to see if she saw anything inexplicable and returned, shakingly desirous of a cigarette.

Once only, righting hair-pins in the crackled mirror at one side of the hall, I caught our shadow-man clearly for an instant, outlined at my right shoulder – ash-blonde hair, flushing features, a scar running from just below the left eye to just above his upper-lip, dusky uniform from the last shout, and the scar's pulled skin recalling Grannie's story of premonition. Had some girl wept for him during that war to end them all, hiding her tears within a pantry's familiar confines? Thinking back, I'm pretty sure his eyes were differing colours, one blue, one brown, calling to mind a dog my Uncle had, whose aqua and hazel gaze produced a permanently distracted air.

Then, just my pinched face in the glass, lipstick too red, eyes questioning their own reflection . . . Sense of being butt of someone's joke.

When our next tea break comes, I'm going to ask you about his presence over a cup of khaki liquid. Perhaps he'll become one of our stories, trotted out at festivities. "Did we ever tell you about our visitor?" But I'm getting ahead of myself, in a way Grannie never would.

If you see him too, it's good, means he isn't only in my head. I'll place my hand on yours, though whether just to give me strength, I won't be sure. I hope you don't reply I must be working too hard, and need rest . . . Or that you "worry the strain of the times is just too much." I imagine explanation: "You know, the light in that hall's really quite strange, the windows were built too high and at odd angles. Some afternoons, I've sworn a bright figure's walked before me, but it was just the winter sun's trick."

Perhaps, as is often your way, you'll say little, returning my touch, your fingers' sudden pressure answering. Don't let me down, though. Don't get up, leaving swinging doors and the echoing of 'Run Rabbit' as you whistle past him and dusk draws on.

Don't leave me trailing, feeling his odd eyes follow –
observing us from every canvas:
   "Peep-bo.
   "I see you."

VANESSA GEBBIE

ED'S THEORY
OF THE SOUL

□ □ □ □ □

Ed is on a beach, alone. He's left his clothes scattered on
the larger rocks at the base of the cliff, back there. Started
to fold them, then stopped, the ocean pulling him round
like a magnet, passing on the tug of the moon. Ed knows
the tide has something to do with the moon. But not the
how or the why, just that it has.

He stops at the water's edge. Maybe it is alive. Like
mercury, all of a piece, finding itself if it divides. Maybe the
movement – a gentle pulse now – is really the sea breathing like everything must, if it lives. There's nothing more
beautiful, so it must live. And if the ocean lives, does it feel?

Ed read a few weeks back, somewhere, can't remember,
about a woman who loved a wall. A wall. That is amazing.
There was a photo, too. She looked perfectly ordinary,
standing next to this crumbling wall, glowering at the

camera like it was intruding. Then a second shot. She'd turned away, maybe thinking the photographer had finished – and was stretching out a hand towards the wall. She was leaning in, her whole body following the hand, her eyes lowered, the fingers flexed, electric. Something in the ether reaching out from those fingertips, reaching out to the wall, and reaching out through the photograph to Ed – and the wall sending back something – something – Ed couldn't fathom it because he doesn't quite . . . but it was there. Ed felt it.

The wall cared.

But this? The water? Ed dips a foot in, the ankle still marked where his sock was tight. The water doesn't care. It's cold. Very cold. So cold the foot begins to hurt.

Ed sits on the pebbles, keeps his foot in the water, waits for it to stop hurting. Doesn't need to look round, see if anyone's watching. There is no-one. Ten miles to the nearest town, signs a couple of miles along the main road – ROAD CLOSED AT BENACRE. More signs if you do turn down past Monk's Farm and the abandoned church – NO ENTRY. CLIFF EDGE UNSTABLE. And the final signs up on the cliff top, where the road stops, sliced, layers of tarmac and hardcore exposed like those things you should keep covered.

DANGER, SUBSIDENCE.

His body's not good, now. Used to be. Used to be hard, firm as a statue. Ed's foot is numb, the cold-ache travelling up his leg.

There was something in the local paper about the church, about Monk's Farm. But like the article about the woman and the wall, Ed can't quite remember it all. Something about the monks taking a tenth of their produce and burying it. Even in the depths of winter, when the stuff was really needed – buried for God. For God, for God's sake. Like God lives under the ground and is going to tunnel to find the stuff, and sit there consuming potatoes, carrots, cabbages, herbs, and turnips? In the dark? Alone?

Ed sits with his foot in the sea and shakes his head. Wasn't it just the same thing? Like the woman and the wall? The monks knowing the very earth felt things, knew things? The monks feeding it? Ed can see them, if he shuts his eyes, and just listens to the sea's heartbeat. Sees the monks in a line, two abreast, in brown. Wicker trays of some sort, baskets. And their cheekbones throwing shadows down their faces. Their brows looming over lowered eyes. Carrying the goods to the churchyard to be buried. Ed will not open his eyes in case the vision fades. Strains his ears beyond the rush of the sea to hear the monks, plainchant.

But that's just imagining, nothing real, a silence in the past for the monks, broken only by the regular sounds of a horse clopping past on the lane, its hooves on the cold ground sounding like a knell. He hears that and feels a swell of something in his chest.

This morning, early, he took a woman to a town and saw her onto a train, and she left. This woman has a name, but Ed doesn't want to think about that. He stood on the platform, the train pulled out of the station, and something in him made him raise a hand, as though he was waving. Like the other woman with the wall. But he wasn't – it was only reflex, and he turned away and drove here.

Ed sits on the pebbles, one foot in the water. His eyes snapped open a moment ago, when the monks got to the place they needed, and tipped the goods into the ground. The horse had gone past with its cart, and all he could hear now was the sound of the monks' breathing, and their hearts beating, and the rattle and jolt of the cart fading up the lane. Like a film, that's all it was. That's where it all came from, his head. Seen it somewhere, must have, on the box, on the screen, not making it up at all, not inventing anything. His head full of other people's images – dragons and mountains, and rockets, plumed horses, jousting knights, stables, tin baths, mines and golden dishes on some distant planet's feast day.

She'd said to him, his woman, that he was hopeless. Treated her like an object, she said, and she was right – Ed loves them all, why should she be different to the rest? But she left. He won't even think of her name, and anyway, the sound of the sea becomes the sound of the train becomes the sound of the monks, the horse, the cart, and the sea again.

As far as he can see, the sea. Right to the horizon, or where the horizon must be – you just have to trust, sometimes – today, it is the same colour as the sea, the sky. It's all one.

Then, by Ed's foot, knocking into it, tapping against his skin, his anklebone, a something, Not sea. Something small, a piece of wood. And Ed's scrabbling in the edge of the water to fetch the thing, a small stick, a piece. Light wood that floats without sinking at all. Can't remember what it's called. Used to use the stuff in models, making planes, with his dad, when he was a lad . . .

And in that single piece of wood, the world disappears and comes back. It leaves a black hole into which Ed can pour everything – how he can't remember what he's read, and where, and maybe he is hopeless, and stupid, and how the photo of that woman by the wall reached out to him, and how there is a soul in the smallest thing, even the stones he is kneeling on, his skin denting with the shapes under his bones.

There is a soul in the water, in the tiny drops that separate themselves from the edge of the sea, splitting over the pebbles. Soul in the pebbles. Ed is wide-eyed at the simplicity of this truth.

He stands, holding the piece of wood. The wood that came from somewhere out there – and he points it towards the horizon – and it is as though the wood remembers the cold, and settles back into his hand, digging into his palm as he grips it tighter, tighter. As though the wood wants to bury itself into his flesh, deeper, deeper, so that when Ed wants it, this feeling, he will have to dig.

And he wonders what that woman in the photo did about the wall. That thing streaming from her fingers was love. How Ed remembers it. How it streamed out of the photograph straight to him, too.

It's the same now – this piece of wood, wood that is not wood at all, and he is digging in his memory – to find his young fingers on another small piece of wood, at home, on the kitchen table, making something with his father. Then his father opening a blade, a blade that caught the light, and he went to bring it down on the piece of wood to make what, a wing of a plane, or a house for a train set? Ed couldn't bear it – "No!" and slid his hand across the table, between the wood and the blade.

Ed remembers. Ed remembers, but doesn't need to. On his palm, wet with sea water, the mark where the point of the blade just pierced the skin, parting the tendons as it came through from the back of his hand, pinning him to the tabletop. And there was something that stopped the world then, the boy pinned to the wood by a blade, his father standing, mute, the air in the kitchen electric. As if it could be the end of something.

Ed turns his hand over to see the bigger scar on the back of his hand where the blade entered. The sea frothing over his knees like snow.

What was the woman's name, this morning? What is a name anyway? A sound we make, learned to make, something that sets one thing apart from another. How do we know the name is what the thing would choose for itself? And what is living and dead? What is animal, vegetable, mineral? Who is to say that the sea cannot feel? Or a wall?

He saw the woman onto a train, in a town. He waited, on the platform, his hand raised, because his hand raised itself. He walked to the gates, standing to one side to let others on to the platform, because they always come, and move, and want to get from one place to another, and shift, and never stay the same.

He went to go home. To his home town. But what was that? A mass of roads, buildings, sewers running beneath them like veins under the skin. Alleys, fences, gateways and tall locked doors.

Walls.

And maybe, just maybe, the things we build have feelings. Maybe, just maybe, the woman with the wall is right. The wall feels, and yearns, and loves her in return. The thing he read said some women marry houses. And another, she married a bridge, and another a great steel tower ...

Ed gets up. He carries the piece of wood back to the base of the cliff, rests it on a fallen rock while he dresses. And on his way back up the lane, he'll pause at the church, may walk for a while among the graves, the tumble of gravestones, all illegible now, covered in lichen. And he'll carry the piece of wood home, light as a bride, thinking that everyone dies, that over there won't be any different to here.

The cliff edge will crumble again in the high night tide, and tarmac, hardcore, will tumble to the beach in great blocks, layered, like chunks of wedding cake.

TELLING STORIES

CATHERINE ROGERS

THE DERBY POET

□ □ □ □ □

—There are many versions of this story. I knew it first as the Peddlar of Swaffham, which is the English story, but there are versions all over the world. This one is inspired by a group of writers I know who live in Derby.

This is the story of the poet of Derby.

Once there lived a man whose name was Joe Michael Jones, 'Jonezy' to his friends. He spent his days and nights working as an educator and inspiring people who some of us might describe as disadvantaged. His work would take him to youth groups, schools, clubs, homeless and community centres and there he would spend all day raising aspirations. But he found it hard to find time to pay any attention to his own aspirations and he could barely rub two coins together to keep himself warm and fed.

He lived in a strange building that was half open to the weather and which had a huge clock, in faded gilt and thrush-egg blue, suspended from its front. The colourful and bizarre history of the building went back to the industrious Victorian age but now birds flew in and out of the broken windows, bats nested in the rafters and mice under the floorboards. Despite being broken, the building also came with a bit of luck – a huge garden stretched out in the back with lots of trees left to grow wild and free and plant their roots deep into the soil. One of these grew with such a curious arrangement of twisted roots that it was a favourite place for Jonezy to sit and write his poems.

One night when he was fast asleep a loud ticking sound disturbed our poet's dreams. It was a clock's beat as clear as bright morning light, and he woke with a start. In the irrational dream state of the night-time Jonezy felt as if some sinister being was letting him know that his time was running out. The sound was so loud that he thought someone or something must have been in the room with him, but when he saw there was no-one there, he eventually settled under his covers and went back to sleep. The next night the ticking began again and this time he sat bolt upright, half expecting a clock to be right up against his face, but there was nothing there, just the cold moonlight streaming in through the broken roof. Returning to a fitful sleep, Jonezy dreamt of all the things he had told himself he must find time to do in his life. When he awoke in the morning, though, the urgency of his daily tasks loomed ahead of him as usual and he pushed the clock and the dreaming to the back of his mind.

This continued for a whole week and on the seventh night of the ticking Jonezy came to the conclusion that dreams, as strange and irrational as they can be, are sometimes worth listening to. He decided he must set out travelling and head to the mountains in Nepal – he knew people were struggling to survive in Nepal, perhaps he could be an educator there? If indeed, as his dream seemed to imply, his clock was really ticking, perhaps he should pursue this dream and maybe that was where his fortune lay.

So he set off and eventually arrived in the hustle and bustle of Kathmandu and found himself a teaching job. Soon he was once more spending his days and nights working as an educator and inspiring people who some of us might describe as disadvantaged. But between you and me, he was expecting more from this pursuit of his dream – nothing hugely significant happened and certainly no big realization that this was where his future lay. The people he met were interesting and sad but he had no idea what he was doing there. Jonezy started to question his actions and his choice to heed the voice of the old clock. He concluded that dreams, as strange and irrational as they can be, are sometimes worth listening to and sometimes they are not.

Jonezy's visa was about to run out so, with very little money, he followed a friend he had met while travelling to Amsterdam, where he rather fortuitously settled into a job writing his poetry for a travel company, who liked his style. The money was okay and the lifestyle was pleasant, if a little directionless. After a few months he found himself wondering again about his dreams. He was drawn to a coffee shop near a park, where he would go and drink coffee and sit and write at the same table every day (under an attractive clock with delicate silver features). He wondered about the path he'd taken and how he'd got to that place. Although now he had more time to pursue his aspirations, he no longer had any dream clock ticking away at him. It was here on one clear and cloudless day that the coffee shop owner called him over and spoke to him.

"I've seen you sitting here writing in your notebooks day after day as if you are waiting for something. Don't you have any home to go to?"

Then Joe Michael Jones told him about the dream and the ticking clock and his feeling that time was running out – how he'd been travelling to the East and then how he had ended up here in Amsterdam writing his poetry for people who wanted to get away. The man laughed and said:

"Now you listen to me, you don't want to go listening to your dreams. I'll tell you something. Last night I had the most ridiculous dream. I dreamt I was in an old clockworks that was half open to the weather, and there was a great big clock hanging off the front of it that had stopped ticking . . . in Derby in England it was, and there I was, and I was digging in the garden under a gnarled old tree where the roots went deep into the earth. Well, in those roots there was an ancient suitcase and in it was my fortune. But if you think I'm going to follow dream fortunes like that you've another thing coming. If you listen to me . . ."

But at that moment Joe Michael Jones wasn't listening. He'd picked up his notebook and was on the next bus back to England, back home to Derby. And he didn't waste any time when he got there either. He gathered his friends together who were still living and working away in that old building, and together they dug in the garden under the tree where he used to sit, with the crazy roots. Sure enough, before long, they struck an ancient looking suitcase and inside were at least one hundred exquisite clocks, worth a fortune in today's market, along with the deeds of that old building and the scribblings of a Victorian clockmaker.

Well, there was enough money from the sale of the contents of that suitcase to restore the clockworks and from that day on the building became a haven of creativity where the ordinary people of Derby (some of whom might be described as disadvantaged) could come to eat, read, play, work in the garden and be inspired. So Joe Michael Jones, 'Jonezy' to his friends, lived happily to the end of his days and they had a plaque, in old gilt and thrush-egg blue, put above the door and on it were the words, *'Dreams – sometimes they are worth listening to.'*

SARA-MAE TUSON

ILL ANGELS
HAUNT ME

▫ ▫ ▫ ▫ ▫

Her voice was crackly on the end of the line. I held the phone in the crook of my neck and tried not to drive off the road. I was still almost sixteen hours away!

"Susie, what's happening?"

Her voice slid in and out with a faint hiss as music insinuated itself down the wire.

"Susie! Speak to me, please!"

"It's like a dream ... but I'm afraid. I ..." I could hear her begin to sob.

Her voice faded, but the music got louder and as it did my head felt light and strange, my eyes closing irresistibly ...

The lights from the truck bearing down on me swam into view. I screamed as I swung on the steering wheel with all my might, driving off into the desert dust on the side of the highway ...

Desert dust?

I blinked and looked around again trying to orientate myself. Around me were the flat green fields of Surrey. A shake pealed through my body like the deep chime of a church bell. The hazard lights from the dashboard winked, persistent. I leaned back and looked at my watch. No more than half a minute had passed. Rubbing my temples, I reached into the glove compartment, scrabbling around for a KitKat. I must have let my blood sugar get too low – with the worry, the rush, I'd forgotten.

For a second I had seen it, like a mirage: *the desert dust, the land stretching out as the highway spooled out in front of me. No cars, nothing except the red evening sky and the elongated tongue of the road lapping at the wheels of the car.*

I ate the chocolate quickly, matching salt to sweet as the sweat from my fear mingled with the heat melting the chocolate.

What's happening to you, Susie? I wondered. The darkness eased itself down around me, as the first white flakes began to fall.

The airport was full of holiday revellers waiting to catch long delayed flights.

"I'm sorry, madam," the woman was saying. "Truly I am, but the snow . . ."

"It's an emergency!" I hated to yell. I lowered my voice. There was a queue behind me.

"Hey, we're *all* waiting for our flights," the man behind me growled.

The woman at the counter smoothed a strand of blonde hair behind her ear.

"I have to leave tonight; it's a matter of life or death . . ."

She looked away from me, keeping her eyes on the computer screen.

"I'm doing my best, madam, but all flights to Nevada have been cancelled. There's nothing I can do," she repeated.

The man behind me pushed his way forward and I was shoved to one side as the other passengers clamoured for the woman's attention. I stood still for a minute feeling numb, until my phone rang and I came out of my reverie with a jolt.

"Susie?" I said, rushing away from the desk.

"Diane, it's me. What's going on? Where are you?"

My heart sank. I had no idea if she was still alive. I'd been almost delirious with relief when I'd thought she'd called me back.

"Pete, I can't talk now," I said absently.

"My God! Where are you? Do you know you've left your insulin here?"

I was casting my eye over the board looking for flights that were still leaving for the U.S. There had to be something.

"Diane! Please, sweetheart!"

The desperate tone in his voice tugged at my heart, but distantly.

"I've got a spare pack in the car." I started to hang up.

"Is this about Susie? If you leave me again to rescue that little junkie . . ."

My finger hesitated and I put the phone to my ear again.

"I have to go to her, Pete. I have to find her. This time it's serious, I know it."

He sighed. I could almost see his thick brows beetling into a frown. I tried to will him to understand but he never had, not really.

When he spoke his voice was bleak.

"What makes this time any different?"

There was a flight to New York leaving in half an hour.

I started to run.

I sat on the plane allowing the sweat to prickle over my face, my back sore and stiff from tension. Taking out my spare kit, I started to check my blood sugar. The woman in the next aisle stared at me in fascination as I lifted my shirt to bare my pale stomach.

"Ma'am . . ." the stewardess began, but I looked up at her and she saw the kit open on the tray in front of me. She swallowed back what she was going to say and eased her face into a smile. Her neat red cravat was a little crooked, and her tightly bound black hair escaped in unruly tendrils around her face, like weeds in a well-tended garden.

"You'll have to put that up again when we begin to taxi," she said in an admonishing tone.

I didn't reply.

Looking out over the wing, I willed the plane to start moving, to take me to her at last.

I took out a picture of her. She is sitting on the old swing that our father hung in the back garden from the massive oak that has been there for over a hundred years. Her red hair is startling, her mouth open as she laughs, kicking her legs up. She looks innocent, so joyous. I never had her relish for life.

Oh Susie, please be okay.

". . . Why America? Why *Las Vegas* of all places in America?"

She was haphazardly stuffing her clothing into a beaten-up leather case. Her long hair hung heavy over her eyes, her full mouth petulant. Bangles clinked on her wrists, disguising the scars. Her jaw was set, stubborn. I lowered my voice, trying to swallow over the dryness in my throat.

"At least wait until I finish my degree, then I can come with you."

"And leave Pete?"

She turned suddenly, folding her arms. Her skin was fresh looking, like a blank page waiting to be written on.

"Yes, no . . . he'll wait for me."

"No he won't, and anyway . . . you love him."

She sighed and came closer. Gently she placed her hands on either side of my face.

"But I need you, Susie," I whispered.

"I know," she said. She took out our lucky penny and placed it in my palm. "We're two halves . . ."

"Of the same coin," I finished.

"Always," she said and she kissed me.

She broke away and I thought my heart would break.

"You can't come with me, Di."

15 Cherry Hollow on the Hill, she'd whispered. *It's the most beautiful party I've ever seen . . .*

🐦

My eyes close and I'm turning the corner in a low-slung saloon. The car slides through the dark wetly as we follow the winding road towards the lights ahead. The low pulse of music is hypnotic. I turn my head to the man sitting next to me. His blond hair is thick and shiny, pasted back on his head. I can't tell what colour his eyes are but he smiles at me and something tightens low in my gut. I lick my lips and look down at my lap. I'm wearing a green silk dress.

He puts his hand on my knee. A car flashes past us and I blink as the headlights blind me for a second. As I turn again to the man beside me a scream rises up in my throat because I see what has been hidden. A skull, the jaw hanging limp, rotting flesh dangling in strips from the bone . . .

"What's wrong, honey?" his deep voice is beautiful, lilting and sweet. I look down and see that his hand on the gearstick is green and rotting as well. I am paralysed with fear so I squeeze my eyes shut. My heart lurches in terror but I force myself to look again.

His face is perfect, serene, with only a hint of concern for me. I look down and see his strong, tanned hand. The nails are well manicured. He squeezes my knee and slides his hand up my thigh.

"I'm a little hot," I say, trying to dazzle him with my smile. I open the window, feeling sick.

It's happening again. The visions.

As we turn in at the drive I can hear shouts of laughter and the low buzz of talk. Suddenly a beautiful brunette runs across the gravel in a yellow slip, shrieking with laughter as two men pursue her around the corner. After a second or two we hear splashes and more shrieks. I grin at him and he smiles wolfishly, his teeth white, glinting in the darkness.

He comes around to my side and opens the door, leaning in to kiss me first.

"You'll enjoy this, I promise," he says and I glance quickly up into the mirror to check my lipstick. Pursing my lips, I brush a strand of scarlet hair back from my eyes. I can feel him watching me as I smooth a finger around my bottom lip, smacking them together. I feel the weight of his eyes on me, not like the other men I've been with, not with ownership, but indulgence.

"You're beautiful," he says. "You'll fit right in here," and the shadow on my heart from my morbid vision leaves me. I want to feel nothing – he will help me to feel nothing.

No fear. He promised me that.

I smile as I take his hand and we go up the wide stone steps into the house.

I feel someone prodding my arm gently. "We're here, Miss," a low voice is saying softly. I open my eyes. The young man's brown hair is faintly ruffled. His face is far too close. For a second I blink, staring at him in panic, not knowing where I am. And then I remember. I whip my seatbelt off and grab my bags, shoving past him.

"Hey!" he yells, "You forgot your . . ."

From New York I catch a flight to Nevada.

The house is richly decorated and ornate, if a little cold. I shiver as we cross the threshold and then the music hits me and I'm carried away in the rhythms and the sway of it. He pulls me into his arms and whispers, "Wouldn't you like it to go on forever?" His cool breath lingers on my hot flesh like a caress. I look around at the swirling dancers. They all move with a grace and sinuous swing that almost looks choreographed. Richly brocaded curtains hang heavily, whilst the furnishings look like they belong in an antique shop, or one of the old National Trust estates back in England. The thought of England makes the light seem to fade, the glamour and the colour seem to dissipate a little. The dancers near us slow down and turn to look at me. Their eyes are blank and staring like a flock of ravens.

"Excuse me," I say, squeezing his hand, suddenly feeling claustrophobic, "I just need to make a call."

I stumble outside and as I try to cross the porch I feel a thickness to the air. I can't seem to step beyond it and out into the garden. I think about pushing forward, but a strange reluctance seizes me. I start to fumble in my purse.

A dog, old and mangy, shuffles out from the shadows and stands just at the edge of the pool of light. "Come here, boy," I whisper, but he doesn't move.

"Here, boy!" I say, a little more urgently. For some reason it seems important that the little dog acknowledges me. But he doesn't move, only sniffs the air and starts to whimper softly. I take my mobile out of my gold clutch bag. I realise my hands are shaking. A small bag of coke falls out when I take out the phone. Swearing softly, I drop down to pick it up. The dog yelps.

"What?" I whisper. He turns suddenly and scampers away. I dial Di's number.

It's been nothing but desert for ages. Finally, I see the sign and I turn instinctively. As the car wheels bite gravel I remember the smell of desert dust from my hallucination and speed up.

I turn back and he's standing right behind me. From somewhere far away I hear the dog barking fiercely, madly.

"Let's go back in, shall we?" His eyes are deep-set. He is so beautiful in the moonlight. I try to look closer, to concentrate, because I realise I still don't know what colour they are.

He draws me up the stairs and I see them all waiting at the top, the music pulsing in the background. They are looking at me. Everyone has shadows in the hollows of their eyes.

I feel a sense of panic as the crowd closes in around me, putting their bony hands on my arms, but the music seeps into my brain and all I want to do is dance.

In the past when she'd passed out, a needle in her arm or blood seeping from her nose, I'd sometimes get flashes of what she saw, and I usually knew how to get to her quickly, especially when she was near death. Blinking back tears, I thought about how long it'd been since the last time I'd heard from her.

The road was old and rutted, with cacti bristling alongside it, peopling the sparse landscape with their abstract forms. I knew I was close. For a second I thought I heard music and the bright yellow light blurred as I felt my head going down. Then the loud bray of the car horn shocked me back into consciousness and I slammed on the brakes as the car skidded in the gravel.

Ahead of me was an old, dilapidated house. Huge and empty, the front door long since collapsed in on itself from age and heat. The loud squawk of a carrion crow startled me. I thought I'd rest here a while before going in.

When Susie was a little girl she'd often crawl into bed with me. Our beds were identical, like most of our clothes, even though we had totally different personalities. Mum always insisted that we match. Susie would climb in, clutching me with her cold little hands, her feet shimmying up my legs, icy and clammy with sweat.

"You see them again?" I'd whisper. She'd shake with fear, unable to talk.

"Shhh. You're safe with me, Susie, I'll keep you safe."

And because I knew it made her feel better, I'd shatter the late night calm with my strongest voice, "Go away and leave my sister alone!"

After a while her body would slowly warm up and her grip on me would loosen as she slept. But I'd stare into the dark for hours wondering why they never came for me.

I look up at dusty steps to the long, wide porch. The house is dark and empty through the hole in the doorway. I hesitate at the top step, reluctant to go in. Suddenly I hear a whimpering noise and I feel a dampness spreading on my leg. I jump, only to see a small, mangy dog scrabbling at my ankles trying ineffectually to pull at my jeans.

Kneeling down, I push him away, keeping him at arm's

length. "What's the matter, puppy?" The dog looks half starved.

Responding to my low, calming voice the dog eases back a step or two and shudders from the tip of its nose to the end of its dirty brown tail. It shuffles a few steps towards my car and then stops and looks at me enquiringly. With my back to the house I feel a cold shiver travel up my spine like a breeze. Only . . . the sky is cloudless and the sun beats down on the little dog, on the wide open desert around me and on the distant highway like a shimmering ribbon on the edge of the horizon. Night will fall soon. I can feel the faintness that I get when I haven't injected, when my sugar level drops. I watch the sun boiling a wide swathe through the ruddy clouds. I can feel her close by.

Serene at last.

The dog edges back towards me and licks my hand. As the dark brushes its fingers across the land and the light bleeds away I start to hear the music, faint but there. I think I hear the tinkle of her laugh.

"Go home, boy," I say to the dog. "Go home."

GEMMA SELTZER

MY SISTER
LIKE THIS

□ □ □ □ □

When she finds me, I am wondering what would happen if I move forward and actually step over the yellow line, the thick lump of colour that marks the boundary between safety and danger. My train arrived exactly eleven minutes ago.

Stop it, she says. Whatever you're about to do. Stop.

I turn. Lila is wearing a jacket printed with cherries; she's pinned a cherry brooch to the left lapel and it sags under the weight. Her red dreadlocked hair is gathered into two bunches which burst from the back of her head like twigs.

Nice coat, I say, before returning to the railway tracks. I lean forward. I'm showing her I could do it.

She looks down at herself and plucks at her sleeve. I don't care if you hate it.

I choose not to reply, because I feel the conversation must end before she notices that the t-shirt I'm wearing was stolen from her wardrobe.

I haven't got much food in, Lila says. Are you staying for dinner?

Maybe, I say.

That's really helpful, she replies. Then, I thought Jack might be around, but no. He said he'd have loved to see you. He's at some botany conference all weekend. Last minute invite to speak, which is a great opportunity for him.

I watch her grope for items in her handbag. Lila and I look alike. People have always said so. Our mannerisms mirror each other, our tone of voice. I see myself in her, how I could be if I chose another way of living.

She stops her fumbling to say, Get away from there.

Whatever she was searching for, it isn't in the bag.

I'm not doing anything, I say, but retreat from the edge anyway. I'm facing her now. I feel my eyes prickle but I tell myself it doesn't matter. Not everything needs to be a battle and besides, there's no-one else at the station to witness my surrender.

She sighs. I think you wanted me to find you like this. That's why you asked me to come right onto the platform.

I just didn't want to search the endless rows of cars for your rusty one.

I think you're desperate for attention, she says.

I say, I was actually going to hurl myself onto the tracks. There's hollow ringing inside of me.

I doubt you're brave enough.

You couldn't possibly know, I reply.

And how's everyone's favourite poetic genius coping? she asks.

I tell her that Ralph is in our flat, painting the walls and watching them dry, noting down ideas that strike him as he works. I say, I don't doubt it will keep him occupied for some time.

Lila snorts. How clever.

A man in a trilby hat makes his way across the platform with two young boys in tow. He lets go of their hands and raps on the station office window, but it's clearly unstaffed. He jabs at the machine, grabs his tickets, shreds them into tiny pieces and throws them upwards. The children watch as orange and white confetti momentarily fills the air.

My sister pulls a cardigan from her bag and tells me to put it on. As a small rebellion, I wrap it around my neck like a scarf. It smells of Lila, both soapy and soupy. She motions with her head and we both walk towards the exit.

On the stairs, she elbows me in the ribs. You are so annoying.

So are you, I say.

We're both over thirty but this is how we talk.

In the hospital, I told the nurse that there was always two of us – even when we were many – and that I didn't speak until I was eight. To me, Lila represented time: when I came along three years later everything had already started. My sister had the words; she used them, and how.

'Countries' was a game we liked to play. Lila was always Italy – we'd been to Rome once – a country which slapped sunshine on bodies and was shaped like a boot thrust into the knees of Sardinia. Perhaps because our imaginations were limited to the images we saw on television, I was Ethiopia and would sit in mournful silence as my sister sang about feeding the world, brandishing chocolate bars I was forbidden to eat.

I had another game: 'Babies.' I made the rules and chose the participants. I was the mother, and I would spend hours dressing, teaching and pacifying all my dolls, until it was time for dinner. I had prams, bonnets and bottles to assist in the endless task of looking after the babies. But despite my dedication, I never was a good enough parent.

Why don't you sit forward for me? the nurse said, plumping my pillow.

I'll tell you about Sea Pony Sarah, I said. I described the plastic toy, which was the size of my six-year-old hand, and how I carried her in my pocket for nine months until, on Yom Kippur afternoon when all the adults were fasting and resting in armchairs and the house smelled of stale breath, I felt a prod in my belly and knew the time had come.

We had our cousins with us that day. I found them too loud and snarling, just a series of arms and feet and mouths in motion. My sister would gather them around her, performing and distracting them from probing at my silence. With her as a diversion, I ran upstairs, closed the door and lay on my bed. Then, I spread my legs wide, pressed my palms on my knees and clenched my teeth. I pushed Sea Pony Sarah right up there, as far as she would go, twisting and twisting, her hair poking out. I think it was painful but I was lost in my head, my mind taking a stroll through fantasy streets. It seemed plausible that life had changed direction and I was giving birth. I remember panting, as clammy women under white sheets did in films, and breathing and making little huffing sounds at the back of my throat.

That's when Lila walked into my bedroom.

Get that out, she said, her face red. Now.

She could have laughed, or run to tell our parents. But she didn't. Once I was dressed properly, my sister took me by the wrist, led me to the living room and never spoke of it again.

Little girls and their ways, the nurse said.

A pair of heels dashed in a quickstep along the tiled floor of the ward.

On the way to her house, Lila stops the car to show me how the salads are growing in her allotment. I have to feign interest because I'm too self-involved to care.

She says, I'm sorry I didn't come to see you. I know mum and dad did, so I figured it was okay.

I search inside for the right response. I say, I won't be able to have children. Lazy ovaries. Saying it aloud is not as hard as I anticipated.

Lila fills a red watering can that she passes to me. Aim for there, she says, gesturing to a dry patch.

I stand and pour, looking at her neat labels by every row. Don't you get bored of all this? I ask.

Lila hesitates before saying, Jack and I used to tend it together. She pulls at her bracelet, decorated with cherries. She sees something in the charms, her eyes narrow. She says, But now he can't be bothered.

Too busy touching up plants?

I don't expect an answer. I can live with her silence. Besides, Ralph always says I should allow Lila more space in our relationship. I watch the wellies march about and Lila pull or pat green things.

After a while she says, So, adopt. It's much easier than you think. I have friends who have done and they love the child as much as they would their own. She sounds like she is reading the words from a script, but I do want to believe her. If you and Ralph are serious about wanting kids, then you have to consider the alternatives, she says. You can't put yourself through any more of this.

I'm quick to reply. I could.

She puts her muddy hands on my shoulders. Look, you have to stop now. Your body won't take another round of tests and treatments. A finger on her right hand bends permanently to one side, a consequence of years of childhood sucking. She says, And you will be absolutely okay.

Will I?

Yes. You're just too sensitive. You always have been.

I just want a baby.

Does she flinch? I think she does. But all she says is, I know you do. Then, I'm done here, shall we go?

And I nod and say, Yes, but it's with the same tone that I could have used for no.

Back at her house, Lila plays the part of a good wife and mother, though she is neither. Jack, the botanist boyfriend, is in Wales discussing rare orchids or trunk rot. His daughter, who usually lives with them, is enjoying time with her other parents. My sister tells me this as she picks mint leaves and makes us tea. I think she is angry, but I can't be sure.

Lila offers me chocolate biscuits from a tin and does not

react when I grab four, break them apart and fill my mouth until I cannot breathe. As I cough through the crumbs, she hands me a glass of water and watches me with tight eyes. When I finish, I look at her through the bottom of the tumbler, the drops of liquid sliding over her.

My sense of curiosity is awakened as I see my sister ticking items from a list on the kitchen table. The Post-it note has lost its stickiness and moves around as she tries to mark the paper. Eventually, she uses a finger to keep it in place. I wonder if my name is there and I consider how she would write about me, how she would put me into words.

Without looking up, my sister says, So, what are you doing here?

I lower my head. Nearby, someone is hammering frantically, desperate to finish the shed, affix the trellis or whatever it is people do around here.

She chooses a different approach. I just can't believe you went through it all again. We were all so worried.

It's nothing to do with anyone else, I say.

She folds her arms under her breasts, making a shelf for them. They rose when I was still in junior school and now they sit firm on her body, her armour against the world.

I used to find you on the window ledge. The one on the landing, do you remember?

Yes, I say.

Well, mum never did! Imagine. For God's sake, the station? She slams the heel of her hand against the table. Look, do you know how many people die each year by falling under trains? You wouldn't go instantly either. Your life would ebb away slowly and painfully.

Don't.

Lila says, When you finally did die, no-one would collect the pieces of you until the police were called and evidence taken.

I wonder if there are other people like us, having this type of conversation, in this city. I look for something to focus on and choose a space on the sideboard where a photo frame must've sat.

You'd just be lying there in gross, misshapen chunks, she says with finality in her voice.

The doctor left after he listened to my chest. He handed me a referral letter and an envelope of flimsy X-rays. I decided Ralph should look first. There was an elderly woman walking by, I remember, pushing a frame forward then pausing for her feet to catch up. The nurse arrived.

I said, I was seven when I fell into our paddling pool.

Get some rest now, she replied.

I was in our back garden and the pool had Disney characters on it, frolicking in a circus design. I remember enjoying the sensation of weightlessness as I tripped and flew head-first into the water. I heard sound around me, but muted, far away.

I was happy in the quiet. My world had been filled with my sister's dancing and singing spectacle, my mother's cross-stitch and my father's moussakas. I felt the liquid rush through my nose, down the back of my throat, into my lungs. The pain came from my stomach, where the ground hit like a rising punch.

Then I felt a wave through the water, a thick arm underneath me and I was being scooped upwards, I was flying, and my face was out of that clear, lovely place. My sister held me to her as I barked water. Before my desperate mother reached us, Lila and I sat together by the pool, chests heaving, wet bodies touching. I told the nurse I had been overwhelmed. I remember the feeling: I had not known my sister could be like this.

Lila takes me back to the train station that evening. On the way, I play with the window controls, making the glass go up and then down, over and over. It's raining. The buildings flicker in the headlights and the car throws up water onto the windscreen as it slides through the streets.

She stuffs her foot onto the brake and stops the car. Glaring at me, she says, You'll let the rain in if you keep doing that.

A flower of panic blooms inside of me, but I swallow it down.

Lila slowly bends onto the steering wheel, rests her head on her arms. Then she jerks her head and sneezes twice into a closed palm.

Always prepared, I dig into my pocket and pull out a pack of tissues. Kleenex Balsam, no less.

Here, I say, passing them to her.

She looks at me, eyes shiny.

Thank you, she says. I appreciate it. She pulls at a tissue, presses it to each side of her nose, then her eyes.

I notice how thin my sister is, and pale.

I speak quietly. Anytime.

Yeah?

I step up to the moment and say, Yeah. Only the best for you. These ones have a layer of protective balm. Isn't that good?

She nods. That's great.

Lila starts the engine and we sit in silence. I take myself to the edge of places; clarity comes when I look down and see the things I can't anywhere else. I've wanted to do something for my sister for a long time.

It's late but not yet dark. As we drive, we watch a group of teenage girls use their handbags for cover as they run shrieking through the streets. They splash through puddles together, two of them holding hands.

PANOS KARNEZIS

AN AFTERNOON OUTING

□ □ □ □ □

The lake was a large reservoir serving the capital some distance away. There were firs and pines on its banks and steep slopes that ascended towards a public road tracing the rim of the stone dam, which was built in an arch like the seats of an ancient amphitheatre. On the side of the road, commanding a splendid view of emerald placid waters and dense forests, was a small coffee shop. A few iron tables and some chairs were set on the gravel under the sun, while under the eaves of the tiled roof, in the shadow, hung a cage with a pair of canaries. It was a quiet afternoon. Very rarely a car drove down the public road. When it did it passed the sharp bends slowly, crossed the narrow rim of the dam and disappeared in the darkness of the trees on the other side. The birds chirped and sometimes the cicadas joined in, but the canaries in the cage always slept, balancing their bodies side to side on a little plastic swing. There were only two people in the coffee shop at that time. They were sitting on the same side of a table on the gravel in front of the shop itself, as far away from the adobe building as possible.

"Have you made up your mind?" the man asked.

The boy raised the price list. It was a laminated piece of faded card soiled with dried coffee rings. The coffee markings were like rubber stamp impressions on some official document.

"Orange," he replied.

The man nodded and snapped his fingers. The waiter appeared at the door of the coffee shop and looked at the raised arm. Then he went back inside. The man lowered his arm and elbowed the boy.

"You can have beer," he said and winked. "I promise not to tell."

"Orange," the boy repeated.

The afternoon heat had begun to silence the birds, but the buzzing of the cicadas increased: it sounded like a repeated telegraph broadcast. The shadow of the two people, of their chairs and of the table in front of them, stretched out on the gravel and fell off the edge of the precipice descending towards the reservoir.

"Go on," the man said. "Have a beer. At your age I used to drink a grown man under the table."

He had a thick growth of dark curly hair that had begun to turn grey down the sides, a long straight nose, narrow lips, and the absolute determination of one intending to be a decorated veteran of life rather than another of its casualties.

"Is it because of your mother?" he asked.

"She would smell it."

The man gave the boy the side look of an accomplice and grinned.

"Boy, oh boy."

"Orange juice," the boy said.

A loud sizzling came from inside the coffee shop and soon the smell of fat reached the noses of the two afternoon customers. The man licked his lips and remembered he had had nothing to eat all day.

"How old are you?" he asked.

He wore a shirt with short sleeves, a pair of immaculately pressed linen trousers and newly bought espadrilles. A sharp crease ran down each trouser leg: it was the latest trend in fashion. The sizzling abated and a radio went on inside the coffee shop. After a careful search its needle came to rest over a sponsored broadcast of popular songs. The cicadas stopped to listen to the music. The quiet afternoon was not so quiet anymore but not noisy either – it was as noisy as lying next to a sleeping partner who snores a little. The man noticed a stain on his shoe. He immediately placed his foot on the strut of the table and began to rub the dust with his thumb.

"Sixteen," the boy answered.

The waiter now arrived with the tray under his arm. He was not much older than the boy but his few years of employment had already set his young face in an expression of universal indifference. The man gave their order and the waiter nodded and walked slowly back to the coffee shop, rapping on the tin tray and whistling the tune that played at that moment on the radio. The man watched him return inside the adobe building.

"Sixteen," he echoed. "Yes. Of course."

He went back to rubbing his espadrille until the stain was gone and the fabric was neat and white again. After giving it a final inspection, he reluctantly placed his foot back on the gravel. The surface of the reservoir was as flat as a metallic sheet and shone in the sun. Some seagulls arrived and circled the reservoir and screeched and sat on the shining surface. The boy began to rock in his chair. Slowly its iron legs sank deeper into the gravel. He was dressed in a shirt of some premier league football team and an old pair of jeans. His elbows were chafed and his hands rough. His skin had a copper tint. It was the colour of someone who spends time in the sun – not a sunbather; more like a builder or an athlete.

A hot wind blew and the tree branches shook. The pine needles fluttered like ornamental tassels and let out a hissing sound. The waiter returned with a bottle of orange-ade and a large coffee on his tray. He placed both on the table, tucked the tray under his arm and fished a brass opener from his pocket.

"We asked for orange *juice*," the man said.

The waiter shrugged.

"We only sell bottled."

The man picked up the laminated card on the table.

"It says it here." He put his finger on the list and read out: "*Orange juice.*"

"That's old. The business now operates under new management."

"This is fine," said the boy.

"You should update the price list," the man said.

"I like orangeade," said the boy.

The waiter looked at the boy and nodded respectfully. He put the opener on the bottle on the table, and took off the cap using only one hand. He threw the cap to the gravel, pulled a plastic straw from his pocket and left that on the table too.

"Want anything to eat?" the man asked. "Are you hungry?"

The boy shook his head.

"But it's lunchtime," the man said.

The boy put the straw in the bottle and began to suck the orangeade.

"Does the new management toast bread?" the man asked.

"Egg mayonnaise or ham and cheese?"

"Cheese and ham."

The waiter tapped his fingers on the tray and turned to leave.

"Bring two," the man called after him.

A moment later he was eating the toasted sandwich. He ate with great appetite, interrupting his chewing only to sip coffee. He had finished when he looked up from his plate and saw that the boy had not touched his food. He was about to say something when he saw a snake cross the road. He jumped off his chair.

"Did you see that?" he asked. "Did you see?"

The boy turned his head slowly, with his lips still on the straw in his bottle.

"Did you see the snake?"

"There is nothing."

The man pointed to a thorny shrub on the edge of the dusty asphalt.

"An adder," he said. "Big one. Grey. I saw the stripes."

"I didn't see it."

"Wait."

They waited for several seconds but nothing happened. The boy drank his orangeade while the man held his breath and watched. Finally he sat down again.

"It was there," he said.

The road was empty and silent. It traversed the hills and the forest like the bed of a dried-up river that once sprang from a secret cleft in the mountains and moved downwards, always downwards, eroding the ancient rock, carving out little valleys and shallow gorges or simply slipping over the polished stone, slowing down at a flatland, speeding up at a rapid, carrying away wood and gravel, meandering like an endless snake.

"It is venomous," said the man. "But it rarely bites."

An engine was heard and a moment later a small car drove past the coffee shop and headed in the direction of the dam. As soon as it came to the narrow part of the road that ran across the rim of the dam it stopped. Only one car could drive across the dam at a time. A stoplight at either end of the dam directed the traffic. When the light turned green the car started and drove until it reached the middle. There it stopped again and this time the driver switched off the engine. A young couple jumped out. For a while they took in the view before they began to take photographs. From the coffee shop, some distance away, the man and the boy watched in silence. The couple talked and laughed and posed for each other, then set the camera on the roof of their small car and embraced. They turned quiet and kissed for a long time.

"How are you doing at school?" the man asked.

"Fine."

"Do well and you can go to university. Do you want to?"

The boy shrugged his shoulders.

"Engineering is a good degree," said the man.

Another car came to the opposite end of the dam and started sounding its horn. The couple stopped kissing and laughed. They waved at the other car, took the camera from the roof of theirs and jumped in. The small car drove off and the other one crossed the dam. It did not stop. It drove to the other side, past the coffee shop and down the hairpins that descended the hill. Far away were the sea and the faint outline of an island. The view from the coffee shop was truly majestic.

"As an engineer you could work in a factory," said the man.

The air smelled of petrol. When the music ended on the radio inside the coffee shop and the commercials started, someone turned it off. The cicadas began again then. The hot wind was still blowing and the man found his handkerchief and wiped his forehead. He looked at the soaked square cloth with misery, folded it in two and put it back in his pocket. Then he had a quick glance at his watch.

"There is some shift work if you work in a factory but nothing like being . . . a doctor, let's say," he said.

The boy was finishing his drink. His toasted sandwich was still on his plate, untried. The bread was burned round the edges and the melted cheese had trickled out into yellow brittle tongues. The man looked at it: he was still hungry.

"But if you don't like maths, you could always study Law."

The road was empty, the air clear and silent apart from the cicadas, and in the reservoir the water still reflected the sun, when the canaries woke up and immediately began to chirp. The waiter walked out of the shop and filled their bottle with water and their cup with seed. The man at the table checked his watch again and sat up in his chair.

"Your mother will be waiting," he said.

While the boy sucked the last of his drink the man arched back his spine, stretched his shoulders and sighed. A line ran along the length of the steep banks of the reservoir, where the water had been all winter. But the summer drought had long started and every week now the level dropped a little, exposing long stems of reeds and thick beds of mud, where worms and frogs and beetles buried themselves.

"Let's do something again soon," the man said. "Is Sunday fine?"

"I have football."

The man nodded.

"Fine. Some other day; I will talk to your mother."

He snapped his fingers and found his wallet. When the waiter came he opened it. Then he hesitated.

"You want another orangeade before we go?"

"I'll have a beer," the boy said.

SALMAN RUSHDIE

GOOD ADVICE IS RARER THAN RUBIES

□ □ □ □ □

On the last Tuesday of the month, the dawn bus, its head-lamps still shining, brought Miss Rehana to the gates of the British Consulate. It arrived pushing a cloud of dust, veiling her beauty from the eyes of strangers until she descended. The bus was brightly painted in multicoloured arabesques, and on the front it said 'MOVE OVER DARLING' in green and gold letters; on the back it added 'TATA-BATA' and also 'O.K. GOOD-LIFE.' Miss Rehana told the driver it was a beautiful bus, and he jumped down and held the door open for her, bowing theatrically as she descended.

Miss Rehana's eyes were large and black and bright enough not to need the help of antimony, and when the advice expert Muhammad Ali saw them he felt himself becoming young again. He watched her approaching the Consulate gates as the light strengthened, and asking the bearded lala who guarded them in a gold-buttoned khaki uniform with a cockaded turban when they would open. The lala, usually so rude to the Consulate's Tuesday women, answered Miss Rehana with something like courtesy.

"Half an hour," he said gruffly. "Maybe two hours. Who knows? The sahibs are eating their breakfast."

The dusty compound between the bus stop and the Consulate was already full of Tuesday women, some veiled, a few barefaced like Miss Rehana. They all looked frightened, and leaned heavily on the arms of uncles or brothers, who were trying to look confident. But Miss Rehana had come on her own, and did not seem at all alarmed.

Muhammad Ali, who specialised in advising the most vulnerable-looking of these weekly supplicants, found his feet leading him towards the strange, big-eyed, independent girl.

"Miss," he began. "You have come for a permit to London, I think so?"

She was standing at a hot-snack stall in the little shantytown by the edge of the compound, munching chilli-pakoras contentedly. She turned to look at him, and at close range those eyes did bad things to his digestive tract.

"Yes, I have."

"Then, please, you allow me to give some advice? Small cost only."

Miss Rehana smiled. "Good advice is rarer than rubies,"

she said. "But alas, I cannot pay. I am an orphan, not one of your wealthy ladies."

"Trust my grey hairs," Muhammad Ali urged her. "My advice is well tempered by experience. You will certainly find it good."

She shook her head. "I tell you I am a poor potato. There are women here with male family members, all earning good wages. Go to them. Good advice should find good money."

I am going crazy, Muhammad Ali thought, because he heard his voice telling her of its own volition, "Miss, I have been drawn to you by Fate. What to do? Our meeting was written. I also am a poor man only, but for you my advice comes free."

She smiled again. "Then I must surely listen. When Fate sends a gift, one receives good fortune."

He led her to the low wooden desk in his own special corner of the shanty-town. She followed, continuing to eat pakoras from a little newspaper packet. She did not offer him any.

Muhammad Ali put a cushion on the dusty ground. "Please to sit." She did as he asked. He sat cross-legged across the desk from her, conscious that two or three dozen pairs of male eyes were watching him enviously, that all the other shanty-town men were ogling the latest young lovely to be charmed by the old grey-hair fraud. He took a deep breath to settle himself.

"Name, please."

"Miss Rehana," she told him. "Fiancée of Mustafa Dar of Bradford, London."

"Bradford, England," he corrected her gently. "London is a town only, like Multan or Bahawalpur. England is a great nation full of the coldest fish in the world."

"I see. Thank you," she responded gravely, so that he was unsure if she was making fun of him.

"You have filled application form? Then let me see, please."

She passed him a neatly folded document in a brown envelope.

"Is it OK?" For the first time there was a note of anxiety in her voice.

He patted the desk quite near the place where her hand rested. "I am certain," he said. "Wait on and I will check."

She finished the pakoras while he scanned her papers.

"Tip-top," he pronounced at length. "All in order."

"Thank you for your advice," she said, making as if to rise. "I'll go now and wait by the gate."

"What are you thinking?" he cried loudly, smiting his forehead. "You consider this is easy business? Just give the form and poof, with a big smile they hand over the permit? Miss Rehana, I tell you, you are entering a worse place than any police station."

"Is is so truly?" His oratory had done the trick. She was a captive audience now, and he would be able to look at her for a few moments longer.

Drawing another calming breath, he launched into his set speech. He told her that the sahibs thought that all the women who came on Tuesdays, claming to be dependents of bus drivers in Luton or chartered accountants in Manchester, were crooks and liars and cheats.

She protested, "But then I will simply tell them that I, for one, am no such thing!"

Her innocence made him shiver with fear for her. She was a sparrow, he told her, and they were men with hooded eyes, like hawks. He explained that they would ask her questions, personal questions, questions such as a lady's own brother would be too shy to ask. They would ask if she was virgin, and, if not, what her fiancé's love-making habits were, and what secret nicknames they had invented for one another.

Muhammad Ali spoke brutally, on purpose, to lessen the shock she would feel when it, or something like it, actually happened. Her eyes remained steady, but her hands began to flutter at the edges of the desk.

He went on:

"They will ask you how many rooms are in your family home, and what colour are the walls, and what days do you empty the rubbish. They will ask your man's mother's third cousin's aunt's step-daughter's middle name. And all these things they have already asked your Mustafa Dar in his Bradford. And if you make one mistake, you are finished."

"Yes," she said, and he could hear her disciplining her voice. "And what is your advice, old man?"

It was at this point that Muhammad Ali usually began to whisper urgently, to mention that he knew a man, a very good type, who worked in the Consulate, and through him, for a fee, the necessary papers could be delivered, with all the proper authenticating seals. Business was good, because the women would often pay him five hundred rupees or give him a gold bracelet for his pains, and go away happy.

They came from hundreds of miles away – he normally made sure of this before beginning to trick them – so even when they discovered they had been swindled they were unlikely to return. They went away to Sargodha or Lalukhet and began to pack, and who knows at what point they found out they had been gulled, but it was at a too-late point, anyway.

Life is hard, and an old man must live by his wits. It was not up to Muhammad Ali to have compassion for these Tuesday women.

But once again his voice betrayed him, and instead of starting his customary speech it began to reveal to her his greatest secret.

"Miss Rehana," his voice said, and he listened to it in amazement, "you are a rare person, a jewel, and for you I will do what I would not do for my own daughter, perhaps. One document has come into my possession that can solve all your worries at one stroke."

"And what is this sorcerer's paper?" she asked, her eyes unquestionably laughing at him now.

His voice fell low-as-low.

"Miss Rehana, it is a British passport. Completely genuine and pukka goods. I have a good friend who will put your name and photo, and then, hey-presto, England there you come!"

He had said it!

Anything was possible now, on this day of his insanity.

Probably he would give her the thing free-gratis, and then kick himself for a year afterwards.

Old fool, he berated himself. *The oldest fools are bewitched by the youngest girls.*

"Let me understand you," she was saying. "You are proposing I should commit a crime . . ."

"Not crime," he interposed. "Facilitation."

". . . and go to Bradford, London, illegally, and therefore justify the low opinion the Consulate sahibs have of us all. Old babuji, this is not good advice."

"Bradford, *England*," he corrected her mournfully. "You should not take my gift in such a spirit."

"Then how?"

"Bibi, I am a poor fellow, and I have offered this prize because you are so beautiful. Do not spit on my generosity. Take the thing. Or else don't take, go home, forget England, only do not go into that building and lose your dignity."

But she was on her feet, turning away from him, walking towards the gates, where the women had begun to cluster and the lala was swearing at them to be patient or none of them would be admitted at all.

"So be a fool," Muhammad Ali shouted after her. "What goes of my father's if you are?" (Meaning, what was it to him).

She did not turn.

"It is the curse of our people," he yelled. "We are poor, we are ignorant, and we completely refuse to learn."

"Hey, Muhammad Ali," the woman at the betel-nut stall called across to him. "Too bad, she likes them young."

That day Muhammad Ali did nothing but stand around near the Consulate gates. Many times he scolded himself, *Go from here, old goof, lady does not desire to speak with you any further.* But when she came out, she found him waiting.

"Salaam, advice wallah," she greeted him.

She seemed calm, and at peace with him again, and he thought, *My God, ya Allah, she has pulled it off. The British sahibs also have been drowning in her eyes and she has got her passage to England.*

He smiled at her hopefully. She smiled back with no trouble at all.

"Miss Rehana Begum," he said, "felicitations, daughter, on what is obviously your hour of triumph."

Impulsively, she took his forearm in her hand.

"Come," she said. "Let me buy you a pakora to thank you for your advice and to apologise for my rudeness, too."

They stood in the dust of the afternoon compound near the bus, which was getting ready to leave. Coolies were tying bedding rolls to the roof. A hawker shouted at the passengers, trying to sell them love stories and green medicines, both of which cured unhappiness. Miss Rehana and a happy Muhammad Ali ate their pakoras sitting on the bus's 'front mud-guard,' that is, the bumper. The old advice expert began softly to hum a tune from a movie soundtrack. The day's heat was gone.

"It was an arranged engagement," Miss Rehana said all at once. "I was nine years old when my parents fixed it.

Mustafa Dar was already thirty at that time, but my father wanted someone who could look after me as he had done himself and Mustafa was a man known to Daddyji as a solid type. Then my parents died and Mustafa Dar went to England and said he would send for me. That was many years ago. I have his photo, but he is like a stranger to me. Even his voice, I do not recognise it on the phone."

The confession took Muhammad Ali by surprise, but he nodded with what he hoped looked like wisdom.

"Still and after all," he said, "one's parents act in one's best interests. They found you a good and honest man who has kept his word and sent for you. And now you have a lifetime to get to know him, and to love."

He was puzzled, now, by the bitterness that had infected her smile.

"But, old man," she asked him, "why have you already packed me and posted me off to England?"

He stood up, shocked.

"You looked happy – so I just assumed . . . excuse me, but they turned you down or what?"

"I got all their questions wrong," she replied. "Distinguishing marks I put on the wrong cheeks, bathroom décor I completely redecorated, all absolutely topsy-turvy, you see."

"But what to do? How will you go?"

"Now I will go back to Lahore and my job. I work in a great house, as ayah to three good boys. They would have been sad to see me leave."

"But this is tragedy!" Muhammad Ali lamented. "Oh, how I pray that you had taken up my offer! Now, but, it is not possible, I regret to inform. Now they have your form on file, cross-check can be made, even the passport will not suffice.

"It is spoilt, all spoilt, and it could have been so easy if advice had been accepted in good time."

"I do not think," she told him, "I truly do not think you should be sad."

Her last smile, which he watched from the compound until the bus concealed it in a dust-cloud, was the happiest thing he had ever seen in his long, hot, hard, unloving life.

CRYING STORIES

KATE PULLINGER

ESTRANGED AND UNANTICIPATED

□ □ □ □ □

The urge to phone my father, and end our estrangement, did not go away.

In the past, before we stopped talking, my father was one of my landline-only people. Of course he didn't have a mobile himself, and he only made phone calls when he was seated at the phone table in the hallway, with his address book, and his landline, a plastic push-button model from the 1970s that was so old and crappy it had become retrospectively cool, like Pot Noodles and Ford Cortinas. Landline people like my father demand to be called from landlines; in his case, this was literal, as he found the idea he might be rung up by someone who was, in fact, in the middle of doing something other than ringing him – like taking a train, or walking down the street, or, heaven forbid, shopping – intensely annoying.

"What are you doing, ringing me from there?" he would shout, once I confessed my location. "Ring me when you get home." The line would cut off abruptly and I'd picture him getting up from the phone table and walking down the hallway.

In our house, our landline had become the opposite of useful. It sat there beside the TV, unloved, receiving calls from robots and insurance agents and loan sharks, costing me money. Well, not me, of course, but costing my wife money. Ruthie's money *is* my money, really, but that's another conversation.

The first step toward phoning my father involved refusing to go along with his landline-only policy, and programming his number into my mobile. That done, I was theoretically able to phone my father from wherever I wanted, whenever I wanted. Secondly, I decided it would be a good idea to make this call in a public place. That way, I would be less likely to lose my temper and start shouting. That way, once the call was over, I'd be less likely to cry. And the third step was to decide where and when: on the bus, on the way home from work. I'd be tired and so less likely to rise to his bait; I'd have dealt with mad people all day so I'd have more perspective; I'd be sitting down; and, perhaps most importantly, I wouldn't be taking time out from any other aspect of my life. Hard to know which of these things would make my father more angry, so I decided not to speculate.

The phone call went like this:

"Hello, Dad."

It was a cold January afternoon, raining, so the windows of the bus were fogged up and I couldn't see where we were

– somewhere on Regent Street, I think, in slow-moving traffic. I was sitting beside a very large man who smelled of damp wool.

"It's me." Of course it was "me," there isn't anyone else in the world who calls my father "Dad," at least as far as I know.

"I thought I would call."

The reception was clear, I didn't have to talk too loudly, which was a relief.

"I'm on the bus. On the way home from work."

"Yes. I'm fine."

"They're fine too."

"No, no-one has died."

"How are you?"

"I'm sorry to hear that."

"I'm sorry to hear that too."

The large damp man sitting next to me gathered together all his many belongings and left. I wiped the window with my glove: Piccadilly Circus.

"Yes, I'm still working there."

"Yes."

"No."

"Yes."

"No."

The questions, and all that they implied, stopped. We both sat in silence. I pictured him in the hallway. I wondered if he'd had the radiator fixed. I realised it is possible to hate someone and worry about them at the same time.

The bus had picked up speed. We were south of the river now and as I got closer to home, closer to my boy and my wife and our house, and our TV, and our landline, I wanted to stop talking to my father and concentrate on the rest of my day. I'd go to the butcher on the way home, pick up a nice pie or two for tea. The conversation had gone all right.

"What really happened to Mum?" I asked. I hadn't planned this; the words just came out, unanticipated. I laughed and said, "Don't worry, I don't expect you to reply."

But he'd already put the phone back into its cradle, got up from the phone table, and walked away, down the hallway.

AILSA COX

WHAT'S THE WEATHER LIKE?

□ □ □ □ □

What's the weather like? Not so bad. Trouble is, this wind. The wind. There always is a chill breeze or the threat of a shower. In a heatwave, he says, "Is it hot enough for you?" as if the sun's been playing nasty tricks. He makes a sound I can't spell, a bitter "k" that marks disgust or disenchantment.

The outlook is not good. My dad's looking chalky white, as if dusted by flour or talcum powder. I have a picture from my last visit, Mum and Dad sitting on a bench in the railway arches by the beach at Dawlish, the two of them bundled up in padded jackets, their Reactolite lenses blacked out by the sun, the two of them housed in that alcove like figures in a mausoleum. His monthly appointments are jotted down in my diary, next to deadlines and birthdays and stick-on reminders to deflea the cat.

How are you? *Not so bad. What's the weather like up there?* I'm standing by the phone, two hundred and seventy miles up north, looking out at the rain, my garden bulbs waiting to be planted, the fallen leaves clogged like papier-mâché. *Is it?* He is astonished. *You should see it here. Not a cloud in the sky.* So – how did you get on at the hospital? *Smashing,* he says vehemently. And my mother backs him up. *They're very good.*

What's the weather like? Terrible! Shocking! The days grow darker as we move through November, the bright blaze of late autumn suddenly turned ashen. I talk about coming to visit, but he says, "It's not worth it. Wait till the weather gets better."

My parents have retired, like so many people from the Midlands, to the place we used to go on holiday when they were young. The English Riviera. They go to dances and play bingo, meeting other pensioners with shared memories of the Delves, Palfrey or the Pleck, and go for cheap breaks at hotels in Weymouth or Newquay.

Their days are ordered, like their working lives, by strict routines – mealtimes and trips to the shops and carefully spaced cups of tea, the tablets ordered in sequence next to the saucer. For Dad, these mealtimes are now a formality; he can manage maybe half a tin of soup or a couple of shortbreads. On Sundays, I call at the regular time. He'll be sitting in his chair, she in hers. He has the one by the window, so he can watch the neighbours' comings and goings, twisted in his seat, poised between the net curtains and the TV screen. She'll plod over to the little table to answer, and she'll say, "Do you want to speak to your dad?" and he'll say, "What's the weather like up there?"

What's the weather like? He bruises easily. His hands are flushed with storm clouds, purple, indigo and violet. But he still follows his timetable and carries out his chores. Washes up. Cleans the car. Shaves every morning, takes a pride in his appearance.

What's the weather like? Freakish. Weather always is. Hailstones clattering like a truckload of gravel; winter lightening; and the wind, the wind, waking me in the middle of the night, ripping at trees, overturning plant pots with a clatter. He's going for regular transfusions, driving himself to hospital, because it would be a waste to pay for a taxi when you've got your own car.

One day I look up and see the snow falling like a thick lace curtain. Bent by its weight, the bamboo is bowed down to the ground. Soon the streets are blanked out, pavements and side roads obliterated, the TV showing monochrome shots of cars stuck in blizzards. The entire country's paralyzed, the worst winter, they say, since 1947, and I give them a call just to check they're okay, even though today is not a Sunday.

The phone keeps ringing, right up to the point when the answering machine kicks in. They are slow to pick up, and she often doesn't cross the room in time, but she'll know it's me and ring back in a minute. But she doesn't. I try again and there's still no reply. I don't know what to do. They can't have gone out, not in this weather.

Finally, he calls, his voice brisk and jocular. "Have you been trying to ring? What's the weather like up there?" And I ask him how he is, and he says, "It's not me, it's your mom."

She slipped on the ice, trying to put the bin out, and he's

driven her to the hospital, but not to worry, they're keeping her in overnight, just to make sure, but not to worry, she'll be right as rain.

"What about you?"

"Not so good. It's this pain."

I don't know what to say.

"You get on with your life. Don't worry about us."

"I'll come down."

"What, in this lot? Wait till the weather gets better."

"I'm coming down this weekend."

"You're better off waiting."

The snow keeps falling silently, like words not said, covering the humped back of the bamboo, and the first blades of early bulbs and the dormant summer flowers. It seems as though spring will never come.

MARIA TAYLOR

A DAUGHTER'S WEDDING

□ □ □ □ □

THE GIRL HAD NO mother. She had vanished at the time of the invasion and no-one had heard or seen anything of her for a year. In her mind Thekla vowed to her missing sister that Despina would marry soon and well. After all, Alexia was probably dead, lost in the confusion of war and its silences. Despina needed a solid family member to marry her off and, after a lifetime of respectability and family banquets, no-one was as solid as Thekla.

Her ideal choice of groom was Michalis, a young man who had recently taken over from his father in the running of the family's restaurant. He was handsome and would become more attractive the wealthier his business made him. Thekla told her niece how their first meeting would run:

"So you meet at the restaurant and you see Michalis.

Look shy and be polite. I will be there. Next Tuesday after-noon is a good time. I have nothing planned. Anyway, you sit with him and we all have a Nescafé or something. Then you can go off for a walk together and who knows, another meeting or two and he might ask you to marry him."

"That quickly, aunty?"

"Yes! Everything is so *moderniko* now."

It had been just under a month since she saw Despi-na's eyes widen in Michalis's direction at a wedding party. Thekla had been chewing on a rather gristly piece of meat and had been cursing the groom's father for economising on his son's own wedding feast. In between lengthy chews she had noticed Despina and Michalis trying not to notice each other. Then it all clicked together pleasurably in her mind; she would get the pair married. Why not? The union promised to be respectable and profitable to both families. Her face had lit up with excitement as she envisaged her niece's future. She swallowed the stringy remains of her meal and rose to have a quiet word with Michalis's parents.

When the day of the meeting arrived, Thekla was buzzing industriously around her flat. She put on a light blue dress and jacket, neatly curled her hair and put on her largest gold cross. She inhaled the intoxicating fumes of hair lacquer as if she were downing a stiff drink and headed out.

Despina lived with her married sister Andri, her husband and their children in a cramped flat. Thekla knocked purposefully on their door and looked in through the letterbox.

"Ah, welcome, aunty Thekla," said Andri, "please come

in, sit down. I'm so sorry the house is a mess, but you know what children are like."

Thekla ignored Andri, zooming past her into the hall.

"Despina, where are you? Are you ready yet?" she shouted.

Andri followed her dutifully and called faintly, "Would you like some tea or coffee, aunty? I have some baklava fresh from the bakery. I bought it specially."

"You don't make your own?" snorted Thekla, "Tsk. Despina, Despina! Where are you?" Suddenly she felt tiny pincers in her stubby ankles, "Oh, what do we have here, ah, it's young Christala! Give me a kiss!" The toddler stood flicking her tongue in and out, "and who's this? Little baby Gavrilli! Oh, his little rattle, we never had such things! When are you going to give us a baby Alexia named after your mother?" Thekla paused and turned to Andri. "Have you heard anything about *her*?"

"No," came the reply.

Thekla sighed and walked straight into Despina's room where the girl was putting on a dress, her bra showing.

"Oh aunty, I'm not dressed."

"Let me zip you up. Now let me take a look at you. Turn around. No stay still. Yes, beautiful. You'll be married by the end of the year, I'm sure." Thekla gazed sweetly at her niece, but her expression soon changed when she noticed something which met with her disapproval.

"You're not wearing that tiny cross, are you? Don't you have a bigger one?"

"I like this one, aunty."

"*Kori mou*, my girl, it's too small. Do you want him to think you're a heathen or something?"

Despina moved robotically to her drawer, "I think I have a bigger one somewhere in here," she fumbled around and pulled one out.

"Tsk, it will have to do, now come over here and I'll put it on." She yanked the cross around Despina's neck as the girl was awkwardly trying to remove the other one.

"What a tidy short hairstyle you have. Long, loose hair makes a girl look like a whore. There are a great many of those around in London, but thankfully none in my family, thank God, although I sometimes have doubts about your cousin Soulla, always covered in lipstick." She raked her chunky fingers through Despina's hair, and their eyes met in the mirror. "He's a very lucky young man."

Despina felt tired; she hadn't slept much the night before and for once it wasn't Gavrilli's howling keeping her awake. She'd lain in the heavy darkness wondering about her prospective husband. What if he wasn't as handsome as she remembered? What if he was rude and aggressive? Then the question that froze her: what would her mother think? *But she's not here*, replied a voice.

Now and then Despina and Andri had strange phone calls. They'd pick up the receiver expecting a voice, but they would only hear crackles and hiss. The sisters would pass the phone back and forth saying "Hello" in English and Greek. Eventually, they would give in to their secret wishes: "Mother," they'd say, "is that you, ma? Talk to us, mother!"

Andri's husband would appear scratching the back of his neck: "Silly girls, it's just the phone lines going wrong. Your mother is dead. She was killed." If he were right then she had to marry without her mother's blessing – *if* he were right.

Despina's eyes began to widen and Thekla instinctively knew what the problem was, although she wouldn't remedy it with any sensitivity.

"My sister Alexia would be very pleased with this marriage. She was my sister, so I'm nearly your mother anyway. Oh, the time. Let's go! Before you know it, the time goes." She moved her hand in a tight circle as if to demonstrate the swift passing of life.

They went back to the living room where Andri was desperately trying to remove a pen that Christala was chewing on, but the little girl's grip was strong. *Don't grow up*, thought Despina.

Andri had managed to produce tea, plates, forks, and a tray of baklava cut neatly into little diamond shapes. "Please, aunty, have something."

"We have no time." Thekla looked down at the pastry smothered in honey and pistachios, "but we don't want Despina passing out. Five minutes then!"

Half an hour later they were on the bus. Thekla was lost in a monologue about which grocers had the cheapest prices, mumbling like a priest. Despina found the mutterings comforting and the warmth of her aunt's plump body felt cosy against hers. Suddenly Thekla burst into life.

"The bridge! We're here, they told me get off at the railway bridge! Ring the bell!" and she flapped her arms dementedly. She barged down the aisle, knocking over the shopping bag of a woman who looked so ancient her skin appeared translucent.

"Bloody foreigners," she said, staring at Despina.

"So sorry," she replied, but the old woman gazed into nothingness, as if she'd given up on facial expressions.

Thekla was the first to see the restaurant.

"Now," she said, with all the bursting joy of a nun who has just seen the face of Christ, "there it is! It's very *classico* don't you think? One day you will be in there with your husband Michalis, babies everywhere, me too, eating souvlakia, meatballs," she continued wistfully, "macaroni, fried potatoes with coriander, olives, a little drink maybe." Then her face turned sour, "but don't get fat. It's no good for a girl to look like an overstuffed pepper. It doesn't matter about me. I've been married for years, my children are grown-up now. You need to stay slim, until you are least forty, forty-five maybe. It doesn't matter so much then."

The restaurant's name was written in tall plastic letters, *The Lantern of Lambri*, and it certainly looked smart to Despina.

"The name of our village, here for all to see, here in London!" gabbled Thekla. "Quickly, go inside. No, don't go inside, stand still. Let me look at you, yes you're beautiful."

Despina caught sight of Michalis through one of the windows. His head was lowered and he was writing something. He seemed a few years older than her, maybe five, maybe six, worldly perhaps. She noticed how he kept brushing his dark hair out of his eyes. Unexpectedly he lifted his head and they looked at each other. Despina felt naked. She dropped her eyes to the pavement.

"You know, he might give us some cake," Thekla continued. "I've heard his cakes are wonderful. That's what your aunty Loulla said, do you remember?" The words evaporated into the air and Despina wondered if it was possible to fall in love with someone who made her jump. She couldn't even look him in the eyes. But he could hers, and he gestured towards her with an open hand as if to say "Come in."

Thekla stepped back.

"You first, Despina. Walk towards him as if you were his bride."

Her aunt stabbed her in the back with a pointed finger, and she felt like a baby being forced to walk by a pushy parent. But Despina's father was dead and her mother was missing. In those few steps from her aunt to the man who would become her husband, she was alone. At that moment she did not belong to either. She could have turned around and ran if she wanted to – but where and to whom?

Oh mother, I miss you, she thought.

Michalis smiled, but Despina couldn't smile back.

"Go to him, Despina," her aunt whispered. "Do what he tells you."

KATHLEEN BELL

THE MARRIAGE-HEARSE

□ □ □ □ □

I REMEMBER THE SMELL of hot leather, the stale air in the car and the dark bristles on the back of the chauffeur's neck. Would you call him a chauffeur? Not exactly an undertaker, though he came from the firm. The man who drove the car behind the hearse.

How do they decide who drives which car? Do they take turns? Hearse-driving – that must be the most important job. You get the coffin, flowers, head of the queue; you catch people's eyes before they look away, embarrassed, or settle in for a good stare. Could be a prestige job, or a long-service award. No sniffly relatives. Not so good if you get hay-fever.

They wouldn't let me up front with the coffin. I tried asking. There's a fixed price for the cheapest option: hearse plus one car. That's enough without the trimmings. Coffin, duty minister, cremation and I'll be paying off till 1982. Barry would have had a fit, told me to leave it – no relation, none of my business – that's Barry all over. Old Mr Upton deserved something, though I never knew what his first name was. He was good to our Tom, even after the trouble started. Asked after him every visit. That has to be worth something.

The woman at the funeral parlour looked down her nose. Nothing you could put your finger on but I know contempt when I feel it. So I held out for the date. "I don't think . . ." she said. I got insistent. Told her it would suit me. Told her I needed the holiday, couldn't get time off work – not as if he's a relative. They're stingy like that. It had to be the day of the Wedding.

At first I felt sorry for the driver. Perhaps he loved the Queen or wanted time with his family. I tried not to mind when he tutted as the hearse ahead took an awkward turn to avoid the bunting and tables of another street party. Chairs and long tables. Sandwiches, cakes, crisps and jellies under clingfilm. The streets were silent. People were all indoors watching TV.

Something about the way that driver looked at his watch got to me. Both hands on the steering wheel so he crooked his left wrist to see the watch face – he did it every time we paused and when we went slowly along a stretch of road. There was a clock on the dashboard, in perfect working order. He didn't have to check his watch. It was directed at me.

I almost expected bunting at the crematorium – or banners to congratulate Charles and Lady Di on their special day. I wouldn't have been surprised at trestle tables where staff and undertakers could have their own celebration when work was over. Fair enough, and better than getting cross with the bereaved.

It was just me, the undertakers and the minister. I did my best for Mr Upton, once the police and council told me there was no next-of-kin. Neighbours didn't want to know. Not after that thing with the dog and the squirrel. People pulled away. Even the lady from meals-on-wheels. He kept putting his hand up her skirt and that wasn't nice, especially when, to be honest, he started to smell. Of piss. But the skirt thing – it was his way of staying alive – taking an interest. Nothing personal – he put his hand up everyone's skirt, even Jehovah's Witnesses'. I'd slap him away. "Not now, Mr Upton" – and he'd give his dirty, toothless laugh and put his hand between his own legs instead. He was just . . . old.

The minister looked as if he'd rather be at the TV and the street parties. I had no time for him. This was his job – not just a job, a vocation. I kept it easy. He had a couple of facts about Mr Upton – the sort you can put in a memorial address – and I said he could choose the hymn if he liked. He probably wanted more of an audience. He had to make do with me and the men in black.

The minister and I sang 'The Lord's my Shepherd.' I joined in the Lord's Prayer and said "Amen" in the proper places. When the minister made his little speech about Mr Upton and how he'd be eating a banquet with Christ in eternity right now, I remembered how things had been when Barry left and Tom had his trouble.

Most of the neighbours looked the other way, as though I should be pitied or deserved everything I got. But Mr Upton came right up to me and said, "Don't you worry about Tom. He's not a bad boy. You visit him when you can. Whatever he's done, he loves his mother."

I couldn't tell that to the minister. But it was the nicest thing anyone said to me that year. If Mr Upton had slid his hand up my skirt just then I'd have welcomed it, and a lot more too.

After the service I didn't want to get back in the big black car to watch the bristles on the driver's neck. I told him to go away, I'd go home on my own, that it wasn't far. But when I checked my purse I only had one pound note, there were no buses and I wasn't sure that would pay for a cab – not on Royal Wedding day.

So I walked. After a while my feet began to hurt because my smart black shoes were for parties and show, not walking. I could hear that the Wedding was over because every so often the air buzzed with laughter and chat and children's tears, which meant the parties had begun. I wanted to think about Tom and my next visit and what I would say. So I took the shortcut over the Common where there weren't any parties. No-one was even walking a dog. Then my foot caught on something.

It was a small plastic doll – like Barbie, but you could see from the hairstyle and clothes that it was meant to be Lady Di. It wasn't very like her – not shy or plumpish or awkward – just a glossy pretence of a princess. You could see the child who owned it wasn't impressed. She'd scribbled on the nails with red biro, as if she thought a princess should be fancier than that.

I felt a bit sorry for the plastic princess. I thought if I left her on a wall a child might find her, so I started to carry her with me. Then a blister burst on the back of my right heel and my foot started to bleed through my tights.

The doll was still in my hand when I reached home. Home was emptier than usual, now that Mr Upton was being burnt and couldn't possibly return to the flat upstairs. I found myself looking at the picture of Tom – the one when he was ten and had what people called his "cheeky grin." Back then he was up and down stairs all the time, popping up to see Mr Upton, calling out to him, me and Barry. He would dart into the kitchen, sneak bits of cheese, ask if he could lick the bowl – normal boy things. Sometimes Mr Upton called in for a cup of tea – he was a gentleman then.

I saw that plastic doll in my hand and suddenly I was overcome by something like rage – which was strange because I'm not usually an angry person. I took a map-pin from the chip-board and suddenly I was attacking the doll. I stabbed her in the chest – not once but again and again – and then, for good measure, I slammed the pin sharply into each plastic eyeball.

She didn't look much different when I'd finished but I was ashamed. I shoved the doll in the dark cupboard where Tom's toy cars waited for his return. I never looked at her again.

JUDITH ALLNATT

HIDING IN THE CRACKS

□ □ □ □ □

THERE WAS ONE SAFE place in the playground – a narrow passageway between the holly hedge and the back of the shed. Dan crouched on his heels listening to the noises outside, squeals and shouts, and in the background the flat thump of a basketball hitting the tarmac, at first loudly, then further away. He sat back against the shed and began to pull off the holly leaves, bending and folding the bright yellow-green ones and touching the soft, pliable points.

Thump. The basketball hit the side of the shed with a force that shook it and jarred his back.

"Catch it, banana brain!"

"Get lost."

"Get lost yourself."

Dan let out his breath; they didn't know he was here.

He picked up his stick: it was his best one with good

knobbly prongs, and he started work. Since he'd started coming here every break-time, he'd cleared such a big patch he had to stand up to do it now. He breathed in the linseed smell, as little curls of brown paint came off the wood, dusting his shoes as he picked and peeled.

Then he saw it. Almost hidden in the joint between the planks and the upright was a small, brown chrysalis. Carefully, he prised it off and held it in his palm. It was light and papery, like a tiny Chinese lantern. He thought of giving it to Mrs Thomas for the nature table. She would check it every day; they all would. The butterfly would be curled and folded inside, and then one day they would look at it, and it would be split, and the butterfly would come out. They would feed it with sugar water, just like in the book, and it would be white, or even red and purple, and have feely bits at the front.

He stepped out into the sharp air, and holding it in cupped hands, walked towards the classroom.

"What have you got?"

They stood round him. Slap, slap, slap went the ball on the ground as the tallest one bounced it, her hair damp and her cheeks flushed. She tucked the ball under her arm.

"Show."

Dan held it closer. The girl held up the ball in front of her, close to his face. He looked at the lines round it and the orange peel texture of it. He opened his hands.

The girl stepped forward and held his wrist. She glanced at the chrysalis, and with a quick movement tipped his hand over.

"Disgusting." She prodded it with her toe – then slammed the ball down.

The others jostled for the ball and Dan shot away, dodging the groups of children, making for the cloakroom.

He leant against the cool wall, breathing in the smell of damp and plimsoll rubber. There was the whole afternoon yet. The bell rang and he filed into class with the rest of them, and took his place.

Mrs Thomas held cards up for them to read. Dan shook his head when it was his turn. He sat with his hands under the table, holding his thumbs, his fingers curled up tight around them.

KATY DARBY

THE DOOR IN THE WALL

□ □ □ □ □

MR BRIDGE DINT SHAVE this morning. There's dusty light comin through the classroom blinds an it makes his blond stubble glint as he sorts through our essays. Mine's on top. I lean over to see what Mr Bridge has written an nudge Santos by mistake.

What you pushin me for, ho? yelps Santos. His voice is all high an disgusted, like he never been so insulted in his life.

I aint even *touchin* you, freak.

Mr Bridge, Maz is feelin me up!

Settle down, Santos, and don't call her a ho. Madeleine, leave him alone.

I want touchin him, I mutter. Mr Bridge gives me a warnin stare. Oh my days, those blue blue eyes, like a gas-flame. He can stare at me all day.

Mr Bridge's bin taking us for English since Miss Allister fell downstairs or whatever an went on long-term sick. Under Miss Allister I got straight Ds because basically I dint give a shit. But since Mr Bridge come in, I bin actually takin an interest in the book we're readin, because *fuck* me, he is *fit*.

He's quite old, probly like 23, but oh my days, he looks like Orlando Bloom or summink (when he was in *Lord of the Rings*, not when he was that bellend in *Pirates* tryin to bang Keira Knightley). His voice is quite posh an normally I hate that cos they sound so up their own arses, don't they? But it's soft too: not quiet, or weak, just soft, an when I hear it, when he speaks to us, it makes me wanna (this sounds stupid, yeah, but don't laugh, or I *will* deck ya) wanna sort of look after him.

So that's what I bin doin pretty much since he come. Though on his first day I wanted to smack him. He told us straight off that this was his first teachin job, which was *bare* stupid. Licence to mug him off because he aint got a fuckin clue. I could see their eyes just shine *right* up, Cheree an Linna an Santos, thinkin fresh meat. New toy. This little lamb tryin to teach a pack of wolves. Seriously now? An then he opened the book.

Basically *Brideshead Revisited*, which you probly aint heard of cos it's from like 1910, is this *long* piece of *Downton Abbey* toss Miss Allister bin tryin to teach us for GCSE. There's these two posh twats, Charles an Sebastian (those *names!*), an Sebastian's an alkie an Charles is sort of gay for him, but then marries his sister an goes to war an whatever. An there's these bits where Sebastian goes off on one about wanting to bury precious things in places where he's been happy like a time capsule or summink.

And also, it's total fantasy, like *High School Musical* unrealistic, because

a) who the fuck talks like that?

and b) who the fuck cares?

Mr Bridge asked us where we'd got to with Miss Allister, which was basically middle of chapter one. He asked Linna to read an she just laughed, showin her teeth like a pitbull. Then he asked Kara, who spends her entire life sucking up to teachers, so she tried, but seein as her tits are about ten times the size of her brain an she basically can't read it was *not* gonna happen. Everyone stared at her as she struggled with the words, her eyes praticly crossed, wonderin what Mr Bridge was gonna do.

And then he says, shall I take it from here? An Kara looks *so* relieved it's hilarious an nods her head an smiles. An Mr Bridge clears his throat an reads this bit that I always thought was lame, just complete bollocks, before, but when he read it, it sounded, I dunno. Real.

Just the place to bury a crock of gold, he says in that smooth voice, *I should like to bury something precious, in every place I've been happy and then when I was old and ugly and miserable, I could come back and dig it up and remember.*

An instead of makin jokes about behind the bins at the Rec or the bus stop outside the libry like we did when Miss Allister read it, the whole class just shut up, like it was shocked, like he'd said fuck or summink. An I felt them inside me, the words, the feelin of things bein lost where you can't find them again. The sadness you feel sometimes that's nearly like love.

An then Santos farted an Linna yawned an the bell went an everybody moshed out the classroom, but it took me a while to get my head back in the room, an then everyone was gone an it was just Mr Bridge an me.

Madeleine, is it? he said. No teacher ever called me Madeleine more than once because I fuckin *hate* that name, but in his voice it sounded, whatever, nice. Elegant. I nodded.

Yeah.

Did you have any questions?

No, sir. Sorry. It was nice, what you read.

Glad you liked it. It's really a wonderful book.

Er . . . yeah.

Oi Maz! You comin or what? yelled Linna from outside the classroom an I jumped up like I bin electrocuted.

See ya tomorra, yeah, Mr Bridge? He nodded an smiled.

After that day I decided to protect him. He don't know it, but he's under my wing. Nobody fucks with me so nobody fucks with him. I feel like I'm sort of an angel watching over him, or a bodyguard or whatever. An I don't want him to know because he thinks he's got us, he thinks he's turned us around or some shit, like Samuel L. in *Coach Carter*, but the truth is he's only got me. Christ has he got me.

Lucky for him, that's enough.

So it's Friday, an as usual I got detention, this time for that thing with the bunsen burner in Chemistry, but it's OK cos Grant, my mum's boyfriend, knows the drill an he's gonna pick me up on his way to Anger Management. After two hours of sittin in silence drawin cocks on Santos's French textbook I want a fag so I raise my hand and say I need to go to the toilet for a female issue. Then I go out the back, check round, an force the lock on the door in the wall with my Oyster card.

It aint exactly a basement, really, more like a tunnel under the building, an old corridor with dark rooms off it full of dust an broken chairs. I found it last term when they was throwin out some of the old shit in there. Someone left the door open an so of course I went explorin. Linna taught me how to break into places ages ago so it's bin my place ever since. My secret. It's quiet an dark in there, like an empty church or summink. It's a good place to smoke without getting caught, or just sit. Think.

So I feel my way through the dark to my favourite spot, behind the door in the second classroom on the right. It's warmer cos it's under the canteen an I've made a little nest for myself, with a not-too-broken chair and an old inkwell for an ashtray. I light the candle an then my Mayfair, an cos I'm bored an it's in my bag, I take out my knackered copy of *Brideshead*. Might as well find out what happens, right? I smoke an read by candlelight. I feel like an adventurer or someone out of *Harry Potter* when I'm down here, sort of excited an calm at the same time. An when I read the words now I hear Mr Bridge's voice in my head, saying em like they mean something, like it's real.

I was in search of love in those days, and I went full of curiosity and the faint, unrecognised apprehension that here, at last, I should find that low door in the wall, which others, I knew, had found before me, which opened on an enclosed and enchanted garden, which was somewhere, not overlooked by any window, in the heart of that grey city.

I think about Oxford, what it must look like. Old stone

an secret passages, sort of like Hogwarts I reckon. Boys all in white with blond hair an blue eyes, an green sports fields an old paintings an stuff.

An then I hear the door, an a woman laughin, though it's more of a secret giggle. Like she's bein naughty. Doin summink wrong, like me.

Fuck.

I drop my book an blow the candle out, crouchin in the sudden black, listenin so hard I don't even breathe. Who the fuck is it? If they find me I'm in serious shit. The rage wells up in me like sick, like a scream. This is my place. *Mine.* If they find me I'll fuckin kill em.

What *is* this place? says a voice, a posh quiet voice, a sound I know like my own heart beatin. Mr Bridge. The sickness spreads in my chest.

Secret storage. Got the key from the Head last year but I think she's forgotten about it, says a woman, an I know that voice too. Thin an dreary like Monday detention, eyes like wet tarmac under a concrete sky. Miss Allister.

Footsteps shuffle along the corridor. The door squeaks open. In here, she says. They used this place as a bomb shelter in the war, you know? Her voice is casual like they just met in Morrisons or something. I thought you should see it before you go.

Before he goes? Goes where?

Think you can handle coming back? His voice is soft, like dust, like candlelight.

I'm better now. Anyway, you said they'd been good.

Amazingly, yeah. The girls especially. I think they're really coming on board.

Even Maz? She sounds like she don't believe him, like

he's lyin or boastin or summink. Fuckin cow. Just cos she can't teach for shit.

Madeleine's bright, you know. And very keen. He sounds hurt.

Don't hurt him, you bitch, I think. Tears stab my eyes. I hug my knees an let them soak into my jeans.

Keen on *you*, probably, Miss Allister says, like it don't matter, like she's talkin about a dog or summink, waggin its tail, wantin to play.

Well, he says, soundin embarrassed, one of the hazards of the job, isn't it?

They'll miss you, you know.

I'll miss them, he says. Believe it or not, I've been quite happy here.

She sighs an there's a faint *shhing* sound which I suddenly know is her stroking his face, her fingers on his blond stubble. I dig my nails into my ankles until the flesh burns, concentratin on how much it hurts.

I should like to bury something precious, she says, *in every place I've been happy*, an he laughs. I know what I should like to do, he says, an there's the soft thump of a body against the wall an a wet loose sound like a dog lappin. A rustle an a silvery noise like zips. Hard breathin. I stuff my fists in my ears as she starts to moan. They're pantin like dogs. I can smell their sweat.

I think of Mr Bridge's blue, blue eyes in the dark.

When I'm sure they're gone I light the candle an look round the room. A strand of hair drifts, snagged on a nail in the bricks. That must be where they fucked. I walk over for a closer look an nearly trip over summink. I bend down an pick it up. It's my copy of *Brideshead*, broke open, with a dirty footprint right across the pages.

I touch the candle flame to the bent cover an watch as it burns. When it's too hot to hold, I chuck it on a pile of broken old chairs, newspapers an textbooks. I don't close the door behind me or look back.

JANE HOLLAND

THE CELL

□ □ □ □ □

My CELL IS THE pillar of fire where God spoke to Moses. It's the furnace I stand in, morning and evening; an intolerable column of flame between me and God. Some days I pack up my meagre belongings in a sack and peer out at the desert. I stand in the doorway and press imaginary footprints into the sand, a journey that stretches all the way back to my old life. My hated cell shrinks in the distance, nothing but a hot dusty hell I've crouched in these seventeen years. When evening falls, I close the door and comb out the sand from my hair. Extinguishing the lamp, I lay down my sack for a pillow and praise God, saying: "Tomorrow, Lord. Tomorrow."

Some months I am visited by one or two of the other Sisters. Often they bring a donkey, carrying sacks of flour and dried pulses, and sometimes a pot of fresh honey for my supplies. I tell them that I intend to leave, and they weep for me. Sometimes the venerable head of our order sends a note with the Sisters, to strengthen my resolve or impart some private information. Once or twice a year, Abba Macarius comes to me in person, a shadow falling over the stone lintel in the late morning. It is an honour to receive his visits. We sit together in the shade and I offer him honey cakes. He relates an anecdote or points to a phrase in the scriptures, asks me to consider it. Sometimes we kneel, side by side, and make our personal devotions. When I look up some time later, I find that Abba Macarius has gone as silently as he arrived. My stone cell yawns in the afternoon silence, as hot and stifling as ever.

I am never sure if these visits help or hinder my progress. I am glad of them, for sure; my soul leaps for joy at the sound of a human voice, and my foolish vanity enjoys Abba Macarius's flattering attentions, however fleeting. But afterwards, in the long stillnesses of the night, I recall each word spoken and regret them all. My pride asserts itself after these visits. It presses vicious thorns deep into my flesh, making me imagine, dream, recast each meeting until it shows me to best advantage, the least worldly of our order, the most pious, the Abba's favourite. Mostly, though, peace falls from my mind and I begin to remember how it feels to be alive in the world. My desire increases and pains me. The struggle to cage it becomes harder, almost impossible to bear. Some days the lure of the shimmering, heat-haze horizon burns my eyes like the desert burns my feet through my sandals. It can take weeks for equilibrium to return, for will to exert itself over my dizzying desire. Yet even will can corrupt the unwary. For it is the individual will, not the will of God, to which the body bows.

By speaking I weaken myself. Silence is the narrow way.

The days stretch out in this manner, my conscience knocked this way and that. Following a visit, I keep the cell door closed during the cooler hours when walking outside would be possible, afraid of my own weakness. Gradually, the stirred air of my cell settles. The humble stone walls and floor are my own again. Soon I find myself able to pray without distraction, and begin to follow the prayer cycles and meditations Abba Macarius has recommended for such trials. I sit cross-legged for days on end, examining one solitary word of the Lord's teaching until it becomes as vast and complex in my understanding as Creation itself. At such miraculous times, I feel His presence so near to me, it seems incredible that almost three hundred years have passed since He gave His life for mankind.

Finally the day comes when I can open the door once more in daylight and breathe the fresh air, staring out at the sand dunes and distant ridges without regret. My peace improves as I focus on the searing fire of God's presence in my life. Some days I eat nothing but dampened leaves. Other days, I take only sufficient water to keep me conscious and able to pray. I find the less I consume, the greater my resolve. Each morning, I examine my arms and legs for spare flesh. My body should be a bird's skeleton cupped in a stone palm, to be hollowed out by God's purpose and played upon like a flute, as His Will demands. This is what I struggle towards as I try to meet Him in everything.

I forget that my feet work, I am so often on my knees in prayer. When I stand, my body lists and drifts. But I ignore physical weakness. Spiritual strength is all that matters in this world. My spine is a ladder where sin may clamber up or vilely descend, and I am determined to conquer my own primitive urge to accommodate it. Some days I wake to find myself on the floor of my cell, when I cannot remember having made the decision to sleep. But a sip or two of water soon returns me to prayer and the path. I am a handful of sand on the desert wind, anchored to this world by nothing but the fine cord of contemplation; sometimes, it is all I can do to prevent myself from floating as I cross from one side of my cell to the other.

Yet I know that I must take no pride in the extremity of my position. The Abba warned us all of this before we left to seek solitude. Extremity of any kind, even in devotion to God, is the work of the Devil. When I sense pride rising at my own severity, I strip down to bare skin, kneel on the sand under the midday sun and beat myself across the back with a bundle of dry sticks until blood comes. My skin burns and I cannot lie on my back for days afterwards. But the pain steadies me. I praise God with every blow, and beg His forgiveness for my vanity.

The sense of humility that follows such chastisements is quite astonishing; I thank the Lord for the blessing of their solace.

The way is never easy, though. Sometimes visions come, terrible in the great solitude of the desert. I fear the visions but know it is part of our testing to watch and learn from them. A bird lands on the stone threshold of my cell and stares in at me, a black-hooded vulture, its wing feathers tattered from a fight. Its eye seems to know me as only God can. It grows taller and taller, blocking out the light, until I look up and see the silhouette of Abba Macarius in the doorway. He watches me from beneath the cowl of his hood but neither of us speaks. The Abba comes in and sits down opposite me, his face unreadable in shadow. I find myself burningly conscious of not being fully clothed, having stripped down for the heat, but I know this womanly awareness is part of my test. We sit there for days, both determined not to weaken, my back and limbs sweating with the rigour of holding myself upright, my mouth still moving in silent prayer. The moon rises and sets three times over silvered sands while we face each other, yet I dare not give in to my physical needs in case the Devil uses my human weakness to corrupt me. On the fourth day, just as the sun is rising to burn away the chill dews of the night, I look up to find Abba Macarius gone and the vulture in his place. It croaks once, then flaps up the step and away into the morning like a tattered robe swirling about an old man's ankles. I sit trembling until midday, to be sure I have passed the test, then take a little water and allow myself to sleep at last.

I can barely remember my old life now. Once I was young and felt proud to be considered beautiful – such folly! I even intended to marry, but the man my father had chosen married another. Then my father died and God spoke to me in the night. That was when I came to the desert and sought the Abba's advice. It was another Abba then, not Macarius. But Abba Amoenus was as wise as he was old, and he soon set me on the path. The first ten years of solitude were the hardest to endure, yet the equilibrium I finally achieved seems more difficult to maintain with every year that passes. Abba Macarius is a deeply spiritual man, and younger than most Abbas, the vital central pillar of our order. Yet my life in the cell feels harder now, and the visions come more frequently to torment me. This shameful weakness is not something I would ever voice, except perhaps in prayer. But I found fewer temptations under Abba Amoenus.

When I awake, evening has fallen again. I close the door to my narrow cell and comb out my hair. Extinguishing the lamp, I lay myself down and praise God, saying: "Tomorrow, Lord. Tomorrow."

LAUGHING
STORIES

TANIA HERSHMAN

"WHAT DO YOU DO?"

□ □ □ □ □

HE MEETS HER AT a party. She has a drink. She asks what he does.

"I work in a lab," he says.

She has a drink. She looks at him.

"What do you do?" she says.

"In a lab," he says.

"What does that mean?" she says.

She has a drink. He has no drink.

"I work. In a lab," he says. "Laboratory."

"Lab-oratory," she says. She has no more drink. "What, sorry? What is that?" He has no drink too. He forms the word again and it feels silly in his mouth. Lab, lab, lab, labrador.

"Dog," he says, "like a . . ."

She has a drink,

    "What do you do?" she says.

    "Science."

    "Science," she says, with her drink.

    It is a party. They are both there. She moves away. She comes back. He has a drink.

    "I do," she says. "Lab," she says. She smiles.

WILL BUCKINGHAM

THE LAKE

◻ ◻ ◻ ◻ ◻

THE DINERS LOOKED OUT over the lake, talking quietly over their food. The restaurant had a kind of pontoon at the back, made of slatted boards, large enough to take thirty tables, which is to say one hundred and twenty diners; and there the guests could sit and gaze out over the lake in the evening, and dine on seafood, and conduct their affairs or their various kinds of business, or stumble their way through the awkwardness hanging in the air after the argument that had blown up during the course of the afternoon, on what was only the third day of their honeymoon. It was a peaceful place. The waiters moved with silent grace. Glasses chinked softly. Nobody raised their voice. The wavelets lapped at the shore. The fish lay silent on the plates, their mouths open, their eyes gazing up at the deep blue of the evening sky where the stars were just becoming visible. There was no music, for the gentle wind over the lake and blowing through the pines was music enough. No motorboats disturbed the silence. Sometimes a bird called to its mate, or a flight of ducks quacked their way overhead, but that was all.

The honeymoon couple were sitting at the furthest extent of the pontoon. They were toying with their food, trying not to make eye contact. It was a quiet night, even when measured against the quietness of all the nights in that most peaceful of restaurants, and there were only twenty, perhaps thirty diners on the pontoon. The honeymooners had finished their first course, and were now picking their way through the fish, removing flesh from bone. As they were engaged in this delicate operation, they heard a cry.

"Woohooo! Woohoohooo!"

They looked around. Some distance off there was a man by the shore of the lake, in his forties perhaps, pot-bellied, in shorts and very little else, a beard on his chin and abundant hair on his chest, wading into the water.

"Woohoohooo!" he called, as the water rose up to his calves, his thighs, his belly. "Woohoohoohoo!"

The honeymoon couple tried to ignore him. The woman – properly we should call her a wife, but she didn't feel herself a wife, just at that moment – looked at the man – who by the same reasoning we should call a husband – and gave a tight smile.

"Hoohoo! Hoohoohoo!" the bather cried. He was hopping up and down in the water, and it seemed as if it was cold, for it was evening, and this was not the warm part of the year.

The waiters began to frown. They swept into the restaurant to talk to the manager. The man in the lake ran back up to the shore, and did a little dance – not as a display, not to show off to the diners, but because he was cold and the water was fresh, and the lake was peaceful and beautiful. And then, to the sound of disconcerted murmuring amongst the diners, he pulled down his shorts, stepped out of them, and proceeded to perform star jumps, as naked as Adam in the Garden.

"Hoop!" he said with every jump. "Hoop! Hoop! Hoop!"

The wife looked at his waggling cock, then she looked down at her fish and felt as if she was losing her appetite. The bridegroom pushed back his chair. "Really!" he said under his breath. "Really!"

"Oooh! Ya, ya, ya, ya . . ." The naked man was crying out, swinging his arms in the air, touching his toes. "Ya, ya, ya, ya, ya . . ."

Two or three waiters had now gathered outside the restaurant, a little way along the shore. They looked unsure of themselves. They did not know how to deal with this, how their silent swoops and turns could meet this unexpected foe. They stood and fidgeted, each waiting for another to make the first move.

The naked man ran down to the water again. "Ai, yo, yo, yo, yo," he cried as the cold water touched him. Then he started to swim, and it was a relief, in a way, just to see that hairy back and those buttocks that broke the surface and that bearded head. At least his cock was no longer visible. That was something.

"More wine?" the bride asked, somewhat awkwardly.

"Thanks," said the groom.

And then something terrible happened. The man swam out into the water and when he was some way from the shore he started to somersault, crying out with joy every time he broke the surface, so that now his head, and now his hindquarters broke the surface, head-hindquarters, head-hindquarters, "Pah! Hooo!" *Splash!* he went, "Pah! Hooo!" *Splash!* Hindquarters. Head. Hindquarters. Head.

The restaurant manager was striding out of the front door now, down to the shore-line. He had a serious look on his face. The guests were shifting in their seats. The bather continued to somersault, a hooting, splashing wheel of water and hair and flesh and genitalia and beard: "Pah! Hooo!" *Splash!*

The bridegroom got to his feet. "Really!" he said again. He hurried inside, his bride trailing behind him.

And then, because the water was becoming a little chilly perhaps, the man in the lake stopped his somersaulting, and with a broad, lazy breast-stroke, swam back to the land. The restaurant manager stood awkwardly by as the bearded man pulled on his shorts. Still dripping, the swimmer jogged away into the sunset, chanting, "Hoo! Hai! Ho! Hoo! Hai! Ho!", until his voice faded into the evening, and there was nothing remaining other than the sound of the wind over the lake and the wind in the pines and the chink of glasses and the soft footfall of the waiters.

ADELE PARKS

IT'S GOT TO BE PERFECT

□ □ □ □ □

JEFF THOUGHT, LONG AND HARD, about the perfect place to propose to Jenni. He wanted perfection as defined by big-budget, Hollywood Rom-coms; nothing less than endless tickertape celebrations and soft-focus moments. Jenni with her fabulous sense of humour, honesty and sexiness deserved nothing less.

Jeff's father had not shared Jeff's view. He'd proposed to Jeff's mother over a bag of fish and chips, as they'd huddled close and looked out at the grey English Channel. Apparently, his father's line of reasoning was that if they married, they could have sex somewhere more comfortable than the back of Jeff's Grandad's van. If Jeff's mother thought the wording of the proposal left something to be desired, she must at least have admired his honesty. She'd replied, "Okay."

Jeff would've paid cash not to be privy to this information but his father loved to relay the story and diligently repeated it every wedding anniversary. "Smelt of salt and vinegar, when I kissed her," he'd say with a laugh. There had been thirty-eight anniversaries so far.

Jeff and Jenni had lived together for two years now and they could have (or not have) comfortable sex whenever they wanted. But this seemed to increase, not diminish, the expectation that the proposal had to be something splendid and exceptional.

Jeff bought a square-cut diamond solitaire, set on a platinum band. It was hideously expensive but the jeweller told him to suck it up and pointed out that now he was proposing he could expect his credit card to be bashed on a regular basis because weddings, especially perfect ones, cost. The sobering thought dramatically altered Jeff's fantasy about where to propose. The beaches of Barbados, Maldives and Thailand were all dismissed, as was Venice (smelly), the top of the Eiffel Tower (crowded), and Rome (frantic). He didn't want to do it in a restaurant or anywhere public, come to that. It had to be somewhere personal, unpredictable and well, perfect.

After lengthy agonising he decided to book a cottage in Wales for a weekend break.

"Wales?" questioned his brother.

"Yes."

"Remote cottage, is it?"

"Yes."

"So she can't run away, is it?"

"Do you think she might?" Jeff was suddenly terrified.

"You're punching above your weight with Jenni, mate. But hell, why not? Go for it."

The drive took five hours in Friday traffic but it was worth it. They arrived as the sun was setting behind the rugged, gothic hills, creating a mauve and peach evening sky, punctuated by strong, imposing smudges of scarlet clouds. The clouds looked like those a child would paint with a thick brush. It was breathtaking. Jeff nearly spluttered out the proposal on the spot but didn't; he needed to chill the champagne, find his i-pod (as he'd uploaded a careful selection of romantic love ballads) and put the flowers he'd brought with him in a vase. It all had to be just right.

The cottage was split into two sets of accommodation, which Jeff hadn't realised when he'd made the booking on the web. He was a bit disappointed and nervous; he hoped the other half would remain unoccupied. The last thing he wanted was a forced intimacy with other holiday-makers; for the next forty-eight hours, he wanted Jenni all to himself. Jeff hastily unpacked. He slammed the champers in the fridge but he couldn't find his i-pod and he only had time to pop the flowers in the sink before Jenni called him into the bedroom.

After they'd made love Jenni decided she wanted to explore. Ideal, thought Jeff, he'd ask her as they mooched to the pub, cocooned in the warm evening air. But as he searched around for a place to conceal the engagement ring (maybe he should've packed baggier trousers, why hadn't he thought of that?), Jeff became aware that Jen was talking to someone.

"Of all the places!" declared a male voice, before bursting into a hearty laugh. Jen squealed with excitement. Jeff rushed outside in time to witness his girlfriend enveloping a bloke in a warm hug. A hot embrace, some might say.

"Jeff, this is Daniel Carter," said Jenni, beaming.

Daniel reached for Jeff's hand and shook it firmly. Mutely, weakly, Jeff allowed his limp wrist to be shaken about. *Daniel Carter*, the name slowed Jeff's blood. Dan the Man. Dan *the* Ex in the flesh – toned, tall, tanned flesh, at that. Jeff noted Dan's big blue eyes, broad shoulders and bulging biceps. Really, Jenni had undersold Dan when she'd once commented (casually, as though she didn't think it mattered) that he was possibly the most beautiful guy on the planet. If it stopped with good looks Jeff might have been able to smile and chat but he knew that Dan had completed an Iron Man Triathlon, that he was a human rights lawyer, and he probably had Obama's personal email address.

"What a coincidence. I thought this place was pretty much deserted," said Dan, with a broad, relaxed grin that exposed perfect white teeth lined in a neat row.

"It's a bit secluded," agreed Jenni, nodding.

"Intimate," chipped in Jeff, defensively.

"You must have dinner with us," offered Jenni, spontaneously.

"Dan probably has plans," mumbled Jeff.

"No, not really. That would be wonderful, if you've enough to go round. I haven't packed anything. I thought there'd be a corner shop," smiled Dan as though he was completely unaware that he was ruining Jeff's life.

Jeff had planned delicious menus for the weekend and brought the produce accordingly; normally Jenni did the lion's share of cooking and he'd wanted to indulge her. He'd spent hours in the local deli, elbow to elbow with passionate foodies and fraught, determined housewives who wanted to impress their dinner guests by buying local and organic. He'd bought the best of everything: fresh pasta, ripe cheeses, crusty bread, black olives slathered in virgin olive oil, caviar and smoked salmon. Jenni went inside the cottage, opened the fridge and assessed the contents. The men followed; Dan's step was jaunty, Jeff's demoralized.

"Oh, we've loads. It'll be nice to have someone to share all these gorgeous goodies with." She reached for the pasta, olives and smoked salmon. Jeff bit his lip and didn't point out that the salmon was intended for breakfast. He'd been planning on making Eggs Benedict.

The evening was the worst of Jeff's life. Instead of proposing to the woman of his dreams Jeff was forced to watch her as she zealously flirted with her ex-lover. Dan was undeniably interesting, engaging and charming. His anecdotes (under different circumstances) might've even made Jeff smile, but tonight Jeff wanted to gouge his eyes out with the cheese knife. Was it really necessary for Dan to be so well-informed about *every* subject broached? No, Jeff thought not. And even though Dan ostensibly tempered his galling good looks with a sprinkling of self-depreciating stories, Jeff wasn't fooled. He knew the man was an arrogant, seducing, champagne-guzzling jerk. He could absolutely tell by the way Jenni laughed at everything he said.

Yes, champagne-guzzling! After they'd consumed two of the fine bottles of wine that Jeff had bought, Dan spotted the champagne and suggested opening it. He promised he'd replace it tomorrow but it was unlikely; there weren't any shops nearby, and besides Jeff didn't want to toast his engagement with champers bought by his fiancée's ex.

That was assuming there was to be an engagement.

The more Jeff drank, the more he doubted there would be. He became increasingly morose as he watched sparks fly between Dan and Jenni, sizzling and cracking in the air. As he downed more Merlot than he knew was sensible Jeff asked himself why had these two ever split up? She clearly thought this man was perfect. Had she ever said? Maybe but it was a long time since they'd had that sort of conversation. Why it doesn't work with an ex is something discussed in the first month of a new relationship or not at all. Jeff couldn't remember why Dan and Jenni hadn't made it and judging by Jenni's animated manner right now, she couldn't recall either. Eventually, Jeff stumbled upstairs. He'd leave them to it. It was less painful.

The next morning Jenni crawled out of bed then returned with two large tumblers of water. Their hangovers were so severe that sex was out of the question, but her bringing water was a comfort, not just because his mouth was as dry as the Sahara desert but because the act was considerate and domestic. Maybe he was getting things out of proportion, being a bit paranoid. The birds were singing, the sun was slicing through the gap in the curtains – it was a good sign. Jeff would stick to his original plan; they'd go for a walk, eat a picnic and he'd propose on the Brecon Beacons, where lush green hills rolled out in front of them, like possibilities.

Jeff moved the dead flowers out of the sink. He hadn't taken the time to look for a vase – he'd forgotten all about it when Dan arrived on the scene. Jeff did his best to cobble together a picnic, fighting his irritation that the wholemeal crusty bread had been eaten and they'd have to make do with basic white sliced – *and* after he'd gone to bed, Jenni and Dan had obviously helped themselves to the organic lemonade, no doubt in a effort to abate the onset of hangovers and gorged on the chocolate fudge cake, probably to quell the munchies. Jeff took a deep breath; it was far from ideal – not what anyone would call perfect – but at least he'd have Jenni to himself all day.

Jenni entered the kitchen. She was bleary eyed and pale from last night's excesses yet still beautiful. She'd paired up a flirty, floral summer dress with big Wellington boots. It was a good look for her, she had gorgeous skinny knees and smooth thighs, and the outfit somehow suggested vulnerability and femininity combined with a practical resourcefulness.

"Will you throw in another sandwich? Last night Dan told me he's recently been through a nasty break up. They were meant to be coming here together, I feel so sorry for him. I said he could tag along today," said Jenni.

Jeff took a deep breath. So the demi-god was single too. "You should put on a pair of jeans. It might turn cold," he muttered darkly.

Dan offered to carry the picnic hamper. No doubt he'd hitch it up on one shoulder, as though it weighed nothing; Jeff couldn't allow that, it was a matter of pride. Martyrlike, he clung to the wicker box but it slowed him down. He trailed behind, forced to watch as they laughed and joked, as Jenni touched Dan's arm, as they tilted their heads close to each other. Jeff thought he might be sick and it wasn't the hangover. Normally, he was not the sort of man to wrap himself up in angry, spiky knots of bleak, evil imaginings. Jealous judgements and cruel conclusions ruined people's lives.

"You've been really quiet today," said Jenni as she linked her arm into Jeff's on the walk back to the cottage that afternoon, "Everything okay?"

"Great," replied Jeff, in a tone that suggested he was anything but.

"Is your hay-fever kicking in?" she probed.

"No."

Jenni looked bemused. Dan was a few feet behind them, locking a gate they'd passed through, mindful of the country code. "You just don't seem too happy and I can't think why." She gestured to the endless fields covered in merry buttercups, "I mean this place is wonderful and Dan being here, well it's *perfect*. It's been so long since I saw him and . . ."

"You know, I think my hay-fever *is* kicking in a bit. I'm going to give the pub a miss tonight," cut in Jeff.

"Oh, right. Well, as you like."

Jenni and Dan set off on the two mile walk to the local; Jeff watched from the window. It was a gorgeous evening, the setting sun spilt pink light on the country road, a cat circled Dan's legs; it was disgustingly idyllic. Jeff pushed his hand deep into his trouser pocket and felt the ring box, nestled forlornly there. Did jewellers do returns, he wondered? It didn't matter; getting the money back on the ring wouldn't help.

Jeff planned to drive straight back to London first thing tomorrow. Dan could drive Jenni. He'd get out of the way; retire with what was left of his dignity.

Or he could hide in Dan's cottage until they returned, catch them at it and cause a big, ugly but ultimately satisfying scene.

Jeff plumped for the latter. Dan's cottage was unlocked. Jeff mooched about, unsure what he was looking for. It felt bleak. Dan hadn't unpacked anything other than his washbag and there really wasn't any food (Jeff had doubted this). The only personal touch was a framed photo of him and some other guy, his brother presumably, which sat on the bedside table.

Suddenly, Jeff heard Jenni's voice through the open window.

"Thanks for coming back, Dan. I couldn't enjoy myself in the pub knowing Jeff's ill and alone."

Jeff swore to himself and looked around for somewhere to hide. He hurriedly scrambled into the wardrobe. He listened to Jenni's footsteps as she ran up the stairs in their cottage and then came outside again.

"He's not there."

"Must've gone for a walk to clear his head," suggested Dan. "Look, while we're here, I'll grab that photo of Joe to show you."

Jeff didn't dare breathe as he heard them come into the cottage, climb the stairs and then come into the bedroom; their footsteps tapped the wooden floorboards, making it easy to track their movements. Jen sat on the bed.

"Joe's a looker," she commented. "But Dan, you deserve more. You caught him having sex with your personal trainer. End of. You need a man of integrity, like Jeff."

At that moment two things happened. One, Jeff remembered why Jenni and Dan had split up and why she'd never felt any animosity or longing for her ex, and two, the wardrobe door swung open and Jeff fell out on to the floor by their feet.

"Looks like I'm not the only one coming out of the closet," laughed Dan.

"What are you doing in Dan's wardrobe?" demanded Jenni.

Jeff wondered whether he could pretend to be looking for antihistamines to ease his hay-fever, but the words, "man of integrity" stopped him. Instead, he muttered, "Would you believe I'm planning the perfect surprise proposal?"

"I see."

"Marry me?"

"Okay," said Jenni.

And when they kissed (after Jeff got up off the floor, obviously), he noted she smelt of salt and vinegar crisps, a detail he planned to tell his kids.

IAN MCEWAN

COCKER AT
THE THEATRE

□ □ □ □ □

THERE WAS DUST ON the boards, the backdrops were half painted and they were all naked on the stage, with the bright lights to keep them warm and show up the dust in the air. There was nowhere to sit so they shuffled about miserably. They had no pockets to put their hands in, and there were no cigarettes.

"Is this your first time?" It was everybody's first time, only the director knew that. Only friends spoke, softly and not continuously. The rest were silent. How do naked strangers begin a conversation? No-one knew. The professional men – for professional reasons – glanced at each other's parts, while the others, friends of friends of the director and needing some cash, regarded the women without appearing to. Jasmin called from the back of the auditorium where he had been talking with the costume designer, he called out in Welsh Camp Cockney,

"Have you all masturbated, boys? Well done." (No-one had spoken). "The first hard-on I see and out you go. This is a respectable show." Some of the women giggled, the unprofessional men wandered out of the lights, two ASMs carried a rolled carpet on stage. They said, "Mind your backs," and they all felt more naked than before. A man with a bush hat and a white shirt set up a tape recorder in the pit. He was scornful as he threaded the tape. It was the copulation scene.

"I want GTC, Jack," Jasmin said to him. "Let them hear it first." There were four large loudspeakers, there was no escaping.

> *'Well, you've heard about the privacy of the sex-uu-aal act,*
> *Let me tell you people, just for a fact,*
> *Riiiight acroooss the nay-ay-ation*
> *It's the in-out one-two-three Grand Time Copulation.'*

There were soaring violins and a military band, and after the chorus a march in exultant two-time with trombones, snare drums and a glockenspiel. Jasmin came down the aisle towards the stage.

"That's your fucking-music, boys and girls." He undid the top button of his shirt. He wrote this one himself.

"Where's Dale? I want Dale." Out of the dark came the choreographer. She had a stylish trenchcoat on, tied in the middle with a wide belt. She had a small waist, sunglasses and a sticky-bun hairdo. She walked like a pair of scissors.

Without turning round Jasmin called out to the man who was leaving by a door at the back of the auditorium.

"I *want* those wigs, Harry dear. I *want* those wigs. No wigs, no Harry." Jasmin sat down in the front row. He made a steeple under his nose with his hands and crossed his legs. Dale climbed on the stage. She stood in the middle of the large carpet spread across the boards, one hand on her hip. She said, "I want the girls squatting in a V shape, five on each side." She stood where the apex was to be, moving her arms. They sat at her feet and she clipped up and down the middle leaving a trail of musk. She made the V deeper, then shallow again, she made it a horseshoe and a crescent and then a shallow V once more.

"Very nice, Dale," said Jasmin. The V pointed backstage. Dale moved a girl from the middle and replaced her with a girl from the edge. She did not speak to them, she took them by the elbow, leading them from this place to that place. They could not see her eyes through her glasses and they did not always know what she wanted. She guided a man across to each woman and pressed on his shoulders to make him sit down opposite. She fitted the legs together of each couple, she straightened their backs, she put their heads in position and made the partners clasp forearms. Jasmin lit a cigarette. There were ten couples in the V shape on the carpet, which really belonged in the foyer.

At last Dale said, "I am clapping my hands, you are rocking backwards and forwards in time."

They began to rock like children playing at ships. The director walked to the back of the auditorium.

"I think closer together, darling, it looks like nothing at

all from here." Dale pressed the couples closer together. When they began to move again their pubic hair rasped. It was hard to keep time. It was very much a matter of practice. One couple fell sideways and the girl banged her head on the floor. She rubbed her head and Dale came over and rubbed it too and reassembled them. Jasmin skipped down the aisle.

"We'll try it with the music. Jack, please. And remember, boys and girls, after the singing you go into two-time."

'Well, you've heard about the privacy of the sex-uu-aal act...'

The boys and girls began to rock while Dale clapped her hands. One, two, three, four. Jasmin stood halfway up the aisle, his arms crossed. He uncrossed them, and screamed,

"Stop. Enough." It was suddenly very quiet. The couples stared into the blackness beyond the lights and waited. Jasmin came down the steps slowly, and when he reached the stage he spoke softly.

"I know it's hard, but you have to look as if you are enjoying this thing." (His voice rose). "Some people do, you know. It's a fuck, you understand, not a funeral." (His voice sank). "Let's have it again, with some enthusiasm this time. Jack, please." Dale realigned those units rocked out of position and the director climbed the stairs again. It was better, there was no doubt that this time it was better. Dale stood by Jasmin and watched. He put his hand on her shoulder and smiled at her glasses.

"Darling, it's good, it's going to be good."

Dale said, "The two on the end are moving well. If they were all like that I would be out of a job."

'It's the in-out one-two-three Grand Time Copulation.'

Dale clapped to help them with the new rhythm. Jasmin sat down in the front row and lit a cigarette. He called back to Dale,

"Them on the end . . ." She put her finger to her ear to show him she could not hear, and walked down the steps towards him.

"Them on the end, they're going too fast, what do you think?" They watched together. It was true, the two who had been moving well, they were a little out of time. Jasmin made another steeple under his nose and Dale scissored on to the stage. She stood over them and clapped.

"One two, one two," she shouted. They did not seem to hear Dale, or the trombones, snare drums and glocken-spiel.

"One fucking two," screamed Dale. She appealed to Jasmin. "I expect them to have some sense of rhythm."

But Jasmin did not hear because he was screaming too.

"Cut! Stop! Turn that thing off, Jack." All the couples creaked to a standstill except the couple on the end. Everyone watched the couple on the end, who were rocking faster now. They had their own sinuous rhythm.

"My God," said Jasmin, "they're fucking." He shouted at the ASMs. "Get them apart, will you, and get those grins off your faces or you won't work in London again." He shouted at the other couples. "Clear off, back in half an hour. No, no, stay here." He turned to Dale, his voice was hoarse.

"I'm sorry about this, darling. I know just how you feel. It's disgusting and obscene, and it's all my fault. I should have checked them all first. It won't happen again." And while he was talking Dale snipped up the aisle and disappeared. Meanwhile the couple rocked on without music. There was only the creaking of boards beneath the carpet and the woman's low moans. The ASMs stood about, not sure what to do.

"Pull them apart," Jasmin shouted again. One of the ASMs tugged at the man's shoulders, but they were sweaty and there was nowhere to hold on. Jasmin turned away, tears in his eyes. It was hard to believe. The others were glad of the break, they stood around and watched. The ASM who had tugged at the shoulders brought on a bucket of water. Jasmin blew his nose.

"Don't be pathetic," he croaked, " they might as well finish it now." They juddered to an end as he was speaking. They pushed apart and the girl ran off to the dressing-room, leaving the man standing alone. Jasmin climbed on stage, trembling with sarcasm.

"Well, well, Portnoy, did you get your little poke? Feeling better now?" The man stood with his hands behind his back. His prick was angry and gluey, it let itself down in little throbs.

"Yes, thank you, Mr Cleaver," the man said.

"What's your name, dear?"

"Cocker." Jack snorted in his pit, the closest he ever came to laughing. The rest sucked their lips. Jasmin took a deep breath.

"Well, Cocker, you and the little man stuck on the end of

you can crawl off this stage, and take shagging Nellie with you. I hope you find a gutter big enough for two."

"I'm sure we will, Mr Cleaver, thank you." Jasmin climbed down into the auditorium.

"Positions, the rest of you," he said. He sat down. There were days when he could weep, really weep. But he did not, he lit a cigarette.

ALEXANDROS PLASATIS

CONFESSIONS OF A GREAT LOVER

□ □ □ □ □

WHEN I FIRST ARRIVED in England in the late nineties, I was lucky enough to share a house with another Greek man with whom I became good friends. A man much older than me, in his late thirties. A man who kept bringing women to our house, women of every nationality, size, age, or religion. Single or attached, these women wore long dresses and short skirts, jeans and tracksuits, or, sometimes, just a fur coat – naked underneath. Well, maybe I wasn't *that* lucky, because all I could do was listen to the moans of pleasure from the other room and then watch them go, with their warm, moist and freshly-satisfied eyes.

But late one evening, after a jolly blonde planted a smacking, slobbery kiss on my friend and shouted goodnight to me, the great lover knocked on my door, said, "Stop masturbating, I'm coming in," and broke into long and uncontrolled laughter. With a mischievous smile he entered my dimly-lit room, a bottle of red wine and two glasses dangling from his hands. He grabbed a chair, brought it next to my bed, sat, and, pouring wine into our glasses, he said:

"I've got some stories to tell you. Listen."

The Very Relaxing Massage

I want to clear something up. During my great sex life, only once my willie didn't work. I was twenty-five years old and had the body of a Greek God. I was going to the gym every day and then I was running up and down hills for three hours. Each morning I was doing three sets of one hundred and fifty sit-ups followed by seventy push-ups and then for breakfast I had fruits, yogurt, honey and hazelnuts. I'll put it this way: my dick was getting so very hard, that I could penetrate the toughest metal.

And so, one day, this woman comes to my house. I don't really remember where we met, but what I do remember is that she was a trainee masseuse.

It was the first time we were going to fuck.

"You want a relaxing or a refreshing massage?" she says.

Now, I told you, I was so fit I could get a hard-on in a sec, I mean, I knew it, I was sure about it. So, I say, "Take off your clothes and give me a relaxing one."

"Shall I take off my knickers, too?" she says.

I turn around and see her red knickers. "No, keep them on," I tell her (I love red ones, you see).

And so, mate, she starts the relaxing massage. The bitch was doing it so well that I almost fell asleep. After a while she asks:

"Aren't we going to have sex?"

Now, what I really wanted was to take a nap. Anyway, I turn around and she mounts me. But the relaxing massage was so fucking relaxing that after a few seconds I feel my dick going flaccid.

"Get off, get dressed and go," I tell her.

She asks why, what happened. I tell her I want to sleep. She leaves and I begin snoring.

Next day I call and ask her to drop by my house.

"Come to your house? You must be kidding!" She sounded very angry.

"No, I'm serious, come, but, this time, give me a refreshing massage."

"You treated me like a whore yesterday!"

Like a whore? I didn't treat her like a whore. What else could I say but "get dressed and go"? How could I know that the relaxing massage would be so fucking effective? So, mate, yes, that was the first and only time my willie let me down.

The Strange Sound

. . . oh, yes, yes . . . There *was* a second time. But that time doesn't really count. I was with this chick, on our first date. We go to a bar and after the bar to her place. We get undressed and jump on her bed. She gets down on all fours and I'm behind her. I push it in and she goes, "Ah . . . oomb!" I pull back and push again: "Ah . . . oomb!" I start getting confused. I say to myself, "What the fuck is going on in here?"

Then, naturally, I get quicker: "Ah . . . oomb! – ah . . . oomb! – ah . . . oomb! – ah . . . oooomb!" This can't be possible, I say. I think I'd better double-check. So, I stop and decide to do her slowly and wait to see what happens. I push in, slowly, as slowly as possible: nothing, no sound. That's it! I say, I did it! She needs to be fucked very slowly, that's all. Then, I pull out, slowly and carefully, very slowly: ". . . ooooooooomb." And then again, push in slowly – nothing. I pull out, very slowly: ". . . ooooooooooooomb."

I continued for a couple of minutes hoping that she would stop making this noise. She didn't. She kept going, "Ah . . . oomb!" I mean, seriously, every single time I pulled out she was making this strange sound. It put me off. Could *you* keep it up listening to this *ah . . . oomb* all the time? I couldn't. My willie went floppy.

Little Red Riding Hood and the Big Bad Wolf

. . . you have to know, my young friend, that a great lover has to be – sometimes – a great story-teller. I must tell you that many women I've slept with – especially Mediterranean ones, English not as much – like to listen to dirty stories.

I had a girlfriend, back in Greece – well, not really girl-friend, we went out together for some time – who would get very horny when listening to dirty stories. Now, I knew very well about all this stuff and had a huge selection of tales to tell. Each fuck, she was asking and getting a different story. She told me she never met anyone as creative as me. She was so happy with my stories that she used to call me The Prince of Fantasies.

Okay, I said I had a great variety of stories, I also invented completely new ones, but I reached a point when I had run out of stock. I had exhausted everything and couldn't think of anything else to say.

"Come on now, babe," she says, "tell me."

"Err . . . Me? Err . . . Tell you what?"

"Tell me these little filthy stories of yours. Tell me, you dirty pervert."

So, I tell her the first thing that comes into my mind:

"I want you to be Little Red Riding Hood."

"Really?"

"Oh, yes . . . You are Little Red Riding Hood . . . and you walk through the forest . . . on your own."

"Oh . . . And who are you?"

"You want to know who I *really* am?"

"Yes, yes! Who you really are?"

"I am the Big Bad Wolf . . ."

"Oh . . . I'm getting scared here in this wild forest all alone . . . Please don't hurt me, Big Bad Wolf!"

"I won't hurt you. No . . . Not yet! Now I'm hiding behind a tree and am watching while you bend down to pick up the flowers."

"What are you going to do to me, Bad Wolf? I'm just an innocent little girl, please don't hurt me!"

"I am going to eat you, you dirty Little Red Riding Hood slut!"

"Eat me? Oh, you're a very bad, Bad Wolf. And you have got such a big mouth, and such big teeth."

Now, I didn't know how to take this last one, because these two front teeth of mine are a bit crooked. But, anyway, I thought I'd better continue with the fairytale. So, I say:

"But first, I'm going to eat this stupid grandma of yours."

"What do you mean, Bad Wolf?"

"I mean, I'm such a Bad Wolf, that I'm going to fuck your grandma really hard and then fuck you even harder, you silly-dirty-foolish-Little-Red-Riding-Hood-slut . . ."

"Are you serious now? She's seventy-nine!"

I think she got a bit upset. Well, we kept fucking, but silently. I didn't say anything more about her grandma. All I wanted was to push the limits a little bit further – that's all. I mean, you know, I never *really* wanted to fuck her grandma. I didn't even know her.

The Blue Nightie

... what's the time? Oh, God. It's late. I've got to get going. That was good wine, wasn't it? Pinot Noir. I like Pinot Noir. And you? Did you like the stories? I think you did, my young friend. Right then. I'll tell you a last one and then I'll go. That's the best one. It's called 'The Blue Nightie.'

I've told you before about Katerina, right? We met in England but a week later she had to go back to Greece. I've paid thousands of pounds to BT having phone sex with Katerina. Every day we would spend three hours talking and fucking through the phone.

First few days we had 'normal' phone sex: "What are you wearing now? Take it off. Now I'm fucking you like this, later I'm fucking like that," and so on and so forth. But, one, two, three, five, ten times, you get bored of it. Then, we moved on to the second stage: I would tell her that I was fucking her while other people watched.

After that, it's the third stage. Stage three has got two versions. Version one: "Now I'm doing this and that to you, and suddenly, your female housemate opens the door and joins us." Stage three, version two: "I'm fucking you on the kitchen table and a builder who is passing by joins in and we fuck you together."

So, we'd tell each other these kinds of stories and would

slowly-slowly progress to the final stage – don't get scared, my young friend, these are only fantasies, next morning you forget them. Well, the final stage is this: while she and I are having sex, five men come in the room and rape me. So, during those long phone calls with Katerina I was getting fucked by hundreds of men, and this idea would make her very horny. She kept saying that these stories made her pussy so wet that she couldn't stop herself from coming again and again . . . and again.

Then one night, she calls and I recognise from the tone of her voice that she's horny. So I ask her what she's wearing.

"I'm wearing nothing, babe," she says. "And you?"

"I'm wearing a blue nightie," I say.

"What are you wearing?" she asks again.

"A blue nightie," I repeat. You know, after all these rapes, I thought the idea would make her horny.

"A blue nightie?! What do you mean a blue nightie? Are you gay?" She was serious.

"I said that I'm wearing a blue nightie," I explain, "because I thought you were going to like the idea."

"Look, darling," she goes, "you cannot do such things when you come to Greece. My parents are very conservative. If you're gay you have to tell me. I have to know."

In her fantasies I had been fucked by half of the Greek population – not to mention the torture and rapes I had to go through in the Turkish army-camps, or our trips to Africa where whole tribes of black men had tied me down and took me really violently, while she was watching from her wooden throne, giving them orders how to fuck me better – and her only problem was the blue nightie.

LOUIS DE BERNIÈRES

FATHER PAPER LION, AVITA CRESSIDA JAY, AND THE TRUE CONFESSION

□ □ □ □ □

FATHER HUGH DE PAPELION was an exceedingly jolly priest. He owed his French name to a Huguenot ancestor who had come over to England in the time of Louis XIVth in order to escape the persecutions and dragonades of that profligate, warmongering, and reprehensible monarch. This ancestor had endured and suffered much, but his sufferings had effectively been rendered nugatory by a descendant, who had converted the family back to Catholicism at the time of the Oxford Movement.

Father Hugh de Papelion had trained at a monastery in the West Country and had then been sent to a parish in Suffolk, an anomalous parish in the sense that it was one of many in that area that was Catholic rather than Church of England. There were enough Catholics thereabouts to cause many a Protestant to raise an eyebrow, but no Papists had recently been involved in any plots to blow up the Houses of Parliament. In England one is allowed to be eccentric, up to a point, and so, over the centuries, the country's security forces had downgraded the Catholics of North Suffolk from Threat to Anomaly.

Father Hugh's jollity was not diminished in any way by the fact that no-one in his parish had ever mastered the correct pronunciation of his name, and he was universally referred to as Father Paper Lion, much to the puzzlement of the children, who thought that he was nothing like a lion at all, even a paper one.

Lions are not as rotund as Father Hugh, nor do they do they find coins in your ears, nor do they come to dinner and get into jovial arguments with agnostics about whether or not there is a god. Neither do they smoke cigars that their parishioners lay by for them specially.

Father Paper Lion was composed in the very image of Friar Tuck, with his capacious figure enclosed in equally capacious black robes, his roaring laugh, and his robust enjoyment of life, but he was also a conscientious and compassionate priest of the kind who is prepared to come out at three o'clock in the morning to attend a death, and leaves presents of food outside the doors of the exceedingly poor. The most remarkable thing about this priest was that he was well loved by everyone in his parish, including the atheists, the agnostics, the Methodists, and the junkies. He was disapproved of solely by the hierarchy of his own church, because no priest had the right to be so publicly happy.

Roughly at the same time as Father Paper Lion had been appointed to the parish, a world famous actress had decided to retire there, at the age of seventy. Thanks to good surgery she seemed to be about forty years old, but with an extraordinarily rigid face, out of which stared a pair of perfectly round and slightly wild eyes. Her hair, once lush, long, and blonde, had been replaced by an exuberant ginger wig that really should have been made out of something a little finer than horsehair. No doubt it was a relic of one of her roles. She draped herself in wondrous costumes, so that one never knew from day to day whether she would appear in the street as Joan of Arc, Ophelia, or Scarlett O'Hara. She wore astoundingly high stilettos, which gave her very good posture, but which meant that her progress was prodigiously slow as she processed carefully down the street to the minimarket. On sunny days she wore a pair of sunglasses with preposterously huge red frames. She lived on cream crackers, cream cheese, and sherry, and did not get up before noon. The hours from midnight until half past three in the morning were spent playing Beethoven Sonatas very raggedly on the piano, with the sherry bottle close at hand. She always made exactly the same mistakes at exactly the same points in the music. Her sleepless neighbours would be on tenterhooks with exasperation as they listened through the walls for the predictable and inevitable crash landing.

Avita Cressida Jay (*née* Dorothy Brass) had led an exu-

179

berantly scandalous life ever since the age of nineteen, when she had married a sixty-year-old tycoon who had soon afterwards died at Cannes when he fell off his yacht whilst drunk, urinating over the side in the dark. Avita had not heard his cries because she had passed out whilst listening to Caruso on the gramophone.

The grief-stricken, and now fantastically rich, widow found true love once more six months later, when she married a charismatic man in his mid thirties, who turned out to be a gangster, who, to do him justice, only ever murdered other gangsters. After he had been jailed for life for being involved in the murder of a doorman who was also a murderer, Avita Cressida Jay proceeded on an extraordinary sexual spree that did not really end until there was almost no-one of consequence that she had not slept with, and she had reached an age when not many still wanted to sleep with her. Her conquests included a minor member of the royal family, a poet laureate, an Iranian general, a dustman from Kerrymuir, a defence minister, a prominent French left-wing intellectual with a funny eye, a German conductor, a man from the Soviet Embassy who defected in the hope of marrying her, an art critic whom everyone had hitherto believed to be homosexual, a Brazilian cocoa baron, and all the usual Hollywood stars. For a while she had lived in an infamous *ménage à trois* with a couple of bisexual leftists in Hampstead. She had occasionally tried lesbianism, in the hope that she might like it, but she never really did, and eventually stopped trying. At the end of it all, in her little house in North Suffolk, she lavished her abundant affection on Valentino, a large Persian cat with a squashed-up face, that loved her as much she loved him.

She acquired an old-fashioned perambulator, padded it out with quilts and cushions, and she and the cat were often seen out together on pleasant days, processing slowly through the streets and along the towpath of the river on their way to the playground, where Avita and the cat would sit and look a little sadly upon all the children playing there. Despite her sexual generosity she had never managed to conceive, even though she had never taken any precautions against it. There were particular little children that she came to adore, and she would tell their parents how simply lovely and adorable their child was, and that she wished she had been able to have one herself, but her career had made it impossible. When it got dark she and the cat would go home, and she would usually watch one of her old films, at first on video but eventually on DVD. She loved to look back on her younger self and remember fondly all the leading men she had so playfully seduced. It appalled and saddened her to think that so many of them were dead, and she would hug the cat to her breast and leave tears on the sweet-smelling fur of its neck.

The onset of old age and the imminence of death often have the effect of focussing a person spiritually, but in the case of Avita Cressida Jay the spiritual was approached with the same promiscuity as her love life had been. She had not been too old to be affected by the half-baked and vapid spirituality of hippy times, so she had swallowed LSD in the hope of meeting God, she had chanted in front of Buddhas until her head reeled from the incense, she had collected polished stones during the time when there was a craze for pet rocks, she had spent all night naked in the woods dancing round a fire with a coven of self-trained witches who mainly worked in the council offices, and once she had even made love on a mossy bank with someone who wore a pair of antlers on his head. She tried many yoga positions but was not really flexible enough to do any of them, she tried veganism for two weeks and a macrobiotic diet for two days, and she travelled to India in the wake of the Beatles, when any Indian man who could afford a loin cloth could set himself up as a guru, acquire a Rolls Royce quite quickly, and sleep with western girls who thought that in this way they could become enlightened.

In her seventies, Avita Cressida Jay turned to what there was in North Suffolk. She went to Norwich and declared in front of an imam that there was no God but God, and Mohammed was his prophet, but soon found it impossible to get up at dawn in order to pray, since her own natural dawn was at midday. She went to a little parish where the nonconformists and Anglicans worshipped together, but she could never remember which of the five churches the services were scheduled to be in. She would drive from one to the other in her gold Nissan Micra, usually arriving too late.

Interested to know a little about the afterlife, she joined a circle of spiritualists in Beccles (sadly now defunct, but delivering messages to other spiritualists elsewhere), and received heartening but vague messages from dead people who claimed to know her, but who she herself could not recall at all. Having been told by her doctor that her many years of avidly smoking Black Russians had greatly compromised her lungs, she went along to Salvation Army meetings in the hope of improving her respiration by finding someone who was willing to teach her to play the tuba. It turned out that she had no talent for it, but she continued to go anyway, and helped them on their collection days in Ipswich and Bury St. Edmunds, where she enjoyed being recognised occasionally by people over sixty.

Avita Cressida Jay also went to the Catholic Church, where she buttonholed the priest and asked to go into the confessional, where she confessed to Father Hugh de Papelion she was not, and never had been, a Catholic. She knew how to confess, however, because she had once played a nun who had had a vision of St. Francis and had consequently turned down an offer of marriage from a handsome Renaissance prince who was one of the few that was not a poisoner.

Father Hugh looked at her through the grid and listened to her sibilant, husky voice. What was he supposed to say? "Go, my child, and do not not be a Catholic no more?"

Instead he said, "We can find ways of making you one, my child."

"I would like to be an honorary Catholic, Father."

"An honorary Catholic? I am afraid there is no such thing."

"The Jews have the Righteous amongst the Nations, Father, and Mormons even baptise people who are dead."

"That is true my child, but we have no equivalent, as far as I know."

"How can I be a Catholic without being one, then, Father?"

"You may come to the services, but you may not take Communion."

"It's all right," she replied, "I can get communion with the Anglicans."

Father Hugh harrumphed to indicate that an Anglican Communion could hardly be considered the real thing.

"Can I come to confess, Father?"

"You can confess to an Anglican, I think," said Father Hugh, "if you make a special request."

"I want to do it properly," said Avita.

"I think it may not be allowed," said Father de Papelion, "so it can only be done if you absolutely promise not to tell anyone. I feel that the Lord may allow it even if the rules do not."

"I promise," said Avita. "Oh, and another thing. When I am dying, and if it is convenient for you, I would very much like you to come and hear me confess, and perform the last rites. I do think one should try to die traditionally, in the best possible way. You know, like King Charles the Second."

"I really don't think I should," said Father Hugh, "but I will come, and afterwards I shall pray, and possibly give myself a penance."

"No cigars for a week," suggested Avita, adding, "Thank you, Father. Oh, and Father, I am leaving you a pot of gentleman's relish in the confessional. Everyone says you are very fond of it."

"Thank you, my child. It's the anchovies. Go and sin no more."

"I haven't sinned for ages," she said. "One has so few opportunities these days. What about a penance?"

"What penance, my child? A penance for not being a Catholic?"

"Yes, Father."

"Hmm, how about saying one *Salve Regina*?"

"I beg your pardon, father?"

"I said '*Regina*.' One *Salve Regina*."

"Is it difficult?"

"Not at all. You can say it in English, if you like. There are translations. It's not really much longer than a sonnet."

"Oh Father, I'd much rather do it in Latin. Where can I find it?"

"On the internet. I'll print one out for you and drop it off, if you like."

"Oh thank you, Father. You're very kind. I find the internet such a bore. I've quite given it up. You look up 'rash' and then you go from one thing to another until you think you're ill with every disease that ever was."

"Very true, my child."

"Where can I get a rosary, Father?"

"If you don't like the internet, you can get some very nice ones in Walsingham, I believe."

Nothing could have delighted Father Hugh de Papelion more than the prospect of confessing Avita Cressida Jay on her deathbed. He was a naturally sybaritic man who had never managed one day's real debauchery in his entire life. He had always had to enjoy most of the sins of the flesh vicariously, since his monastic vocation had prevented him from doing so at first hand. When given the opportunity, such as in doctor's waiting rooms, he avidly devoured the red topped scandal sheets that detailed the exploits of minor celebrities of whom he had in fact never heard. Once, in a bus stop, he had found an abandoned pornographic magazine whose explicitness had almost caused his eyes to pop from his head. He had furtively crammed it into his briefcase, and then burned it in the grate after half an hour's goggle-eyed perusal. He still dreamed about it at night, and woke up ashamed and embarrassed.

The reason that he wanted to hear Avita Cressida Jay's last confession was that she had been involved in a spectacular scandal some thirty years before, in which she and a cardinal had been accused of an undue attachment to each other, and of visiting each other in the small hours when respectable people were not usually in search of spiritual refreshment. It had made all the newspapers, not least because she had been publicly going through one of her pagan phases, and had been photographed dressed in a blood-spattered white robe, holding a decapitated chicken that had been allegedly sacrificed by a postman who was in his spare time a druid in ownership of a golden sickle that was really only gold-plated.

The unfortunate cardinal had been despatched to a closed monastery on an inaccessible island in the North Atlantic, where it is assumed that the almost perpetual ice may have cooled his ardour, and Avita Cressida Jay had evidenced her grief at their enforced separation by spending a week at a private clinic in Virginia Water.

Father Hugh de Papelion could not help it; he was desperate to know what, if anything, had occurred between herself and the cardinal. One reason for wanting to know was that the cardinal was a second cousin twice removed, and the whole family had been buzzing for years with arguments about whether there had been anything in it. Father de Papelion knew that whatever he heard in the confessional, even from an honorary Catholic, must remain forever secret, but still he wanted to know. It seemed very likely to him that it might be a suitable topic for a deathbed confession. It would not be too uncharitable to say that he looked forward somewhat to the death of the raffish old actress.

There came a day one sunny autumn when the falling leaves put Avita into the right frame of mind for falling off the twig herself, and she decided that soon she was to die. She went to the doctor and informed him of the fact of her imminent death, whilst reassuring him that she needed no treatment and was not depressed. She called in all her spiritual advisors and put them on notice, and she advertised in local shops for a loving owner for Valentino. She interviewed twenty-three cat lovers, observed how Valentino responded to them, and finally selected a Jehovah's Witness who repaired domestic appliances and cleaned windows. She spent a morning writing out an account of all Valentino's likes, dislikes, personal foibles and requirements, and left it on her dressing table, with instructions that the cat should be delivered to the Witness within twenty-four hours of her demise.

Avita Cressida Jay wrote her will, in which she left enough money to the Witness on the assumption that Valentino would need two meals a day for approximately another ten years, plus snacks. Everything else she left to a hospice on the Isle of Wight. Then she took to her bed with Valentino, and willed herself to depart. She gave up eating, and drank as little as possible, so that within two weeks she had already grown very weak. Feeling the valedictory mood growing hourly within her, she sent for her spiritual mentors.

Thus it was that a rabbi found himself face to face in her drawing room with a witch of very striking gothic appearance, only to be met on the way out by an imam in a very dapper robe and a white turban, who in turn came face to face with a saffron-robed and shaven-headed Theravadic monk, who came out and encountered an evangelical whose joy in the Lord was possibly more pathological than philosophic. She saw a shaman from Woodbridge, a crystal healer from Framlingham, a Reiki master from Diss, and an ecologist from Harleston who was to arrange her burial in a patch of woodland in a rapidly biodegradable wickerwork coffin.

On the day of her death she got up painfully and went downstairs to feed Valentino. She felt very woozy, and had to clutch onto things in order to get about at all. She felt her heart fibrillating in her chest and knew that her time had come. She poured herself a large medium dry sherry, and, with immense pleasure and trembling fingers, sat at the kitchen table and smoked her very last Black Russian as she gazed out of the window and watched the wind whip up the golden red sycamore leaves from the lawn. She went to the telephone and called Major Blake of the Salvation Army. She rested for a couple of minutes, and then telephoned Father Hugh de Papelion, leaving a message on his answering machine that he would not pick up until he came in two hours later.

Having heard the message, he gathered his things together, set off in haste, and found the door off the latch. Letting himself in, he found himself in a house exuberantly overflowing with religious ornamentation and impedimenta. There were crucifixes, menoras, philacteries, buddhas, tamata, icons, Green Men, Vishnus, Shivas, Ganeshes, and a corner dedicated to Catholic martyrs, in which there was statuette of St. Agnes carrying her breasts on a platter, and another one of St. Lawrence cheerfully brandishing a grill. There was also a saint with his eyes on a platter, who Father de Papelion failed to identify, and a St. Sebastian with his body and even his halo stuck through with arrows. It occurred to him that mankind owed the whole genre of kitsch to the world's religions, and perhaps especially to his own.

In the hallway stood a life-size teak carving of Hanuman, the monkey-faced god, owner of twenty-eight transcendental divine opulences, who was conceived with the aid of a piece of divine pudding that had been stolen by an eagle and dropped near his mother, Anjara. Avita Cressida Jay had draped the statue with garlands, and the floor about his feet was soft with ash from all the incense sticks that she had burned in his honour. Hanuman was clearly the greatest object of Avita Cressida Jay's devotions, and Father de Papelion was never to find out that it was because she identified closely with him on account of the fact that he had been very mischievous in his youth.

He crept quietly upstairs, and found Avita Cressida Jay in extremis, Valentino clutched to her breast, and her long silver hair flowing out over her breast and pillows. Her exorbitant wig lay discarded on the floor beside the bed. The room did not smell sweet, and Father de Papelion fought back an impulse to open the windows. There were several dead mice in various states of decay about the floor. They had been presents from Valentino who had hoped thereby to contribute to his mistress's recovery.

"Oh Father, it's you," murmured Avita, opening her eyes.

"My child," replied Father Hugh.

"I have to confess," said Avita.

"If you are up to it," replied the priest generously.

"Father, I have sinned," said Avita.

"I know," said Father Hugh, and as the dying woman said nothing further, he added "You are supposed to tell me the details, my child."

"I'm very tired," she said.

"Just the best bits," said Father Hugh, adding quickly, "I mean the gravest sins. Shall we do the worst ones first?"

"I enjoyed them all," she said feebly. "It was so much fun."

"What was?" he asked.

"The cardinal," she said.

"Yes, my child?" said the priest eagerly, leaning forward to hear her better.

"Cardinal O'Fagan. I called him Bumsie. He had the nicest bottom I ever saw. I saw a lot of bottoms, Father."

"I'm sure you did, my child. Please confess if you can. It will get it off your chest, and you'll go to meet the Lord with a clean spirit and a pure heart."

She reached out a trembling hand and rested it on his. She turned her head and looked at him. "Father, I met him at a do in the House Of Lords. I caught his eye, and he smiled. Such a nice smile."

"And then what, my child?"

"I was on my own in the house in Dorking, and there was a tapping on the window. It was a leaded window."

"Yes?"

"I opened it, and there he was in the moonlight, dressed as a policeman."

"A policeman?"

"It was his favourite thing. He couldn't manage anything unless . . ."

At that point Father Hugh de Papelion heard no more, no matter how closely he put his ear to her moving lips. The proximity of his face made the affectionate Valentino purr at double forte.

The cat's raucous purring was the least of his problems, however, for below the window outside Major Blake's rapidly assembled band of brass players were playing a very loud, very mournful, very eloquent, and very long version of 'Abide With Me,' just as she had requested for her last moments.

As the music died away, Avita gasped, held her breath, and died with it. Father Hugh de Papelion looked into those eyes from which the light had suddenly and completely fled, and said, "Damn." Then he made the sign of the cross on her forehead and said, "*Absolvo te*. Depart in peace."

He patted Valentino on the head, and went to her telephone to call the doctor, competing this time with 'For Those In Peril On The Sea,' which had been Avita Cressida Jay's second favourite hymn ever since an escapade with a Lieutenant Commander in Malta who had made love with her in a tiny dinghy in the turbulent channel between Malta and Gozo, during which time they had drifted quite a long way in the direction of Lampedusa.

After the doctor had arrived and set the formalities of death into motion, Father Hugh de Papelion started back to his church, where he intended to pray for the departed. "Oh well, it was better than nothing," he said to himself, and found himself singing "Bumsie bumsie bumsie bumsie

bumsie bumsie bum" to the tune of the 'Battle Hymn of the Republic.' He would never be able to get it out of his head for the rest of his life, and eventually had to accept it as the Lord's just punishment for his prurient curiosity.

FELICITY SKELTON

GEOGRAPHY

▫ ▫ ▫ ▫ ▫

Now, GELS, TAKE OUT your pencils. We're going to draw a sketch map.

Why did these words always bring prickles to my eyes?

After gazing at Miss Colley's chalky lines on the black-board – how she could make that white chalk squeak – my sight was blurred and smudged with tears.

I hope your pencils are nice and sharp!

She probably never said "nice." Nice meant precise; come to think of it, she probably did mean precise and sharp as well.

She was old, maybe thirty-five, wore laced-up shoes with ventilation holes, Viyella shirts and skirts which had gone baggy at the back. She had no shape that I can remember. If she did, it was that of a banana – hunched at the shoulders, with a small head topped with tightly permed hair of no easily determined colour.

We all, I think, felt both pity and contempt for her –

and her good friend Miss Kitching. I don't know how, but we knew that they had never left school. As daygirls they had arrived in the distant past, and as leavers they moved quietly, safely into the staffroom, and never left. We, with our teenage dreams of a future full of sex and cigarettes and beer, and then marriage to some chisel-jawed dark-haired surgeon or executive, could only fear that the truth might be that sideways slip, that creep and dumb acquiescence to the school rules, the school buildings, inside the school gates.

What on earth is that you're doing?

A pasty hand snatched the Geography exercise book from my desk. (Beige, with alternate lined and plain pages, for the drawing of maps. And ears of corn, I seem to remember. They were easier).

Why don't you sharpen your pencil? Erase this mess, and start again.

When the bell went, hell was not done with. Now it would have to be finished in homework.

My pencil was never sharp enough. My pencil sharpener, if no-one had 'borrowed' it, merely snapped the lead through. Once I made such a perilous point that it scratched a tear in the cheap paper. We weren't allowed to leave blank space in our books – every line had to be filled before we were given another – so I drew the map over the gash, hoping I could disguise it as a river or a coast-line. But Miss Colley was never going to let me past.

What's this? Why are you so stupid and clumsy? Get some gum and stick a piece of scrap paper over this and start again.

I gave up Geography, as soon as I could. But I couldn't

give up Biology, and then Human Biology – both taught by Miss Colley's sidekick, Miss Kitching.

Miss Kitching spent every double lesson reading out pages from the text book, or copying pages onto the board. Thence we copied them in our turn into our books. She rarely turned round to face us, and sometimes some girl, braver than me, threw a dart or a rubber. I needed glasses badly, but no-one had noticed, so to keep out of harm's way I sat near the back. But whether they'd discussed me, or whether it was spite, Miss Kitching soon decided that my handwriting and my drawings of frogs were abysmal.

Come to the front! Sit here, where I can see you.

This was really horrid, because she spat when she spoke, and if she did turn round, the two of us at the front desk were sprayed with it. The other problem was that the girl who always chose to sit at the front desk (those double ones, with a bench shared between two) was a vicious little madam who liked to pinch you for no reason. The only time I pinched her back she screamed and I was kept an hour in detention.

Miss Kitching was thinner than Miss Colley, and more tightly strung. She had one of those pinched faces where from the forehead down everything gets narrower and less significant, until the mouth is the size of a bum hole, and the chin recedes so swiftly that you wonder what's holding her bottom teeth up.

Sometimes, I think, she was aware that we hated her. She seemed on the edge of tears, and exhausted. Mostly, she was rude and ignored us as much as she could. One day a girl said she felt sick and Miss Kitching wouldn't let her leave the classroom. She turned her back and went on drawing blackberry bushes on the board – one of those triple boards that you could telescope up and down and across.

Angela was sick, loudly, on the floor between Miss Kitching's desk and the door.

Sit down, at once, Miss Kitching said, without turning round, but Angela was brave and she left. We were aghast. Nothing happened. Miss Kitching carried on until the bell went, then picked her way carefully around the stinking mess on the floor and left the room. We'd been hoping she would slip in it.

When I passed my French GCE with a good grade I went to see Miss Colley, who taught French as well as geography.

"P'tit" she would say, her lipstickless mouth pursed as if she hoped for a kiss. "P'*tit*" – the emphasis on the *tee* and no *-er* sound please. Otherwise it was *Lar maysonn ay darn lar rue*. The only French word she made any attempt with was "P'*tit*."

Please, Miss Colley, may I do French A' level?

She looked me up and down – suddenly, I understood where the expression came from – and gave a contemptuous "huh."

You? *You*? Can *you* really imagine yourself writing an essay in *French*?

For the only time in my life I stood up to her.

I don't see why not. I like French. I've done well in it.

But she made the "*huh*" noise again and turned and went back into the staff room, slamming the door.

As we got older and bigger, and bosoms swelled and hips gave us waists, and we started rolling the waistbands of our skirts till they were *almost* more than the regulation two inches above the knee, Miss Colley and Miss Kitching shrank and receded. They were irrelevant. Miss Colley got more and more bad-tempered, and Miss Kitching more and more weary and irritated if anyone spoke to her.

Then, one day in Human Bilge, we came to the reproductive tract. Tract? Does it have a tract?

What we all must remember, even those of us not close enough to smell the sweat which was seeping through Miss Kitching's nylon jacket under her arms, is that the tube which makes up a human testicle is immensely long. It was a three-board job, and as Miss Kitching drew, first one long line, and then a parallel line to that because after all it was a tube, until the whole wall of the classroom was covered with what looked like unravelled knitting, she kept up a commentary. It went something like this:

And if you took a man's testicles and cut them open and extracted the tube and spread it out it would reach from here (one side of the board) to over here, and to here, and right to here . . . (all across to the other side), and then back again, and up here (squeak) and down and along here, and again, and longer and longer and longer and more and more and more, (squeak), and on and on and on . . . and her face was redder and redder and she moved quicker and quicker, and her arm was a blur as she stretched up to reach the top of the board and then bent to fill the very last inch of the space, even behind the desk, where we couldn't see it.

And it was the only time any of us could remember her not copying out of the book.

SHOUTING
STORIES

HANIF KUREISHI

WEDDINGS AND BEHEADINGS

□ □ □ □ □

I HAVE GATHERED THE EQUIPMENT together and now I am waiting for them to arrive. They will not be long; they never are.

You don't know me personally. My existence has never crossed your mind. But I would bet you've seen my work: it has been broadcast everywhere, on most of the news channels worldwide. Or at least parts of it have. You could find it on the net, right now, if you really wanted to. If you could bear to look.

Not that you'd notice my style, my artistic signature or anything like that.

I film beheadings, which are common in this war-broken city, my childhood home.

It was never my ambition, as a young man who loved cinema, to film such things. Nor was it my wish to do weddings either, though there are less of those these days. Ditto graduations and parties. My friends and I have always wanted to make real films, with living actors and dialogue and jokes and music, as we began to as students. Nothing like that is possible here.

Every day we are ageing, we feel shabby, the stories are there, waiting to be told, we're artists. But this stuff, the death work, it has taken over.

Naturally we didn't seek out this kind of employment. We were 'recommended' and we can't not do it; we can't say we're visiting relatives or working in the cutting room. They call us up with little notice at odd hours, usually at night, and minutes later they are outside with their guns. They put us in the car and cover our heads. Because there's only one of us working at a time, the thugs help with carrying the gear. But we have to do the sound as well as the picture, and load the camera and work out how to light the scene. I've asked to use an assistant, but they only offer their rough accomplices and they know nothing, they can't even wipe a lens without making a mess of it.

I know three other guys who do this work; we discuss it amongst ourselves, but we'd never talk to anyone else about it or we'd end up in front of the camera.

My closest friend filmed a beheading recently, but he's not a director, only a writer really. I wouldn't say anything, but I wouldn't trust him with a camera. He was the one who had the idea of getting calling cards made with 'Weddings and Beheadings' inscribed on them. If the power's on, we meet in his flat to watch great movies on video. He's jokey: "Don't bury your head in the sand, my friend," he says when we part. "Don't go losing your head now. Chin up!"

He isn't too sure about the technical stuff, how to set up the camera, and then how to get the material through the computer and onto the internet.

It's a skill, obviously.

A couple of weeks ago he messed up badly. The cameras are good-quality, they're taken from foreign journalists, but a bulb blew in the one light he was using, and he couldn't replace it. By then they had brought the victim in. My friend tried to tell the men, it's too dark, it's not going to come out and you can't do another take. But they were in a hurry, he couldn't persuade them to wait, they were already hacking through the neck and he was in such a panic he fainted. Luckily the camera was running. It came out underlit of course, what did they expect? I liked it – "Lynchian" I called it – but they hit him around the head, and never used him again.

He was lucky. But I wonder if he's going mad. Secretly he kept copies of his beheadings and now he plays around with them on his computer, cutting and re-cutting them, and putting on music, swing stuff, opera, jazz, comic songs. Perhaps it's the only freedom he has.

It might surprise you, but we do get paid, they always give us something "for the trouble," and they even make jokes: "You'll get a prize for the next one. Don't you guys love prizes and statuettes and stuff?"

But it's hellish, the long drive there with the camera and tripod on your lap, the smell of the sack, the guns, and you wonder if this time you might be the victim. Usually you're sick, and then you're in the building and in the room, setting up, and you hear things, from other rooms, that make you wonder if life on earth is a good idea.

I know you don't want too much detail, but it's serious work taking off someone's head if you're not a butcher, and these guys aren't qualified, they're just enthusiastic, it's what they like to do. To make it work on television, it helps to get a clear view of the victim's eyes just before they cover them. At the end they hold up the head streaming with blood and you might need to use some hand-held here, to catch everything. It has to be framed carefully. It wouldn't be good if you missed something. (That means that ideally you need a quick-release tripod head, something I have and would never lend to anyone).

They cheer and fire off rounds while you're checking the tape and playing it back. After, they put the body in a bag and dump it somewhere, before they drive you to another place, where you transfer the material to the computer and send it out.

Often I wonder what this is doing to me. I try to think of war photographers, who, they say, use the lens to distance themselves from the reality of suffering and death. But those guys have elected to do that work, they believe in it. We are innocent.

One day I'd like to make a proper film, maybe beginning with a beheading, telling the story that leads up to it. It's the living I'm interested in, but the way things are going I'll be doing this for a while. Sometimes I wonder if I'm going to go mad, or whether even this escape is denied me.

I better go now. Someone is at the door.

JOEL LANE

WITHOUT A NAME

□ □ □ □ □

IT WAS THE SIMPLEST of marketing gimmicks. A plain
black label, no brand name or logo, on a frosted glass
bottle. On the back, a tiny label gave the statutory product
information: alcohol content and volume. It was priced like
high-end vodka, maybe £16 a bottle. The drink itself was a
sweetish clear spirit, not unlike kirsch – a shock of intense
flavour with a strangely numbing, blank aftertaste. It didn't
mix well, but there was a purity about the neat spirit that
people seemed to like. Nobody knew what it was called.
Some retailer started calling it Nada, and the name stuck.

After a few months, it emerged that the manufacturer was some small company in the Netherlands run by
a one-time stockbroker who'd gone bankrupt in the
credit crunch. I assumed it was the aura of the unknown
that made Nada so popular. After all, it was a strange time.
The government had broken most of its election prom-
ises and was handing over all the public services – health,

policing, education – to private firms based overseas. And the deepening chill of 'austerity' meant nobody dared to rock the boat. In a climate of fear, the unknown might feel like a way of getting through.

But all my theories about Nada's appeal dissolved in my first shot of the drink. It filtered through my gut like a wave of stillness, making everything in the world seem clear and painless. Then it was gone, and all I could taste was the memory of that quiet moment. I drank half a bottle of it that night, and walked home in a kind of blurred ecstasy threatened by shadows I couldn't make out. For me, it was never a drink to just have one or two of in company or in a hurry. You had to give yourself up to it.

There were rumours that Nada contained some kind of narcotic; but official lab tests confirmed it was just an alcoholic spirit. It was catching on mostly among solitary drinkers and in quiet pubs, not in wine bars or at parties. People who drank it didn't tend to socialise, and they certainly weren't out on the pull – though you'd see couples on dates drinking it, wrapped up in their cocoon of desire. And it made some people violent, especially if they mixed it with other drinks.

I'm not sure why I gave a bottle to my mate Barry for his fortieth birthday, except that I was trying to tell myself it wasn't addictive. He and his wife had recently separated, and I felt he deserved something to escape into. I knew he'd never tried the drink. We were at his house, and he poured us each a shot. I was still drinking a beer he'd given me, so I hadn't touched my glass of Nada when Barry got up to change the CD, then stopped halfway across the room and turned, as if listening to a sound from the road. Then he collapsed silently. By the time the ambulance came, he'd stopped breathing.

The hospital found traces in his bloodstream of some very potent synthetic poison. The police took the bottle of Nada, and confirmed that the drink was contaminated. They kept me for two days. I might have been in major trouble if there hadn't been several more deaths from poisoning that week, all linked to Nada. The unnamed bottles were withdrawn from shops and bars. The police stated that a minority of bottles in the international Nada supply had been poisoned, apparently at random. The manufacturer would have been arrested, but he committed suicide by drinking a poisoned glass of his own product.

Needless to say, Nada was banned everywhere. But there were rumours of a black market, and private Nada parties where the addicted took their chances. At Barry's funeral, all I could think about was having a glass of the stuff. I'd run out at home. Maybe I needed some distraction – I've never coped well with funerals. Don't see the point of turning grief into a ritual when it already corrodes everything. And there was the guilt as well. I'd given him the frosted bottle.

A few weeks later, I lost my job due to a restructuring at work. It was launched by the MD with a lot of inspirational talk about brand identity and modernisation. *Change is the norm*, a memo to staff declared. None of it meant anything – except that the same work would be done by fewer people, on casual contracts. Thirty people who'd been told to think creatively about their role in the company were informed that they didn't have one.

By the end I was glad to leave. But the exhilaration of

freedom didn't last long. I applied for twenty-three jobs and didn't get a single interview. It was November, and my severance package wouldn't last to the end of the year. My flat deteriorated. I lost the will to keep in touch with family or friends. Didn't even have Nada to fall back on, though cheap vodka was an acceptable substitute.

One night I heard a rat scratching frantically behind my bedroom wall. I couldn't stand just to lie there and wait for it to find a way through. I got up and walked out into the rubbish-strewn streets of Balsall Heath. It was two in the morning. Maybe there'd be an all-night bar or off-licence somewhere.

I followed the main road towards the city centre. A few cars drove slowly past, the drivers scanning the pavements for drug dealers or prostitutes. But the recession had affected even those trades. To my right, a side road dipped sharply under a railway bridge; a narrow brick walkway led across to the other side. Under the bridge, I could see a light above a black door. I walked carefully down the steps to the cracked paving-stones of the street's meniscus. On the far side, the upper branches of trees were framed by the moonlight.

The building looked like a club, but it had no name and no sign apart from a black square that stood out from the wall. I had nothing to lose. I rang the bell next to the unmarked door, and was about to walk away when the door opened and a man in a black jacket said: "What are you after?"

"Nothing," I answered.

He stepped back, leaving the door open. I slipped inside. It was an office building refurbished cheaply as a night-club: red lights, dark wallpaper, a small bar with black metal tables. A dozen or so people were sitting there, but none were in groups or even pairs. The bar had no taps or optics, just a line of bottles beside the cash register. All of them were of frosted glass with plain black labels. The middle-aged barman was idly spinning a wooden wheel that rested horizontally on the bar. It held three concentric rings of shot glasses, all filled with a clear liquid.

As I stood there, wondering what to say, a man rose from one of the tables and handed the barman a tenner. The barman spun the wheel harder, then let it slow to a halt. The customer took a narrow shot glass and knocked back its contents in a single gulp. He closed his eyes and then, slowly, returned to his seat. The barman filled a new glass, put it in the gap, then spun the wheel again. He looked at me.

Just one drink, I told myself. For old time's sake. And I couldn't afford more than that. I handed him a crumpled banknote. The glasses spun round. I could smell the faint, sweetish odour of the unnamed spirit. How many bottles was he using? What would happen if one turned out be deadly? The barman looked through me, into the night I'd come here to escape from. He didn't care.

It tasted better than I remembered. Was that just the effect of not having drunk Nada for a couple of months, or was it really different? There was an edge to it, a metallic tang that lingered in my mouth. In that moment I knew. I swallowed the rest of the shot, put the empty glass back on the bar, and nodded to the barman. Then I turned and walked back out into the street.

To my right, steps led up to a broken wall with a few

black trees reaching above it. The moon was caught in a web of twigs, fading.

A CHANGED MAN

□ □ □ □ □

As HE CAME OUT of a deep dawn dream, out of a fiery dream and into his bed, John Munby became aware of a terrible truth: for it seemed that, at some point in the night, he had turned from a person into a voice. A voice without a body.

"Oh," he said, "this is awkward."

But strangely enough, he knew exactly what to do next. He slipped such moorings as he had – the duvet, his light-blue pyjamas – and ascended into the air. Then he bumped into the ceiling.

Eventually, once he had accustomed himself to the smooth mobility of his new form, he made his way to the corner of the bedroom above the closed door. He could see the keyhole below him. He slid down the door, over the white panels and round the silver handle, and let himself out into the world – into Manchester.

Now, in the fresh air and at the start of a new day, he

felt his anxiety itself change shape: it took on the aspect of a grand eagerness to test the capacities of his new-found freedom. "At least I will not die in bed," he announced. His voice filled the air – *he* filled the air.

In an ecstatic spirit of adventure, he crossed the road, and soon found himself at the bus-stop opposite his house. There stood Miss Helen Fairweather.

It had formerly been the kind custom of this lady to stop and talk to John, but she had stopped stopping and talking around the time that he had taken to drinking his red wine during the day as well as the night.

John did not mind; he could see that she had been afraid of him.

"Good morning, Miss Fairweather," said the voice that used to be John Munby. Of course, this voice sounded like his, but its source was, as far as Miss Fairweather was concerned, nowhere to be seen. She looked sharply around her, but, seeing nobody, did not reply, in case it was a sneaking person she did not care to address. She thought she smelt claret. The bus arrived, and carried her away.

The voice flew off in the opposite direction. He had a yearning to see someone he loved.

"Jessica," he said when he had slipped into the appropriate flat, on the seventh floor of a grand tower overlooking the park, "who is this man?"

The man was asleep. Jessica was awake, however, and sat up at once. She fearfully leaned over to look under the bed. There was nothing there except for an old novel.

"Don't look for me now, Jessica. I can see you are busy."

Jessica hid her face.

"It's all right," John said. "Just tell me: do you love him now?"

Slowly, she took her hands away from her face. She nodded.

John Munby said: "Good for you." And then he let himself out.

A little later, perched on the top of the same tower-block, listening to a vigorous argument some way beneath him, on the seventh floor, the voice of John considered its options. Going to see Jessica had not made him any happier, as he had hoped it would. And now he felt himself to be tired of the city. Tired of being 'he.' Enough was, this time, definitely enough.

All at once, as lightly as he had floated up from 'his' bed that morning, he shed his 'he-ness.' 'He' became 'it': just a voice; an ex-John-Munby.

The voice decided that, as it could now travel so freely and so effortlessly over the world, it would embark on a grand tour. It would see the far-flung places. It would swim. It would fly. It would climb every mountain. It would float down Broadway and the Grand Canyon alike. It would speak to strangers, perhaps in foreign tongues – how difficult could it be to pick up a little French and Spanish, not to mention Hindi and Mandarin, along the way?

The voice did not know how long this wonderful condition of complete freedom might last or, indeed, whether it wanted it to. It felt no great urge to return the past, and its old, voice-less life at the bank, with wage-slaves. It felt no great ambition for the future. Above all, it was remarkably complacent, philosophical even, about the present.

"A metamorphosis," it reasoned, having now shaken off

the last remnants of Munby-ish uncertainty, "is not always to be feared."

From Manchester, it headed south.

At Nottingham, it assisted a family of tourists who wanted to be in Northampton.

At St. Albans, it stood in a public library and shouted, "Shush!"

On the beach at Margate, it considered the welfare state with a blind pensioner, while, from a distance, her daughter watched her talking to herself, and concluded that she was now very far gone indeed.

At Dover, on a fine May morning, it spoke all the poetry it knew, and admired the view.

In Paris, at the Musée du Louvre, it crept behind the portrait of a king and, when the tour guide came near with a large group of visitors, interrupted her with corrections and tales of gallantry.

In a Roman palace, it gave the President a piece of its mind.

In Vatican City, it crouched in the Pope's mitre and spouted phrases from the *Book of Common Prayer*.

In Berlin, it went clubbing. But it was too loud there for it to make itself heard.

The voice travelled on.

It debated economics in Geneva, helped tearful twins through a maze in Copenhagen, busked in St. Petersburg (the *politsiya* failed to move it on), stabilized the situation in a certain trouble-spot (the precise location of which must remain forever classified), fell in love with the innocent happiness of a koa-wood ukulele in Honolulu, directed the traffic at a San Francisco cross-roads, met the novelist Richard Brautigan and warned him to stay off the booze, and, in a bar in Los Angeles, stopped to intervene in a dispute between professional killers over which was better, left or right-handedness.

"*No*-handedness," the voice said, "is the one true liberation."

And that settled that.

At last, the voice that used to be John Munby grew weary and hoarse. It had travelled a long way, and all but satisfied its appetite for adventure – adventure such as it had never experienced in its former life.

In Washington DC, nobody paid it attention at all – the people walked down the broad streets with their hands over their ears. This was a new blow of loneliness. Although chiefly taking joy in its immaterial independence, the voice had often sought for understanding too, if not friendship and love. But such things were not so easily obtained. Most people, it seemed, did not wish to linger too long in the company of a voice without a body, however much it strained to be helpful to them. And it did not improve the voice's mood to discover that the people who didn't mind it at all could usually hear other voices, too, that it could not.

They were often unhappy, and made for bad company.

The voice wished that it had been turned into a gigantic bug, stayed at home and not spoken to anybody at all for at least two months.

A tall ship took the voice all the way back to England. It walked – or rather, pretended that it was walking – along the Jurassic coast of Dorset. Blankly staring at the sea one day, from the top of a hill slightly inland, it turned and saw an old man making his way cautiously along a rising path. The man seemed somehow to be an old-fashioned one. He belonged in this remote place, and had always belonged there. The voice thought he had a familiar look. Behind the old man, in a valley, was a village; through the trees could be seen the tower of a church.

The voice hid in a bush, and as the man passed by, called out:

"Theodore!"

The old man stopped, and raised his head.

"Yes, God?" he asked.

In a carefree mood, and in more irresponsible times, the voice might have left it at that – as a good joke, well carried out, on somebody who did not, as far as it was concerned, matter in the slightest. Or it might have carried the mischief a little further. But this time the voice was merely pleased to note with what simplicity and politeness the man, whose name was evidently Theodore, had replied.

Time stood still. The waves of the sea were hushed. The stealthy voice might now say anything it liked – it was God, and could tell Theodore to go and throw himself into the sea. It could tell him that, for his many sins, he must now lie down in the field and tear his clothes. Or that he must do as an ambitious soldier once did, and pay for victory in battle with the life of his only daughter.

But such things have been done before, and will be done again. The lonely voice did not think of them.

"Theodore," it said, "I am curious. Pray tell me, if you

please, what it means for a man to die? I would like to know, for . . . I am curious."

"Death," replied Theodore, "is the final transformation. Beyond there lies nothing, and life is as nothing to the dead, and all things are laid low. A man who is dead knows no time, no eternity, no sleep; no reward or punishment awaits a sinner there, in that great expanse, in that kingdom of the dead."

The voice was both impressed and bemused.

"But there is so much in the world, Theodore, there is so much to see, and enjoy, and do. We should not willingly give up life to enter this fine kingdom of yours."

"It is no more mine, Lord," Theodore replied, "than it is thine."

Was the man drunk? Or was he simply always like this? The voice did not care to find out. For now, it had come to a decision – one that had been made a long time ago, it realized, in a deep dawn dream, only to be forgotten as quickly as it had been made.

"Theodore," said the voice at last, "I thank you for your wise reply to my enquiry. May I impose on you a little longer, to ask your advice on a delicate matter?"

"Yes, God," said Theodore. He seemed to be quite untroubled by the notion of a deity who needed to ask for his advice.

The voice grew serious.

"I wish to know what a – what a God must do, in order to be rid of life?"

Theodore said nothing, so the voice went on:

"Theodore! You must know that I have enjoyed myself greatly, very greatly, creating such wonders as life on earth and the stars in the sky – and I do not now despair of the world and wish to be rid of it, despite its iniquities, which are all ultimately my fault, anyway, of course . . . But I have made a peace with myself that requires me to pass into this place you speak of – this place beyond punishment and reward, beyond sleep, beyond eternity, beyond everything. I wish to go there. Would you, out of your charity and love towards me, be able to tell me what I must do in order to obtain my desire?"

Theodore looked cautiously into the bush, and ventured to say:

"Fire, I believe, Lord, is the element for you."

The bush seemed to meditate on this notion. And then it replied, with a laugh:

"I do believe, my dear Theodore, that you are right about that. But I have left my box of matches in Manchester."

And with that, it flew away, heading north.

The voice had remembered that John Munby, in his cups, had left the gas stove on over-night . . .

On her street in Manchester, Miss Helen Fairweather was almost thrown off her feet – the bus had braked violently, several yards short of her stop. She steadied herself and drew breath to tell the driver to be more careful and take her to the appointed place, when she heard him say: "There's somebody up there." He was looking across the road.

From an ugly brick house, smoke fumed upwards into the night.

Miss Fairweather looked into the flames.

At the blasted window where she had often seen John

drinking his red wine and falling asleep over his books, she could make out the shape of a man raising his arms to heaven.

AIMEE WILKINSON

DOT DOT DOT

□ □ □ □ □

IT WAS THE DAY after their party that he first found one;
floating in a plastic cup in the dregs of a vodka and tonic.
A beetle, the smallest he'd ever seen. A mere dot in the
universe. Its legs curled tight underneath its body, it was
a millimetre or two in size with a black exoskeleton. He
presumed someone had left the window open, it must have
flown into the house attracted to the light. He dropped the
cup into the bin bag he was carrying and thought nothing
more of it.

After he'd cleaned the house to a state comparable to
when they'd first moved in, he phoned Claire to see how
she was feeling. He'd thought the party would cheer her up.
But as the night grew long and their friends more raucous
she'd withdrawn into herself, made excuses about popping
to the 24-7 garage for some lemonade and hadn't returned.
Later, he'd found a text on his phone telling him that she'd
gone to her mum's for some 'peace and quiet,' and as word

got round that she'd absconded, the party itself dispersed, and he'd gone to bed alone.

Claire retuned later that day and made appreciative cooing noises at how clean the house was. She didn't mention why she'd left, didn't thank him for arranging her party or discuss how she felt. She switched on the TV and settled down into the folds of the sofa, the cushions enveloping her body as if trying to swallow her. And as the minutes slipped into silence between them, he went upstairs and ran her a bath.

That night, as they were undressing for bed he found three more beetles on the top on their white bed sheets, like an ellipsis on a blank page, the end of a sentence left unfinished. He brushed them onto the carpet and glanced at Claire to make sure she didn't see; he didn't want to upset her further or give her a reason to sleep on the sofa again. They lay with their bodies facing the ceiling, and as he reached out his hand to take hers, she pulled away and turned her back to him.

He went to work the next day with the weight of his worries like a leaden blanket wrapped around him, and he immersed himself in data management. Every now and then he would think about Claire. What would she be doing while he was working? She'd moved past the daytime pyjama phase, where she would forget to brush her teeth, comb her hair, but the melancholy still bubbled on the surface and threatened to spill. He wondered how much time her work would allow her to take off, before wanting to replace her. And he thought about how long it would be before they could resume some resemblance of normality.

She offered him a thin smile when he came home in

return for the white roses he'd brought her. White roses: a small gesture to say the things he couldn't express. The TV was on, some generic cooking programme about the season's hottest recipes, and he wondered why she watched such shows seeing as she hadn't cooked once since it had happened. He opened his mouth to comment on this irony, then snapped it tight shut again, holding back the flash of irritation, as he had grown accustomed to doing.

On the magnolia walls of the bedroom he was greeted with dozens of little beetles, each stationary as if sensing his approach. Surprised they didn't move, he put his thumbnail to one and applied pressure. The body cracked and fell to the cream carpet, leaving a dot of black beetle blood on the wall. He took some tissue and wiped away the beetles, his movements frantic as he found more and more of the little creatures. It was as though, as his eyes adjusted to them, additional beetles kept appearing in the places he had just cleaned. He felt them patter on to his feet like the first droplets of rain, saw them bounce into the ply of the carpet. Claire came in and watched him, her eyes narrowed.

"What are you doing?" she asked.

"I'm getting rid of these bugs, they're everywhere." He shuddered, as if they were crawling on his skin. Claire shrugged but didn't look at the black dots crawling in the carpet. He wiped the last of them onto the floor before checking the other walls. "Can you just get the Hoover for me? I can handle this."

She left the room and returned a second later with the Hoover. Then she went downstairs and closed the door as he began to clean.

That night he tried to touch her again. The doctor had said that they needed to retain contact, to find solace in each other. As they lay side by side he reached out to her, his tentative fingers wide on the cotton sheets like a star-fish, but just as they brushed the tips of her own, she turned her back to him and switched off the light.

In the morning he found a beetle nestled underneath his index fingernail, its legs ploughing deeper into his skin. He picked it out then flicked it onto the floor with disgust. They were all over his bed sheets, on the walls, the window sill, the curtains and the carpet. Scores of them, dancing dots before his eyes. He put a glass of water to his lips, took a long drink then felt something alien move on the back of his tongue. His stomach contracting, he retched back into the glass and counted six bugs bobbing up and down in the bile-infused water. He pulled back the bed sheets, dumped them in the laundry basket and switched on the Hoover.

He found Claire downstairs staring at the TV in her dressing gown. A filmed-over, neglected cup of tea by her feet, her hair unkempt. He watched her for a moment, his arms still trembling from exertion, his chest tight.

"Are you just going to watch TV all day? When are you going back to work?"

She didn't move. She didn't even blink, her eyes fixed only on the screen. "I don't feel ready."

He clenched and unclenched his fists. "Claire, it's been weeks. How long are you going to keep this up for?"

"Until I'm ready."

"I can't keep going like this. You need to face facts. Get over . . ."

She turned round and stared at him. He stopped, his

words choked back, like someone's fingers were wrapped around his throat. And so the sentence remained unfinished. An ellipsis hanging in the air between them, crackling with electricity.

But it was too late. In a burst of energy, Claire leapt up from the sofa and pounded up the stairs. He chased after her and watched as she stripped out of her pyjamas and pulled on a pair of jeans and a t-shirt. Her ears deaf to his pleas, she grabbed a bag out of the wardrobe and filled it with clothes. He followed her from room to room, unable to stop her or explain how he felt. She only turned to face him as she as she opened the front door.

"That's how you feel isn't it? Get over it? Accept and move on? It's not as easy for me as it is for you."

"We can always try again. The doctor said . . ." Claire held up a hand to silence him, turned and slammed the door.

He went back upstairs and lay on the bed as his thoughts spun around him. Should he have told her how he felt? Would that have convinced her to stay? His eyes focussed on the ceiling and he noticed the beetles were back again. There were hundreds of them, and as he watched still more appeared, until the ceiling was engulfed in black. Then suddenly, with one fluid movement, the beetles dropped down and landed on his body. They swarmed up him, millions of little legs scratching his skin as they crawled under his trousers, his pants, his shirt. They were in his ears, in his nostrils, scraping and scampering into his mouth. He tried to close his jaw. Clamp down on them. But there were too many and they were too strong. The force of thousands pushed his mouth open and they piled into his body, down his throat. There was a searing pain and a loud crack as they broke his jaw and split the skin around his mouth. Beetles skirted over his irises, buried their way under his eyelids. As the light faded to black and his body heaved from the inside out with their sheer collective weight, all he could think about was Claire and the things left unsaid.

ROBERT SHEARMAN

COMING INTO LAND

◻ ◻ ◻ ◻ ◻

LADIES AND GENTLEMEN –

We hope that you have taken pleasure in this Air Inter-continental Flight from Los Angeles to Paris, France. That you have enjoyed the in-flight entertainment system, that you have enjoyed our specially prepared meals and snacks. We hope that you've taken the chance to sit back, and relax – and maybe sleep as we've crossed all those time zones.

We now need to inform you that we will soon be beginning our descent into Paris. And we ask you to pay attention to the following information and act upon it accordingly.

We are currently cruising at an altitude of thirty-thousand feet at an air speed of four hundred miles per hour. The time at our destination is 13.25, so do remember to change your watches if you haven't already done so. The weather looks good and with the tailwind on our side we are expecting to land in Paris approximately fifteen minutes ahead of schedule. The weather in Paris is sunny but cloudy, with a high of seventeen degrees in the afternoon, you may need to wrap up warm, there's a chill to the evening. If the weather cooperates we might get a great view of the city as we descend.

We hope that may be possible. The captain says he'll do his best. That would make it easier for everybody. It all depends upon the clouds. We're fighting these damned clouds.

We will soon be locking all toilets prior to our arrival in Paris, so this would be a good time to use the facilities if you have not yet had the occasion to do so. Go now. It's all right. We'll wait.

I'm sorry, that's all the time we have. I'm sorry. If you could all return to your seats. Yes. I'm sorry, madam. I'm sorry. Please return to your seats, and prepare for landing.

We ask that at this time you secure all baggage underneath your seat or in the overhead compartments. Please take care in storing baggage, and know that the contents of the compartments may have shifted during the flight. Please turn off all personal electronic devices, including laptops and cell phones. Smoking, of course, continues to be prohibited for the remainder of the flight, and will not be permitted until after you have cleared customs and left the terminal building. You are welcome to keep drinking alcohol. If you are the sort to find it calming, if you find it an aid rather than a hindrance to concentration.

Please make sure your seat backs and tray tables are in their full upright position. You may fasten your seatbelts or not. It's all the same to us. If you choose to fasten your seatbelt, insert the metal tab into the buckle by your side and pull on the strap until it is comfortable or secure. But many find that the seatbelts don't do any good. For some they are, if anything, a barrier. For some the seatbelts suggest their faith might be lacking.

And, ladies and gentlemen, be advised. It is all a matter of faith.

Air Intercontinental is proud of its safety measures, and our fleet has a survival rating that is one of the highest in the world. Last year an average of eighty-three percent of all our passengers arrived securely and intact, at any one of our destinations all around the globe. Eighty-three percent. That's not something to be sneezed at.

But we know too that faith is a personal thing. And that even with all the support and encouragement from our specially trained staff, not all our passengers are able to sustain that last effort of mental strength necessary to ensure their safe arrival. On every flight there will be those that fail. On any flight, those that will vanish from their seats. That'll disappear completely, and fade into thin air, the moment that the wheels hit the runway.

There are certain precautions that should be taken to give you the best chance this will not happen to you.

We are arriving soon in Paris, the capital city of France. You will not land safely unless you absolutely *believe* in Paris. You are required to have faith in the city, in its culture, and in what it represents. In the very concept of Paris, on a philosophical level. If you have no faith that it's really there, then it won't be.

Playing upon your screens now are certain classic images of Paris to help you in your effort. The Eiffel Tower.

The Mona Lisa. An old man on a bicycle waving a baguette. It is important that these be used as a focus for your concentration, and not as a replacement for actual faith itself. You need to believe in Paris, not merely the images put before you. The man on the bicycle will not be there to save you.

Some of you will be returning home to Paris. For you the ideal of Paris should be easier to hold. But be warned. Simply knowing something exists is not quite the same as having *faith* in it. We know tales of French couples, perhaps disillusioned with their lives, disillusioned with each other, who have lived in Montmartre for years, perhaps, who have more *evidence* than most of Paris's existence – and who, nonetheless, didn't make it through touchdown with all their body parts in place. Maybe they got complacent. Maybe, at the crucial moment, they took their minds off Paris altogether. So even if you've lived in the destination city of your flight and feel you've no doubts at all, we ask you still to pay attention and focus. Focus upon what your home *means* to you, right deep down in your soul.

Do not fall asleep or doze during the landing. Heaven knows where you might end up.

For those of you who have never even visited Paris before, your task is necessarily harder. But do not be unduly alarmed. Concentrate on what Paris means to you, too, and why you booked the ticket there to begin with. Why you paid so much money. What it was that drove you to so risk your very existence, and give such anxiety to the loved ones you've left at home, just to visit the place. There must be a strong idea of what Paris is in your heads in order for you to have done that. It doesn't matter how idealised or inaccurate, not if you truly *believe* in it. Faith isn't a spelling test. Just hold on to that inner Frenchiness you have, hold on to it tight, and you'll be just fine.

For those of you who have visited Paris, but have never lived or worked there, you may be in the greatest danger. You may only half remember a city you once visited when you were small. You may be hanging on to happy holiday memories from when you were a kid – that time when your Mummy and Daddy smiled at you, when they took you to that park, when they let you feed all those pigeons and eat that ice cream – are you really *sure* that was Paris after all? That you're not getting your holidays mixed up? Think. As you ate your choc ice, can you remember whether it was really the Eiffel Tower that was looming above you? Wasn't it just a common or garden electricity pylon? Be sure.

It is estimated that false nostalgia is responsible for most of the deaths and vanishings on transatlantic travel. False nostalgia kills.

For me, when I need to have faith in Paris, I always think of my time there with Jacques. Jacques and I walked along the Seine hand in hand. We drank Beaujolais and we smoked Gitanes, and he was the perfect lover, we made love right there underneath the night sky of Paris. With the sound of Paris in my ears and the smell of Paris up my nose, and yes, all those people watching, and some of them were tourists, but most of the peeping toms were Parisians through and through. And as he drove deep inside me, "Mon Dieu!" he cried, and I squealed loud and shrill, I squealed loud so the noise would bounce off the Notre Dame, ring right round the Arc de Triomphe, all Paris could hear our rutting, and Paris delighted in it, because that's what Paris is, Paris doesn't care, Paris is a whore, I squealed like a little pig, *une cochonette*, that's what Jacques called me, I didn't know what it meant at the time, afterwards I had to look it up, frankly I was a little disappointed, "Mon Dieu," cried Jacques, "cochonette, merci beaucoup!" So, as the plane descends, as we near the ground, I think of Jacques, it's the thought of Jacques I hold on to, and I think of how afterwards he held on to *me*, so tightly, and how his French peasant sweat tasted.

Some of you may prefer to think of the Louvre, or of croissants.

Please do your best to keep your children calm during the landing procedure. You will have seen how we distributed amongst our younger passengers at the beginning of the flight little picture books of Paris, along with simple but convincing explanations of the city's importance in commerce and the arts. Encourage them now to review this literature, and make sure for their own safety that they have not graffitied flying dragons or similar non-Parisian monsters over the illustrations. We invite you too, if you feel any doubts or weakness, to study the safety card in the seat pockets in front of you. The French translation of what to do in the event of a crash can be very reassuring.

Should the cabin experience sudden pressure loss, stay calm and listen for instructions from the cabin crew. Oxygen masks will drop down from above your seat. Place the mask over your mouth and nose. Pull the strap to tighten it. Then breathe normally. If you are travelling with children, make sure that your mask is on first before trying to help them with theirs.

Should this happen, of course, it might distract your

concentration. Alongside the oxygen mask will drop a headset. Place the headset over your ears. Wiggle the toggle to adjust volume. The headset will be playing a medley of typical French music, from *La Marseillaise* to Sacha Distel. If you are travelling with children, make sure that your headset is playing first before trying to help them with theirs.

If you are travelling with children, there is no point trying to hold on to them. It doesn't work. It doesn't work. Believe me. I'm sorry. Believe me.

We are now beginning our final descent. We hope that you have taken pleasure in this Air Intercontinental Flight. The cabin crew have certainly taken pleasure in serving you, and we hope to see you again on another flight very soon.

I didn't mind that Jacques lied to me about being married. He kept the ring on, after all, and every time he waved to the barman for another drink he flashed it in front of my face brazenly enough. Every time he reached out to stroke my cheek. No, I just wish he hadn't given me a false address. What did he think I was going to do, stalk him? I'm a girl from Louisiana. I knew what this fling was, just a fling, right? But when I tried to visit his home, my next stopover in Paris, I found that the street he'd given me didn't even exist. That's what hurt. I never pretended it was love, not even as we were having sex, but it wasn't just *sex*, was it, there was something more to it, wasn't there? I thought so. I believed so. Yes, that's what hurt.

I wonder if his name were Jacques at all.

Landing positions.

Good luck, everyone. See you on the other side.

Oh, Jacques.

Air Intercontinental thanks you for flying with us. We always remember you have a choice.

Oh, Jacques, hold on tight, baby. Hold on, *mon brave*.

STRICTLY PRIVATE & CONFIDENTIAL

□ □ □ □ □

Strictly Private & Confidential

Mr ____ _____

___ _____ _____

LONDON

___ ____

Dear ____ _____

FINAL WRITTEN WARNING

Thank you for attending the disciplinary meeting on 5th August 2012. The purpose of the meeting was to discuss your work performance; your failure to meet the required standards of work when we believe you are capable of doing so and your negligence in the management of your workload for which you are responsible. In particular, the recent issues with the management of company data.

_____ _____, Managing Systems Executive conducted the meeting; I was present as her witness. You declined the opportunity to have a witness present.

During the meeting we discussed the issues with company data which had occurred in November/December 2011 and had resulted in you being subject to the capability procedure. Under the capability procedure you were set clear objectives in communication, relationship management and company data management. These issues were also discussed in your performance review in February 2011 and as a result of your continued performance we withheld your 2011 salary review.

You explained to us that you struggled updating the spreadsheet on which the management of the company data depended. You said that you had concentrated on assimilating company data, rather than completing the back-up information. You acknowledged that without the back-up information it was not possible to keep track of the company data, and this had resulted in the loss of important data and your inability to be able to respond to senior management's queries. The lack of comprehensive information also affected your ability to be able to produce reports from our company electronic files. You told us that you were able to produce reports for senior colleagues as they had updated the company data files correctly.

You said that the situation you had found yourself in led you to feeling pressured. You had spoken to _____ _____ and she had been supportive, but you found it difficult to meet her expectation. You were also given support by _____ _____ who spent time with you on managing your inbox. You told us that you felt suited to a support role. You thought that your key strengths were around the relationships with other members of the team and helping them.

We discussed the capability review meeting that took place in April and July and you advised us that you felt that both meetings had been fair and accepted that the problem was on your part. We talked to you about issues that came to light in July, whilst you were on holiday, around the managing of company data. The issues seemed to be created because you did not maintain an up-to-date overview of this data. There were numerous occasions when you requested information that had already been passed on to you and uploaded in to our system, and there was an instance where the same report was sent to the same member of staff on two separate occasions.

You told us that you had been feeling a "deep set feeling" that you were "suspended in dread." That you felt "reality, with its commonplace ebbing and flowing, was slipping away" from you and you were "spiralling into a void, a non-place of self-doubt and misunderstanding."

We outlined your failings and reiterated to you that they

had caused much embarrassment for the company and a considerable amount of time for your managers and colleagues in trying to determine where this company data had disappeared to. It prompted _____ _____ to make the decision to take the responsibility of data management away from you. Evidently, this is not a decision that has been taken lightly; it is now necessary for one of your colleagues to take on the workload. Furthermore, it leaves us with a situation where it is increasingly difficult to justify your role. It is through these actions and as you have offered no grounds in mitigation that we are issuing you with a final warning. This warning will remain on your file for 12 months.

We discussed that you will continue to assist the team; however you understand that in order that your situation be viable you have a period of 3 months in which you need to win back _____'s confidence, so we feel you are capable of taking back responsibility for company data, and in doing so will not cause any further risk to the good reputation of the business.

You have the right of appeal against this decision to the Managing Director _____ _____ within 5 working days of receiving this letter. You must do so in writing and set out your grounds for appeal.

Yours Sincerely

_____ _____

HUMAN RESOURCES DIRECTOR

Disciplinary Meeting 5th August 2012

Present: _____ _____ (**A**), _____ _____ (**B**), _____ _____ (**C**)

B introduced the meeting and explained that we would review the information about **A**'s performance. **B** checked that **A** received documents and there was nothing he was not aware of.

B: The problems in 2011 reflected in your yearly performance review; were these discussed at your last appraisal?

A: Yes.

B: Okay, I'll now review your performance, chronologically.

A: Okay.

B: Your problems ostensibly started with the management of the company data?

A: Everything stalled and I was not prepared for that impact, it knocked me off kilter and I was not prepared for its impact. I don't think I handled the impact well, and the problems started when information I was receiving began to disappear within a black hole of my own making. Before it seemed to be going so well, you know.

B: Why was this . . . [unable to decipher what followed due to interference] . . .

A: Through my own fault, of course. I had not updated the spreadsheet, it confused me, I concentrated on other tasks, on rather than, you know . . . of equal importance, the back-up information. Others rely on those spreadsheets. I found it missing – it's all my fault – I should have updated those spreadsheets. But I felt like a funambulist, walking a very thin line, balancing across a gargantuan void of meaninglessness . . . Everything was teeming with nothingness, you know, like Beckett said. *Teeming with nothingness.* So I was walking between these two poles: nothingness and those spreadsheets. I failed. I simply failed.

B: Could this have contributed to the problems with communication?

A: Things just got worse.

B: I don't think it was solely the spreadsheet that led to these problems.

A: I took my eye off it.

B: It took a long time to resolve.

A: Yes. I'm not sure I made the connection, or understood the situation. I felt that I was doing a lot of things, but not doing them well. Schopenhauer said: 'Every man takes the limits of his own field of vision for the limits of the world.' I think there is a lot of truth in that, I became myopic, my field of vision narrowed. I dealt with all this by brushing it all under the carpet, metaphorically speaking of course, subconsciously affected by the stress. I didn't, and still don't for that matter, want to cause people trouble.

B: It all came to a head in November/December.

A: I think this was when it was like a snowball rolling, beginning to roll, to accumulate speed and strength, when it began to hurtle downwards away from me, yes. The problem was getting bigger each day, getting out of control. Issues started to surface.

B: Yes, your line manager complained to me at this point. You had caused a lot of problems for your team.

A: The problems I faced with the spreadsheet were

immense to deal with. The loss of company data happened because I'd not updated the spreadsheet. I have repeated this to you countless times already. Work was sitting on my PC that I didn't know about. The amount of emails that I was receiving at that time, well, quite incredible really . . . I found it all so painfully, cripplingly overwhelming. I don't know, it was just a failing on my part. My errors became catastrophic; things began a natural down-turn because of my actions, wait, my inactions. I possess a deep-set feeling that I'm suspended in dread. It's hard to explain, reality, with its commonplace ebbing and flowing, is slipping away from me, like spiralling into a void, a non-place of self-doubt and misunderstanding.

B: We started the capability procedure, concentrating on your communication, relationship management, and data management. Do you have anything to say about this?

A: I knew my reports were not going out as frequently and consistently as they should have been. Administration became difficult. Have you heard of Fernando Pessoa?

B: No.

C: No.

A: Well he was a poet of outstanding beauty. He wrote in various aliases, or *heteronyms* as he liked to call them. Well, here, when I am here, I feel like someone else, you know, I feel like another person. Like Pessoa, I feel immense sadness at the things I see, at everything around me, this office, the people I work with, it's all so sad.

B: Okay. But I don't see the point of this . . .

A: Well, of course there's a point . . .

[**A** leaves the room momentarily. **A** returns after approximately 4 minutes.]

A: Look, I began to panic. I began to feel the weight of time, the time it took me to do things, simple things. I began to feel smothered. Lost. Gone, you know. Some call this stress, but I think it's something altogether different ... I think it's something deeper. Something real. Getting everything up to date would take time and would mean that other tasks would have to be left. I was starting to feel the pressure of this. When under this pressure I made a point of not showing it, so I would complete tasks hoping people wouldn't notice.

B: Did you not discuss this with anyone?

A: No, I simply brushed things aside.

B: But these tasks weren't difficult, you should have been able to manage them.

A: I have been having difficulties. I have this recurring image that haunts me day and night. It's my mother. I see my mother. In the hospice, the tubes sticking out of her, wending their way to machines, the hole in her thorax, the phlegm, the decaying tissue and muscle. The voice box gone. I see her there, dying, everyday and night. It's all I can think about, her suffering, the pain, the way it had to end for her. All that pain. So when I sit in here, in this office, processing all your information, well, it just doesn't compete, you know. It is nothing to me. I have other things on my mind. I don't expect you both to understand this. I don't expect you to even care. I just thought I would speak truthfully with you. I just thought that if I explained everything to you then you might be able to see why I am the way I am. I leave my mark everyday here for you to scrutinise, but that's all you do, like an automaton, you scrutinise the marks I leave behind. And nothing else. It's like you aren't capable of thinking any other way. It's like you don't want to think any other way.

B: Would you say it is fair to say you have been consistent in apologising and then it doesn't change when you say it will happen?

A: I see there are problems. I see there are mistakes. Last year was a wash-out. I've finally come to terms with this. I've been in denial about it. Once when I was a small child I ran away from home, I hid in a tree house we had built near a disused canal behind the houses I grew up in. I hid in the tree house for hours. I could hear my poor mother calling out my name, frantic with worry, I could her crying, each sob. At first I liked it, I liked the power. I liked the fact that no-one knew where I was, like I had just vanished. But then her sobbing, her cries, the worry and pain my mother was going through began to weigh heavily on me and I had to return to the house. I said nothing when I returned and just let my mother's tears pour over me. It took me years to apologise. I hid my guilt away, I hid the pain away.

B: The scale of your problems are large.

A: Yes, I see that.

B: There were instances when managers were chasing you for company information and you said to them you would send it ASAP but you never did. You just ignored their emails.

A: That's correct. I feel dreadful panic every day. The slightest things set me off: it can be losing my favourite pen, or the way someone has intoned something in conversation, or a spelling mistake in an email. I cannot stand the lack of grammar these days, have you seen the emails people send to each other at work these days? Have you seen the lack of basic grammar in them? I cannot begin to describe to you the paroxysms of rage this sends me into, so much so it eventually sends me into torpor. So, it turned me into a zombie and there's nothing I can do except stare at my screen all afternoon, doing absolutely nothing.

[**A** became silent for a good 3-4 minutes.]

A: Have you ever done that? Have you ever done absolutely nothing?

B: No.

C: No.

A: Well you should try it. It's very liberating. It clears the mind of all the awful things that drag you down. It's the best cure for all of my ills. Have you ever heard of Joseph Brodsky?

C: No.

B: Is this really relevant to your appraisal?

A: In 1989 he gave a commencement address at Dartmouth College called 'In Praise of Boredom,' and in that address, to the packed lecture hall, to all those eager students about to step out into the big wide world he said: ". . . you'll be bored with your work, your friends, your spouses, your lovers, the view from your window, the furniture or wall-paper in your room, your thoughts, yourselves . . . You'll try to devise ways of escape . . . You may take up changing jobs, residence, company, country, climate; you may take up promiscuity, alcohol, travel, cooking lessons, drugs, psychoanalysis. In fact, you may lump all of these together; and for a while that may work. Until the day, of course, when you wake up in your bedroom amid a new family and a different wallpaper, in a different state and climate, with a heap of bills from your travel agent and your shrink, yet with the same stale feeling toward the light of day pouring through your window . . . Depending on your temperament or the age you are at, you will either panic or resign yourself to the familiarity of the sensation; or else you'll go through the rigmarole of change once more."

B: I don't know . . .

C: Joseph who?

A: Well, I have finally woken up, and like Brodsky I sing to the world that we should embrace boredom. We should go with rock-bottom. We should sit here and revel in our boredom together. Come on! Celebrate it with me! Come on! You're both bored, too . . . That's why you're here, doing this, come on, you're both bored, too. We are all bored!

B: I really have no time for all of this . . . You have caused the company a lot of embarrassment and wasted a lot of my time. It is why we have reached this point; it is why we are all here.

A: We are here because we must be here, we have to be here, there is nothing else for us but *here* . . .

B: I really can't go on . . .

A: We must go on . . .

B: This is pointless . . .

A: That's why we must go on . . .

B: Do you have anything to add? To me it all seems fairly transparent; things have been raised at meetings.

A: I am always searching for moments of clarity, but these tend to be few and far between . . . Then, I am back in the thick of it. In the mud, the slutch, the shit with everyone else . . . Trying to get a foothold, you know.

B: Thank you for that . . .

[**B** leaves the room.]

A: But we must go on . . . We must go on, right?
C: I'm just here to take notes. I don't know . . . Must we?
A: Yes, we must go on.
[**C** leaves the room, leaving **A** at the table.]

SINGING STORIES

MICHELENE WANDOR

THE SNOW CURL

□   □   □   □   □

—A Story for Lila

ONCE UPON A TIME there was a snow curl. It wasn't a flake, because it wasn't shaped like a flake. It wasn't a snowball, because it wasn't big enough to be a snowball. It wasn't a snowman or a snowlady because it was nothing like packed together enough to be any kind of snowperson, and it wasn't a round shape.

Its job was to come down from the sky and float and swoop and curl its way round trees and through branches, curling its way down to the ground. That's why it was a snow curl.

It was very fussy about where it was going to land. It knew it must land some time, because all snowflakes and snow curls have to land, because they go down from the sky, down to the ground. So the snow curl decided that if it was going to land anyway, it was going to find the perfect place to land. On land, of course. The snow curl wasn't stupid enough to land on the sea or in a river, because it knew it would melt and float away into the water.

It didn't want to land on a roof, because houses are warm, and the roof would be warm and it would melt. It didn't want to land on a car, because people come out and drive cars and they wipe the snow off their cars and windows so that they can see where they are going. It didn't want to land on a window sill, because a bird might come and sit on it with its feathery bottom.

It was night time, and quite dark. Far below, on the ground, the snow curl could see lights. It was floating high in the air, gently going downwards. As it got nearer the ground, it saw there were lights in the street, on tall poles, so it called them street lights. Then there were lights shining out of the windows of houses, where people moved around behind the glass. So it called them window lights. Luckily there was quite a bit of wind, so it could float around, from left to right and from right to left, looking around all the time as it was floating down. It was accompanied by lots of other snow flakes, all of them different from the snow curl, but all of them very friendly. They all smiled at each other and dipped their curls and flake-ends in greeting. You may wonder how a snowflake and snow curl can smile, but they can. So there.

Then the snow curl saw exactly where it was going to land! There was a little garden with a little wooden house with glass windows and a glass door, and inside the little wooden house was a table with two chairs. There was no-one in the little house, because it was too cold for people to sit in. The roof was pointed, and on the top of the roof was a round piece of wood, with a point on the top, just like a pear. The snow curl had never seen a pear, and didn't really know what a pear is, but it liked the funny shaped thing with a point on the top, and it knew as surely as a snow curl can know anything, that this was the place to land.

A gentle blow of wind took the snow curl down into the garden, and carefully deposited it on the top of the roof, right on the tip of the wooden pear. And the wind whispered into the snow curl's ear (because snow curls, unlike snow flakes, have ears): "All the snow flakes will melt, but you will just become invisible. From this little wooden house, you will be able to guide all the other snowflakes and snowcurls down safely onto the ground. And when you are invisible, you will be able to see everything that's happening, all over the world, by day and by night."

And the wind kissed the snow curl behind its ear, and the snow curl shivered with pleasure, because now it had an important job to do.

MICHELENE WANDOR

THE SNOW TUNE

□ □ □ □ □

—A Story for Oliver

ONCE UPON A TIME there was a big flurry up in the sky.
All the snowflakes were getting ready for their big day. They
were going to have a very special snow party, which was
called a snow storm. A storm is usually a little bit fright-
ening, but this storm was going to be gentle and soft and
white, and it was going to fill the sky for miles and miles
around.

The snowflakes weren't quite ready to set off for the
journey through the sky. Every time the snow falls from
the sky, it has a special tune, and every time there is a new
fall of snow, there has to be a new tune. The flurry in the sky
was because every single snowflake had its own idea for a
new tune, so you can imagine the noise!

Some snowflakes were singing very very loud, and other
snowflakes said to them: "Hey, you, you're too loud. Please

sing a bit more quietly." Some snowflakes were singing very very quietly, and other snowflakes said to them: "Hey, you're singing too quietly, sing a bit louder, please. We can't hear you." Some snowflakes couldn't think of a tune, and other snowflakes said to them: "Hey, you, why aren't you singing?" And the snowflakes shrugged their shoulders (because some snowflakes have shoulders) and said: "We can't think of a tune."

After a lot of singing and not singing, the snowflakes gradually fell silent. They looked up, and there, above them, was a new cloud, and the cloud said: "Come on, snowflakes, it's nearly time to go. Are you ready?"

The snowflakes shushed and shustled each other, and finally they all spoke together in one soft voice: "We haven't got a tune yet."

"Well," said the cloud, "gather round me and we'll find a tune together."

So all the snowflakes gathered round the edges of the cloud, and they tuned their voices and they tuned their guitars and they tuned their ukeleles and they tuned their drums, and the cloud swooped and dived and rolled and waved, all in a rhythm, and all the snowflakes started humming to the rhythm, and then they started listening to each other, and some snowflakes sang high and some snowflakes sang low, and some snowflakes sang fast and some sang slow.

Finally, the cloud slowed down its cloud-dance and stayed still in the sky and said to the snowflakes: "There. Now you have a tune, and you are ready to go. Bye-bye! Have a lovely flight."

And the cloud shook itself and all the snowflakes took

off and flew slowly and gracefully down and around each other, dancing to the rhythm, and humming their tune and nodding to each other.

And that is why, when it snows, everything is very quiet, so that the snowflakes can hear each other singing.

Author's note:

Writing with reading-aloud-in-mind can mean a number of different things. I have written commissioned stories to be read aloud (pre-recorded) on BBC radio, and I have read some of my stories aloud at live readings, in the presence of an audience. When my children were very little, I was lazy about making up stories for them, preferring to read books to them. With my grandchildren, it is a little different – influenced partly by the fact that the two for whom the above stories were written live a long way away, in America. So these stories were written for someone else to read out loud to children who (then) were too young to read for themselves. I think that if I were reading them aloud, I would find myself ad-libbing and improvising round the story, to suit the present moment and the child in question. A new, ephemeral story would come into being, by virtue of the written story being voiced.

KAREN STEVENS

WHERE YOU'RE HEADING

□ □ □ □ □

WE HADN'T SPOKEN FOR A YEAR, me and Mrs Neill. Not since our Lee gave her the finger when she'd kept his ball. You went storming round her house to get his ball back, of course – all fire and thunder (*I'll break your door down, voodoo woman!*). Next thing the police were out front and you'd locked yourself in our bathroom, hanging out the window and threatening to jump. Do you remember that, Les? Do you remember putting your bare foot out onto the window ledge? I was thinking: *this is it; this is really it.* I held my breath and waited for you to drop like a shot crow.

Since then, we hadn't spoken for a full year, me and Mrs Neill – but last Tuesday I stood in her green-carpeted hallway with Tom Jones's *Green Green Grass of Home* looping dangerously through my head. Mrs Neill watched me with her tiny psychic eyes. "It's been hard, Mary, watching you watching that road day after day," she said, in the long pause in which she could have turned away. She pulled me into her big soft bosom. *Green-green-grass-green-green-grass,* went her back-patting. "How much can we ever know of our stories as we live them," she soothed.

This afternoon I watched the tap dripping. It's the time of year as much as anything, Les. Just a few cars passing through our road and the boys back at school and that hollow September stillness that makes me feel so empty.

Mary,
Time up.
Les.

That's what your note said a year ago today. I searched the house like a dog seeking another dog's smell, then pushed my face into the dent you'd left in your pillow. I kept saying, *Life will always be unfair.* Every time I said *unfair* I felt as if I was falling off a cliff.

Time up. Just that. After ten years.

Over the past year I have kept watch at the front gate, imagining again and again the time when you will round the curve at the end of our road. I will watch you grow bigger until your dark shape has lines, and I can see your stony Welsh features. You will only stop walking when your breath pushes against my face – *Down the la-a-ne I walk with m-y-y sweet Mary, hair of gold and lips like cherries, it's good to touch the green green grass of home . . .*

That's what you sang to me in The Blacksmith's Arms when we first met. Remember? I told you my name and you were drunk and broke into song and the whole pub stopped and clapped, and I was riding your voice like it was a horse.

Anyway, we started talking last Tuesday, me and Mrs Neill – and on Wednesday she was sitting on my sofa. Her knowing eyes travelled over our coffee table, across the kids' dirty cups and cereal bowls. I cringed because I thought she might mention that afternoon when you threw half of our crockery out of our kitchen window. Afterwards, you went to bed for days because you couldn't stop thinking about the universe and the Earth hurtling through space at 67,000 miles per hour. That's what you said: 67,000 miles per hour. No more, no less.

"I get a lovely smell of violets," Mrs Neill said. "That's how I know a message is coming." She paused for me to ask about the violets and the message, but the air was thickening like porridge and I was scared I wouldn't be able to breathe. You would have gone mad, Les, if you'd found her sitting in our house – *voodoo woman* – but I was like a plant in drought, a year long drought, when leaves curl in on themselves and grass turns tobacco brown. I couldn't face another year of nothing.

It was January 1979, Mrs Neil told me. That was the first time. She was lying in bed and couldn't work it out, the smell of violets. Her John – God rest his soul – was asleep beside her. And then a voice said, *Margaret, this is Charles. I have come to tell you something you should know.* Charles is Mrs Neill's dashing cavalier and spiritual guide. Charles had a message from her beloved dead mother who told her to go out to John's shed and search through his things. Finally, in an ancient wellington, tucked behind the lawnmower, she found a bunch of old letters from his mistress.

Pornographic, they were. Filthy. "Now, I'm telling you this," she said, "because Charles has a message for you too. About your Les."

I lit up a fag with shaking hands and, as always, Mrs Neill was receptive. She saw my fag smoke quivering, and knew I wasn't ready. Her big bosom drooped with disappointment. *Just take the message*, I told myself, but there was a wall that the words kept banging against, and I said nothing.

I often watch Mrs Neill's 'ladies' struggling up her front path. They have the same look, as if the world has fallen away and they are stranded in mid-air. Sometimes, I put a glass to our living room wall and listen out for the guiding words that funnel down from dead people's dried-up mouths. I expect to hear the shrill wail of unhappiness or uncontrolled laughter, but all I've ever been able to make out is the word, *Kevin*. During the long silences, I imagine Mrs Neill is doing something awful, like giving a Chinese burn, but her 'ladies' always leave with a new certainty in their step, as if the world has rolled back beneath them. This is what I wanted, Les. For a year I hadn't known whether the sun still shone or whether the stars still moved on their set courses.

When Mrs Neill had left I went to our front gate and watched the road. The evening light had a strange sepia feel and the houses were flat black shapes – that's how it seemed to me – just shapes. I watched the dark curve at the end until the light had nearly gone from the world. I sat in the boys' bedroom once it was dark and listened to them breathing in and breathing out the powdery dust of everything. *This is it, Les. This is really it*, I told myself.

When our Ashley woke he looked surprised to see me. He launched into one of his long speeches about air crashes and black boxes. He wants to be a pilot because they're trained never to give up. Right up to the last nano-second pilots worry about altitude and technical stuff, even when the plane's breaking up. If they lose faith in their training then that's it, it's all over. *Whoop! Whoop! Boom!*

While Ashley was talking I kept seeing you on that last awful night, Les, standing naked and half-hidden between your two rows of runner beans. Your body was too lean, too grey, as if over the years you'd stopped living.

That night I dreamt you were slipping through blackness with outstretched arms, your hands clutching two tiny stars. I floated towards your voice – *Down the road I look and there runs Mary* – grabbed the heel of your foot, hauled myself onto your leg and crawled until I was grasping the ribbed hump of your chest.

On Thursday Mrs Neill put a note through our door: *I don't like to think of you worrying about receiving your message. Every story needs some sort of direction. Come and have a cup of tea and we'll see where you're heading. Mrs N.*

On Friday, another note. I was hunched below the living room window but managed to summon the courage to peer out. It was a shock. Mrs Neill was standing in our flowerbed, her boiled face just inches from the glass. Her big bosom was pouting, and suddenly I doubted. I read her second note, anyway: *Come round this evening. Charles is not happy, but I had a chat and told him about your pain. The pain that only a man can give to a woman. Mrs N.*

Thing is, Les, since the dream I can only imagine you hanging in space, and that's how I want to keep you –

suspended in inky blackness and ready to sing for me. I don't want to know that your feet are walking up another woman's path or pushing themselves under her table. I don't want to know that you are pinker and fleshier, more solid than when you disappeared.

There are no answers outside of ourselves. *Go away,* I mouthed to Mrs Neill, and she stumbled backwards, over our flowerbed, as if I'd slapped her. I was receptive, and I saw my life laid out behind me: your body recoiling when our skulls were pressed together for that photo . . . your head turning away in shame when I laughed . . . your jokes about how I speak: *We're eating salad, aren't we kids – not salid. Ha-ha* . . . And that time after sex – *oh God* – when you said it was like being pulled into a terrifying tunnel of darkness . . . and later in our marriage, when I put your hand on my wrung-out breast and you'd kept it there, unmoving, like a form of punishment . . . and in The Blacksmith's Arms, right at the very start when you should have walked away, yes, you should have walked away, Les – *Down the la-a-ne I walk with m-y-y sweet Mary, hair of gold and lips like cherries* – but my friend Angie wiggled up like a plump child on display, and held your attention. She ran her hands over the fleshy hump of her breasts and spun around so that her new dress opened like a scented flower revealing the tops of her heavy legs – and that quick red thrill shooting up your neck . . .

And why have you never liked me in that way? Why have you never *burned* for me?

You would always leave, and I have always known this.

There have been times when you have looked at me almost with pleading, begging me to acknowledge it. Year upon year, it has felt as if I have been squeezing the air out of your song, the notes gradually thinning and thinning until they are no more than vibrations. It has been exhausting, and it has felt, at times, as if I have been slowly killing something.

SIMON PERRIL

DUETS

□ □ □ □ □

THAT NIGHT THE CUTLERY misbehaved into the small hours, the small hours distended; and all he could do to accompany this activity was to focus upon the bedroom doorknob. Breaking the knob's gaze to a certain rhythm proved productive. If he looked away and returned – moderately fast – the knob would not flinch in its regard. That the house contents lived a full life at night and mostly slept in the day was no cause for alarm. Alarm is the astute conjunction of idea and music in a corporeal pouch, he thought. When he could.

The holes in his face: five. Three might be voluntarily sealed. One, once open, became a conduit, and he could barely choreograph what passed through, into, and out of this pocket that doubled as a passage.

He never remembered his dreams and so, out of revenge, decided to act out their absence in the daytime. Egg first, fried to the degree to which the eye is gougeable with minimal spillage. At such moments he would be wearing – for once he had seen them – the track marks of these dreams; his body a soft map alluding to territories not consciously visited, and never recalled.

It wants eating, mother would say. He knew this to be true, and it troubled him. Everything awake and wanting. Willing. He was not yet glass. Though shapes swam his flanks, darted within his temperate depths. Soon he would blossom. Fruit.

The guitar in the corner of the room. The lesson it held, the sculpture it was. Of the forest machine it might be when he plugged himself in, and just listened to the wood and tensile branches. It was a prosthetic ear through which he heard the first idea of a forest. He would walk this idea into the open, into the park.

Green. Bench. Path. Green. Bench. Path. Green. Bench. Path. Green. Bench. Path. Swings. Trees meshed, knitted by bird diatribes. He moved through the air, felt the breath of trees on his cheek. Walking over the green humps of parkland, he wondered what lay under them, sleeping municipal dreams. Four dogs, three stick-less, walked their owners round the circuit. Nothing connected, nothing lit. A slight intensification in the luminosity of the grass. Perhaps if he positioned himself elsewhere the whole park would fire like a synapse, ripple like a surface of water; discrete objects curating their own eddies in a civic symphony. But there was the nagging matter of the empty pocket in the pit of his stomach; what was kept there was now lost. Needed replenishing.

The internal organs of the supermarket vibrated in a way for which he had sympathy. And it was comforting to see himself portioned out and cellophane-wrapped in assorted aisle compartments. At the till, the lady brimmed with pride as she told him he could have two for the price of one. Figures. It was like being at work, listening to his boss's invocation to abstract gods of quantity and measurement. He could see his logic. Really see it. Words danced with numbers in perfect formation. Like bees. But in this instance, and others like it, there was never any by-product such as honey.

He clutched the limbs to him as if they formed the rudiments of a body modification kit. He spilled onto the street, saliva on a tarmac tongue, past the penthouse molars to the further reaches of the city's mouth.

It was nearly time, and he had been practising. He couldn't recall the first moment he found he could strum his thoughts with all manner of materials. They wouldn't sing, so much as hum, and this had marked effects: it was an Orphic condition. Today was barely a day at all. It was as if night had been converted to negative. The intensity hurt his eyes. Perhaps he should practise again now. Duets were the way to take the edge off things; to sound that edge and strike up some kind of partnership with the simple objects to which the world belonged. The nearest opportunity for a duet was the intestinal bike chain coiled around the exoskeleton of the BMX. The tarmac scab looked absurd on such a wounded pavement.

BLAKE MORRISON

THE SONG OF
THE CAGE

□ □ □ □ □

RIGGS PICKED UP THE MEN halfway down the autoroute. He hadn't planned to, but the bolder one, who was
Hispanic, stood his ground in the outside lane and the
choice was to run him over or stop. People had been trying
to scrounge lifts since they left the capital. They stood in
dozens by empty sliproads or in the shade of flyovers.
There were many more of them than there were vehicles
on the road.

"Isn't there a bus service?" Riggs asked his girlfriend,
who laughed. The fares were more than people could
afford, she said. The only transport was the odd cattletruck
– or the cars of gullible tourists like him.

"Put your foot down," she said, when the man stood in
his way. And when he came to a standstill, "Don't roll your
window down."

"Ria," the man said, smiling through the open window. Ria was where they were going. Riggs looked at Mariel, who shrugged.

"Gracias," said the man, opening the rear door. A second man, black, appeared and got in the other side, wedging Mariel's son in the middle.

Not for the first time, Riggs felt out of his depth. He didn't know the country and he barely knew Mariel. Her son, for instance: she hadn't mentioned him till their third date. And when she'd suggested a holiday, he'd assumed she meant the two of them, not that her son would be coming as well. For the relationship to work, he'd have to win the boy round. But his presence was inhibiting. What was Mariel like? Riggs couldn't tell. Her familiarity with a country he'd never been to before added to the estrangement.

Picking up speed, he glanced across at her and she shrugged again. Exasperation not fear was the look. Crime figures here were one of the lowest in the world, he'd read – because punishments were severe, she said, and the police force brutal, and the people not so desperate as to hijack tourists. The two men in the back were smartly dressed, in T-shirts and casual trousers. They didn't smell. They even had shoes.

In the mirror the black man introduced himself. His name was Henri, he said. He worked as a quality controller on a tobacco plantation, the plantation was in Ria, he'd learned to speak English in school, one day he hoped to go to the US, it was difficult to arrange with the authorities but it was an ambition of his, the American President was an imperialist aggressor but he had nothing against ordinary

Americans, he was twenty-nine and had three children, the youngest only two weeks old, he'd been on business in the capital but now it was back to the plantation, they must visit it, see how it worked, he could promise them a coffee each and a cigar, yes yes they had tourist sites to see, the Falls, the Caves, the Tilting Rock, but they must see the plantation, ten minutes was all it would take. Riggs wound his window down, letting air blow in, while Henri talked on. He was making efforts with Mariel's son – asking how old he was, and which languages he knew, and did he play sport. The other man said nothing. He had no English, Henri said, but worked for the police, inspecting plantations. Maybe it was stupid to feel more secure knowing a policeman was in the car. But Riggs was an Englishman and he did.

Coming here had been Mariel's idea; he'd have been as happy going to Spain. All he knew till a week ago was the story of the President and his canaries. There were three of them, kept in a cage, each differently coloured – the colours of the national flag. Visiting statesmen were always photographed in front of them. Government broadcasts began with the sound of them trilling and chirping. And every poster along the autoroute, under words like Liberty and Truth, showed the President – beaming and moustached – standing proudly by their cage. Ministers came and went but the canaries had flown in with the President thirty years ago and showed no sign of falling off their perch. Their implausible longevity was an international joke. Exiled opponents and human rights lobbyists liked to contrast their visibility with that of the President's political prisoners, lying unseen in squalid cells. But the canaries remained a colourful emblem. Till he came here, four days ago, they were all Riggs knew about the country.

"You American?" Henri asked. Riggs caught his eyes in the mirror, noticing that one of them, the left, veered off at an angle – a wall eye, or a glass eye maybe.

"English," said Riggs, which was safer than saying American and anyway true. Best not get into Mariel. Her mother was Spanish, her father half-Dutch, and her ex-husband, the boy's father, Greek Cypriot. Or so she'd told him. There was so much he didn't know. About her, about the world. How did a man of thirty-five get to be so ignorant? He'd sleepwalked through his life. And now it had brought him here, with a woman he'd met three months ago, a boy he'd spent four days with, and two strangers.

Henri talked on – about the hurricane that hit last September, about next weekend's cigar festival, about the plantation. They must come. He wasn't asking, he was telling: they were coming. To shut him up, Mariel turned the radio up. A folk song was playing, the unofficial national anthem, as familiar as 'Guantanamera.' Riggs had heard it so often – on the radio, on television, from musicians serenading them in restaurants – he could almost sing along.

"You like?" Henri asked.

"What's the title in English?" Riggs said, into the mirror.

" 'The Song of the Cage,' " said Henri, and explained how the lyrics had been inspired by the President's three canaries: caged birds, the song went, sing more sweetly than birds in the wild. "Very beautiful," said Henri. Riggs scanned his face for humour or irony. There was none. It was tempting to get political, to ask why if caged canaries sing so sweetly no tunes were ever heard from the prisoners in the nation's jails. But what did Riggs care? And there'd be no point. Whatever his real feelings, Henri would exhibit loyalty to his President: "Which prisoners? There are none. The people here are free."

The autoroute petered out just before Ria. Mariel whispered to Riggs that they should drop the two men in town. Riggs kept his eyes on the road and didn't react. Visiting the plantation might be an experience. Common courtesy said they should go. Or was he just too lacking in nerve to refuse? "Did you hear me?" whispered Mariel. Henri, craning forward and picking up the tension, began to talk at manic speed: they must be hungry, he would stop and get them bananas, they could make the plantation tour as brief as they liked, fifteen minutes at the outside. Mariel brandished her wrist watch and muttered under her breath at Riggs: it was nearly two, they'd been late leaving the city, her son was tired and hungry, the last thing he wanted – that she wanted – was to visit a fucking tobacco plantation, it wasn't as if any of them smoked. Riggs feigned distraction at the sudden traffic and ignored her.

"Left here," said Henri. They were turning off the main street, taking a road out of town that wasn't to the Falls or Caves or Tilting Rock.

Riggs drove on. They'd done the men a favour, and now the men wanted to pay them back. It was reasonable enough. Henri would be offended if they refused.

"How far to your plantation?" asked Mariel, seeing Riggs was determined not to stop.

"Not far," said Henri.

Ria was already a speck behind them. Much further and they'd be way off route.

"How far?"

"Near now."

The lift down the autoroute had been a scam, Riggs knew that. But what kind of scam? Stubborn at the wheel, he surrendered to events taking their course. Mariel too had given in. The landscape became flatter and more fertile, away from the hill region where they'd been heading.

"Left here," said Henri, pointing them up a dirt track. The dirt track was ridged and holed – Riggs took it slowly, for fear of wrecking the hire car's suspension.

"Right here," said Henri, directing Riggs up an even narrower, rougher track, more like a footpath than a road. "The hurricane," he added, pointing at the shiny new tin roofs of farm buildings. Maybe the hurricane had caused the potholes too.

The last track was grassy, passing a shed or barn of some kind and ending in a gate of barbed wire. A man appeared and pulled the wire back, and Riggs squeezed through the gap, into a yard. Two other cars were parked there.

"Tourists," said Henri. The tourists, if they existed, were a reassuring sign. Mariel still wore her exasperated look, a how-the-fuck-did-we-get-into-this. But when Riggs got out she followed.

"Come on, hon," she said to her son, "Let's go look." Meaning let's get this over with fast.

At the end of a yard was a low shed, with men milling round, and beyond it a small field. Riggs had imagined vast acres, not a dead-end farm.

"Please sit," Henri said, showing them to a rough bench in the shade, then disappearing. The bench was the hospitality suite, the green room, before the event. Flies buzzed round.

"Now what?" said Mariel.

Henri walked back over, carrying two small coffees.

"I don't drink coffee," said Mariel.

"It's OK, I'll drink it," said Riggs, worried her refusal might look like aggression. Two swigs of bitter grains and the coffees were gone, their blackness descending inside him. No offer of a Coke for the boy. He must be suffering in this heat. The bottle of water in the car was long empty.

Henri introduced them to an older man in blue, Hispanic, who shook hands and led them into the field. The tobacco plants stood in uneven rows, two feet tall, scrappy, mottled, and – so Riggs thought – in need of water. The man in blue had a book with him, some erudite guide to tobacco cultivation, with illustrations to help when he ran out of words. The words were English, just about, as in "Here is more big leafs, for example, but bottom leafs, for example, is baddest for smoking." He was standing by a plant at this point, and waved a knife at each leaf in turn. The blade was sharp and six inches long. Riggs wished he had his old penknife on him, the one he was given as a child. The jack in the boot the car-hire man had shown him was the closest he had to a weapon.

They moved onto the barn. A woman was sewing fresh-picked leaves together. Above, bunches hung from the rafters, in deepening shades of brown. Three children appeared, with big eyes and bare feet. The woman held the leaves for Riggs to touch. Soft but crinkly. He felt all right again, with children around, though Mariel's boy seemed

awkward, shuffling his feet as the kids stared at his train-
ers.

"You want take photo?" said the man in blue.

"We don't have a camera," said Riggs.

After the barn, they were taken back to the yard, where
the cars were parked. No sign of tourists, but round the
shed a dozen men stood talking – one of them scarred,
none conspicuously friendly. At least the tour was over.
They'd been conned into visiting a scabby plantation, that
was all. It wasn't as if they were going to be killed.

"We should be heading off," said Mariel.

"Yes," said the man in blue, "but first one last show
you."

He took them to a hut, in the corner of the yard. Inside
was a table, with boxes laid out in rows, like ammunition.
The man in blue opened a lid. Neat cylindrical shapes, like
bullets or shells. Cigars.

"Five hundred dolour in shop. Here only two hundred."
There were several different brands. Could one small farm
supply all these? So, thought Riggs, this is why they've
brought us here. Harmless enough. But he wasn't biting.
He didn't smoke.

"You na smoke? But friends they smoke. Give for them.
Present. To you, one hundred and sixty dolour."

Did he have friends who smoked cigars? He couldn't
think of any. Mariel tugged his hand. Her son was tugging
hers. The man in blue took a cigar from the largest box –
'Winston Churchill' – and made them touch it as he sucked.
You could feel it swell and contract through the skin.

"Finest in whirl. Special prize. Hundred and fifty
dolour."

Three men stood in the doorway behind them. One hundred and fifty dollars didn't sound so bad suddenly. Maybe it was a bargain. Riggs had two hundred on him; they'd still have enough for a meal, and he'd his cheque card back at the hotel.

"Hundred and forty. Last prize. Like rabbing me, but I give you."

Riggs's hands were in his pocket, feeling the notes, preparing to count them out.

"We didn't come here to buy cigars," Mariel said. "We have to go."

Her voice was firm. The men in the doorway parted.

"Ten dolour for the tour," said the man in blue, clutching Rigg's sleeve. Back in the city you could see three museums for that. It would feed a family for a month. Riggs handed a ten over. The man in blue handed him a cigar. It had come from his pocket and was crumbling, unlike the ones in the box.

By the car, Henri and friend stood waiting. Riggs thought he'd seen the last of them. But finding his way back to Ria wouldn't be easy.

"You want a lift to town?" Riggs asked.

"As guide," said Henri. There'd be a price, that meant.

"OK," said Riggs.

The five of them climbed in, then Henri got out again, to pull open the barbed wire gate. As he opened it, he bent down by the wheel.

"Puncture," he said. "We fix for you."

Riggs got out to look. The front offside tyre was flat. The stony dirt-track must have done it. Unless the tyre had been let down in their absence. Henri got the jack from the boot. It was hot. They had no water. Riggs looked at Mariel and she looked back. The two men put the spare on within five minutes but it felt like hours.

"That work many dollars at the garage," said Henri, shutting the boot.

"Let's get on the road," said Riggs, standing up for himself for once, though he'd decided, when the time came, to hand over whatever it took. The two men fell silent in the back. They were pissed off, that was clear, having earned no commission on cigars. Yes, it was probably them who'd manfactured the 'puncture'; it would turn out the tyre they'd removed just needed reflating. In the mirror Henri looked sullen, one eye fixed out the window. Now it was Riggs and Mariel doing the talking, to lighten the mood – what kind of bird was that hovering overhead, and had the hurricane struck Henri's house, and what were his children called? The questions took them to the edge of Ria.

"Stop here," said Henri, by a settlement on a right-hand bend. "Wait one minute."

No "please" any more. He crossed the road with his bag, at leisure. Riggs turned to Mariel's son.

"You OK?" The boy nodded, bored, and looked out the window. "Is he coming back?" Riggs asked the other man.

"Sí sí," the man said, though it was doubtful he understood. Was Henri making them wait to humiliate them? Or was it an ambush? Riggs looked at Mariel. She was the one with the firm voice and a little Spanish. If she ordered the Hispanic to get out Riggs could drive off. Henri appeared at last, bagless, ambling back. Maybe it had been a harmless errand.

They drove off again. Larger buildings appeared. They came into Ria.

"You want lunch?" said Henri.

"That's kind but no, we have to get on," said Riggs.

"Good lunch, cheap price," said Henri, half-hearted. He wasn't friendly. But the menace had passed.

"Stop here," he said, as they turned into Ria's main street. The two men got out quickly, patting Mariel's boy as they did. Riggs got out as well, and walked behind the car, so Mariel wouldn't see him handing out dollars. Ten each. The men took the money without a word. He watched them walk off up the street, then checked the tyres, playing for time, knowing what she'd say. "Thirty dollars to three strangers for fucking up our day." It was true. But she'd no right. The money was his to waste. She was only his girlfriend. He got back in.

"I'm hungry," said Mariel's son. Breakfast had been hours ago. But they weren't stopping in Ria. The guidebook said there was a restaurant by the Falls, twenty kilometres away. On the road out of town, Riggs saw the posters again, with the smiling President and his canaries.

ADAM ROBERTS

McAULEY'S HYMN

□ □ □ □ □

Lord, I know the cosmos is but shadow thrown off by your light,
And I've learned the truth – man's sphere is *interplanetary* flight.

Once there was a conflict in my heart, I do confess it so:
But to reach the stars is further than the Lord permits us go.

Coupler-snaps to spindle-poles and thrust: I see Your Hand, O God –
Yours the grace and wrath that drives the spinning antimatter-rod.

The Bible's a complex machine, Lord – many million parts intact
And Man can barely ken the myriad ways they mesh and interact.

Every verse and word is placed within the working of the whole
Forms a spiritual motor meant to launch and then to guide the soul

Accelerate escape velocity beyond the pull of sin
And take us to the final airlock-gate where God's Love pulls us in.

Just as an engineer can't pick and choose components of his ship,
Maintain these few, but let those others rust or seize or slip,

Just so a soul can't pick and choose from all these Biblical commands,
He takes the whole book up, or lets the whole book tumble from his hands.

I can't get to sleep tonight; old bones and limbs are hard to settle;
So I'll stand the watch up here – alone with God and spaceship metal.

My engines whirr. A hundred days of thrust and delta-V and strain
Interpenetrating space, around Thy Sun and home again.

It is too much – the driveshaft moans – and all the angle-jets are loose;
Twenty billion miles of thrust has given them a fair excuse.

The perfect dark of God outside: the blackest black that baffles sight
The mystic void, infinity, the Ancient of all Days – at Night.

Here's Ferguson relieving me. Three years since his last planet-pass:
His wife's back there with both their kids; an outdome domicile on Mars.

He yearns towards his planetfall . . . and who of us can blame the man?
It's been a long and homesick while since his contracted time began.

There's none on any world for me: none to fly to, fast or slow,
At least since Mia Chong went on to Thee, Lord, thirty years ago.

And since that time I've found Thy medium's truly neither void nor 'cuum
But a flower of awe and grace, infinite black-petalled bloom.

I recall Mkoko most, whose habitation now is space
And whose corpse, if found, would reignite the interstellar race.

No, God will not let mankind find him! No, I know my work's secure!
His chilled corpse will circulate in darkness and for evermore.

Nor yet alone; the spaceways throng with bodies in grim circulation
Prizeless jetsam of our mortal-danger spaceflight occupation.

When the *New Apollo* burned! What then was our space-age worth?
Venus out to Neptune on a long ellipse, and back to Earth,

What worth? – if soon as docked, locked-on to Orbital's bulkhead,
A flash fire burst and left most of our crewfolk carbonblack and dead?

Not that they are *un*civil in the Merchants! I have heard Ivanov say:
"Engineer, McAuley! How's your Tachyon Thrust machine today?"

True he gets the tech-talk wrong, but at least he leaves me clear
To coax the best from thrust and slew – I am the lead House Engineer,

So they phrase it: "Still with engines? Weren't you top of *Phys* at Cape?
Named 'most promising' and feted, sashed with 'top of class' blue tape?

Planet-beating scientist at school, and Uni star at Thrust?
How did your bright prospects turn to engineering grime and rust?"

True, I won the scholarships; I topped exams and glowed inside
Then I kenned the hook that Satan hoped to snag me with was – *pride*.

So I left the Cape Space School, walked straight out the lecture hall,
Signed a fifty-year full contract with a freightline for space haul.

There I started as a fuel-whelp – regulating engine feed,
In the old-style bucket spaceships, with the old-school pilot breed.

Ten-a-second was the fastest then – eh! – inefficient drive;
Only think that now our haulers manage more than fifty-five!

Soon we'll move yet faster – the advances made since I began!
No, I do not doubt machines: but what about the soul of man?

Faster's good, but there's a limit – set by God and space and time;
And only fools could miss it, only sinners hope to cross its line.

I'm a man that's travelled far, I've sped a fraction fair of c,
Two light years in all I've ventured . . . far, how far, O Lord, from Thee?

You were with me night and day. I still recall that first frag hit,
When the sensors missed the debris and the main compartment split –

All those shards came shooting through us faster than artillery rounds,
Twenty breaches in the hull . . . banshee decompression sounds –

Fire, alarm and panic; Anson lost her leg and then her life
Amputated – half a gram of space ice was the surgeon's knife.

All her lifeblood shot and clouded, filled the cabin with red fog
And I felt Satanic presence, evil breath of Gog-Magog,

So I prayed, and prayed it double: spoke the words, but *acted* too:
For the nearest prayer is labour – words are good but deeds are *true*.

Sealed the breaches, damped the yawing, set the engines to reboot
Lacking even time to wipe my comrade's blood from off my 'suit

Never seen a ship take damage like it and come back again to O:
None of it were possible without that You had willed it so.

And how did I repay your mercy? Entered on that Orbital
Showered, drank a tub of whisky, found a whore and paid her full.

I've still scorch marks from the flare-ups on my arms and on my back
But I've worse than scorchmarks on me – deep inside my soul is black!

All the sun's atomic fire could never burn this sin from me
My one hope: to lose myself in Thy Stellar Immensity.

Sins of five and fifty years: *Apollo*, *Pug* and *Hesperus*
Can the grace of God match these, the orbits of my trespasses?

Voyages I'd wank myself into a stupor all month long,
Years when every dock I stopped at turned my Right around to Wrong.

Nights when I'd observe my crewmates, ire and envy in my gaze,
Hating them for loving, filled with fury rather than Thy Praise.

Blot the wicked hours of mine, Lord! when I spent my time ashore.
Som'd in Pataweyo's Moon-house, thinking less and sinning more.

Worse than all (my crowning sins) were foulest blasphemy and pride.
Stoker ten years, hardened to it: bad without and bad inside.

I saw Saturn's cities built: new fruit beneath the ring's great arc;
And was *dazzled* by those Christmas baubles shining in the dark –

Coming round the darkside – there were miracles to fill my eyes!
All the cosmos's stars were shining weldspot bright in oil-black skies.

I spent all my downtime porthole-gazing, tracing constellations, each
And every star (I thought) should science put within man's reach.

Pride, pure pride! I know it. The whole cosmos only hymns Thy Will
Thou set distances to put the voyage far beyond man's skill!

Blasphemy and disobedience if I doubt the speed of light!
Thou couldst set it otherwise, and Wrong; Thou set it thus, and Right!

The clearest scripture written there: that our lot's Solar – and that's all.
But in Saturn's orbit I heard a silky-spoken devil's call.

Warm as heated milk, beguiling: "See, McAuley! Pick a star!
Set your course now, engineer – *make* it near although it's far!"

Firm and clear and low – no haste, no boast – the ghostly whisper went,
Setting out the evidential facts beyond man's argument:

"Though it takes you twice a generation, you *must* go!
Worship me, God Hyperspatial – spurn the Deity of Slow.

Speed, now, speed! Go faster yet – learn new Elysian mysteries!
The FTL prize hanging low: McAuley – it is yours to seize!"

A spaceship is a million pieces, working all together true,
And the Bible's a machine as complex, made by God *to do*.

Starts off clear: "Let there be light." Just that is what the Good Book says.
God began the universe, and *Light* speed-limited its ways.

Light! It is the *same* as God! It's holy, not to be denied;
And the voice that whispers different comes from mankind's sinful pride.

But I was just in my twenties, head all dazzled with my dreams
And I thrilled to think that *c* was not the limit that it seems.

Shining in my thoughts aurora-like; it racked me through and through:
Tempted me beyond the show of speech, unnameable and new –

Thou knowest all my heart and mind, Thou knowest, Lord, how far I fell –
Second Engineer upon the *Hesperus*, but first in Hell!

It came to me in a lightning strike, the way to make it yield:
Generate a cross-spun singularity inside a Bergson field –

And *counterspin* a *second* shell of strung-grav matter, pitched outside
Using sub-quantum inertia to arc-tune that second's ride,

With both Hawking thresholds moving spinwise close enough to c
Gravitational cross-shearing would work to break a bubble free!

And *inside* the envelope – a ship! A heavy-shielded hull;
Balanced where the shearing forces cancelled each and each to null.

And inside that ship a crew, made up by men and women's souls,
Adams there, and Eves, new-tempted by their far transgressive goals:

Truly they could reach the stars in weeks instead of centuries – or
It were closer to the truth to say: could reach beyond God's Law.

Young and wicked as I was I didn't see behind the mask,
So instead I set myself to *earn* enough to fund the task.

The Merchant Houses had but lately finished all their battles off
Lex Ulanova was a new thing: fair, said some; but harsh and rough.

Either way, I didn't trust to patent office copyright,
Though I worked out all the specs, I kept my notions close and tight.

Dreamt of riches; had no thought to *gift* it to the human race.
At the time it felt like greed; but now I only see Thy Grace.

Now I feel Thy hand about me: and about my feet Thy care –
From cold Saturn to hot Venus, through the transit of despair,

Hesperus came to the fieldlands, hundred-thousand globes of green
All in solar orbit, in God's Sunlight basking bright and clean.

There we worked as mission tug, ten million protein cargo tonne
Up the invisible slope to Earth-Moon docking at Lagrange A1.

Slow work in the old days, in old ships without the Tachyon Thrust
But it gave me time to ponder whether *clever* can be *just* –

And the opening verses of the Bible echoed once more in my head.
"I made Cosmos out of Light, inviolately so," Thou said.

I was drowsing in my billet – sick with self-doubt, drink and tire:
"Better to rip out your eyeballs than watch stars with Sin's desire!"

And the countervoice said: Lo, the universal open road!
Let man be a soaring eagle, and no more a pond-stuck toad!

God and devil battled for my conscience as I lay midship:
And my right hand clutched my whole life's work – upon one data chip.

On that chip and nowhere else: the superluminal data was:
Heresy and sin, all written in the neutral tongue of maths.

Should I just destroy it, or disseminate it all instead?
Would my actions kill the living spirit, or restore the dead?

Then the warning siren sounded, loud – and all was frantic rout
As a stopper-field explosion tore the main drive chamber out

And the guidance software flared and died, and all the ship was seared.
Every scrap of power flat vanished; all the lights just disappeared.

The explosion killed Mkoko; Wei Hu Cho was blast-concussed.
We were venting air and losing heat as fast as we lost thrust.

Everywhere and everything was blacker than a soul in sin;
Space was dark as death outside, but darker still the soul within.

We were coming round about behind the moon's unsunlit face
Not a single photon hit my eyes or pierced the dark's embrace.

Not until we cleared the lunar arc, and sunrise gleamed again
And by Thy sweet grace I had the Light to see my duty plain.

One porthole, bright-lit – no more – but bright as any welder's flame!
Just at the right time to save the ship *illumination* came,

Closed the bulkheads with my muscles (since the pisomotors failed)
Reset mainframes B and C and brace-rebooted core mainrail.

Saved the ship and all our lives – (except Mkoko, scorched and dead) –
And all because of God's good Sun, and the soul-saving light it shed!

Afterward I dressed Mkoko's corpse, for burial in space,
And I slipped my data chip inside his Mortis Carapace.

I sprayed all his body with the stuff, and sealed my chip inside
Because I couldn't quite destroy it – there, alas, you see my pride.

But at least I knew I couldn't keep it, couldn't follow through.
I had seen the light and seen my sin. For that I must thank You.

Thus I wrestled with Apollyon – Ah! – and fretted like a bairn –
Threw away the working-plans at last with all I hoped to earn,

Dropped my years of labour into space's infinite wellhole
Lost the sweat and lost a fortune, but at least I saved my soul.

The human engine is entropic, ruled for sure by waste and slip,
And accordingly mankind will never build the Perfect Ship.

I will never last to judge her lines or take her curve – not I!
But I've lived and I have flown in space. All thanks to Thee, Most High!

And I've done what I have done – Thou'll judge it soon if ill or well –
Not complacent of a place in heaven, thinking hard of Hell.

But when I've outflown the mortal grav-well and my soul is free
I may *hope* to ride the perfect starship, in excess of *c*.

It will fly by Grace – and God will pilot: light years by the billion,
Flitting quickly on towards our true home: sky's Avillion.

Still they pester, still they question: "Where, McAuley, are your notes?
Your ideas – you'll reconstruct them? Plan your interstellar boats!

Start afresh from first positions! Join your dots and sketch the line
Tell at least the core idea, your means for besting old Einstein . . ."

I was prideful, too much boasting, and I told the world my plans;
Would to God I'd cut my tongue instead, and severed both my hands!

"Don't deprive mankind," they plead, "of this new shortcut through spacetime!
Don't steal all our future – the loss of that would be a crime!"

I *could* tell them; somewhere out there is the chip that you crave
Locked inside a corpse's shroud and buried in a vacuum grave;

You *could* seek it, but that's not a quest you ever shall fulfil:
Nothing happens in our solar-country contrary to His will.

Yes, the physics of it *works*: but this doesn't mean the working's *good*.
And a jealous God is best served by a jealouser priesthood –

Engineers – His truest priests! For who else better knows his Law?
We know how it's shaped, and how it tells man: thus far go – no more.

FRANK

□   □   □   □   □

My name is Francis Oliver Patrick. I am twenty-seven years old. There is nothing you can say that will hurt me.

It's Thursday and I'm eating pizza. Pepperoni. Jalepeños. Extra cheese. There's a Corona in my hand which I'd forgotten about. It's only half-drunk and so am I. I take a swig and it's almost warm. The TV is on but I can't tell the difference between one programme and the next. I find myself in the kitchen, running the Corona under the cold tap.

I have to put the bin out tonight.

The beer isn't really cold when I return to the living room, but it's an improvement. I hold it by the neck to avoid heating it up. My hands are always cold, though.

It's Mum's birthday on Sunday.

Some baldy on the TV is yelling at me to buy some product. I know for a fact that I won't buy it, though. Another advert has come on and I've already forgotten what Baldy was yelling about. Oven cleaner. A conservatory. Tampons.

It's Mum's birthday on Sunday.

It's Thursday.

I have to put the bin out tonight.

It's Friday and I'm in the bath. I've loaded it with bubbles, the water blue beneath the foam. The steam rises like a curtain and the room smells like patchouli.

I forgot to put the bin out last night.

I haven't been sleeping well; I lie in bed, clammy, not sure if I'm hot or cold. I'm worried it will affect my appearance. I'm not a movie star, but I like to think I look like one. There's nothing wrong with altering your self-image.

It's Mum's birthday on Sunday.

I pinch my nose shut and sink under the surface, my knees rising up. It must be warm in the bathroom, but outside the water my damp knees feel cold.

It's Mum's birthday on Sunday.

It's Friday.

I forgot to put the bin out last night.

It's Saturday and I'm in my neighbour's garden. I know she's at work so I climbed the back fence. There isn't any room in my bin so I'm stuffing a black sack into hers.

I have always been resourceful.

This garden is leafier than mine. My garden is bleak. It matches the house. My house is semi-detached from this one. Semi-attached to this one.

My neighbour's name might be Sue.

I rang Mum this morning but she didn't pick up. It went

through to voicemail so I hung up. I feel stupid talking to a machine. It doesn't gel with my self-image.

I had a dog once. It was a beagle. It didn't gel with my self-image. I thought I looked like a dog person, but I don't. A dog isn't like a hat, though. You can't just take it back if it doesn't suit you. I took the dog to the seaside, bundled it into a tight, hairy ball and hurled it off a cliff.

I have always been resourceful.

It's Saturday.

My neighbour's name might be Sue.

It's Sunday and I'm outside Mum's house with a bouquet. Mum's name is Sue. She lives in a bungalow on the other side of town. She's lived alone ever since my father had to leave.

It's Mum's birthday today.

I'm pressing my index finger, hard, against the doorbell. I can hear a metallic trill, muffled. Bricks. Wallpaper. Dado rails. There is no other sound from inside. I peer through the window. All I can see are net curtains and one dead fly on the sill.

My neighbour's name can't be Sue.

I place the flowers on the doorstep. They lie on top of the mat, partially obscuring the faded 'WELCOME.' The mat now says: 'COME.' I pick up the flowers and slide them through the letterbox as far as they will go. She'll find them when she comes home.

It's Mum's birthday today.

It's Sunday.

My neighbour's name can't be Sue.

❧

It's Monday and I'm in the town centre. There's a CD out that I want to buy but I can't remember what it is. I'm standing next to a fountain. I don't remember the fountain being here. I remember HMV being here.

I walk around the fountain but can't see HMV. I would ask somebody, but it doesn't gel with my self-image. I pick a random direction and walk. I find myself outside an adult store. The windows are blacked out like an expensive limo, but this place looks cheap. The paint on the storefront is black and flaky. I lift a finger and peel off a flake. It looks like a woman's face.

My neighbour's name can't be Sue.

I walk into the store. It's dimly lit and smells like sweat. There are shelves stacked with DVDs and a whole wall of sex toys. Vibrators. Cock rings. Fleshlights.

It's a long time since I was here.

The man behind the counter is ugly and overweight. I'm not surprised he works at a place like this.

"Can I help you?" he asks.

"Give me a dildo."

"What size are you looking for? Do you want something realistic? We've just got in the new Cyberskin range. They have the most lifelike feel out of . . ."

He's staring at me.

"Just give me something I'll enjoy."

I slide my credit card across the counter and realise I'm still holding the black paint flake. I place it next to the card.

My neighbour's name can't be Sue.

It's Monday.

It's a long time since I was here.

It's Tuesday and I'm staring at my reflection. I caught sight of myself in a shop window and can't tear my eyes from the same pair of eyes staring back. The image is my own face in reverse and that seems to mean something.

Sometimes I wonder who I am.

Something moves beneath my reflection, like a ripple in the image.

"Frank, hi!"

I find myself staring at my neighbour's face. I think of the black paint flake.

My neighbour's name can't be Sue.

"Shouldn't you be at work?" she asks.

I have never worked. I have too many important things to do. I receive a cheque every year from my father. I hate taking his money but I can't work. It doesn't gel with my self-image.

"Are you on your lunch?" she asks, looking at her watch.

I don't know how to respond. I don't wear a watch.

"I'm . . . just heading back," I say.

"Pity," she replies. "We could have eaten together."

I can't tell if this is flirting or politeness. I don't know which I'd prefer.

My neighbour's name can't be Sue.

It's Tuesday.

Sometimes I wonder who I am.

It's Wednesday and I'm wearing shorts. It isn't shorts weather but I bought them yesterday and I like to try out new things. I glance at the unopened box on top of the bedside cabinet. It's wrapped in a paper bag but the dimensions of the box give away plenty.

I open the wardrobe and pull a suitcase from the top shelf. The case is locked with a combination. I unlock the case and lift the lid.

It's worse than I remembered.

I have never been one to stick to convention. It doesn't gel with my self-image. A happy man is one who does what he wants and doesn't care what people think.

I am the only important person.

I stare into a sea of brown-wrapped boxes, their sizes differing, but each one phallic. I place the new addition in the centre. I want to inspect some of the others, like looking through a photo album, but I can't. It doesn't gel with my self-image. My hands are shaking as I zip the case shut.

It's worse than I remembered.

It's Wednesday.

I am the only important person.

It's Thursday and I'm carving beef. I waited outside the butcher's for it to open. The joint has been thoroughly sea-soned and slow-roasted. Salt. Pepper. Rosemary. I'd hoped it would be rare but it seems more medium.

I have to put the bin out tonight.

I'm faced with a platter of thinly-sliced circles, wet with juices and still lukewarm. I pull a sewing box from the cup-board and select a rich, burgundy thread.

There was a dead pigeon on the lawn today.

I thread a needle and push it through two slices of beef. The meat in my hands feels warm. I carry on stitching, the beef juices staining my shorts.

There's a knock on the front door but I don't move to open it. I cannot answer it in beef-stained shorts. It doesn't gel with my self-image. The knock is repeated. I continue my work. I hear footsteps retreating and everything goes quiet.

There was a dead pigeon on the lawn today.

It's Thursday.

I have to put the bin out tonight.

It's Friday and I'm wearing my beef shirt. I heated it in the microwave for a minute or so before I put it on. The juices run down my otherwise naked body as I sit in front of the TV. I have the bottom of the shirt – the hem, I guess – between my teeth and I'm chewing carefully.

I forgot to put the bin out last night.

There is a blonde woman on the screen wearing a thin top and no bra. I can make out the shape and colour of her nipples. Mum is blonde, but her hair is dyed. It must be greying by now. My neighbour is blonde, too, but I don't know if I like her yet.

I've never really been a people person.

The beef is tender and the seasoning adds a necessary depth of flavour. I am pleased with how the shirt came out. It has short sleeves, but the right one is slightly tighter than the left. The whole thing has held together well. It's surprisingly heavy.

A trickle of juice has traced its way down my left thigh. I bite off a chunk of beef and lean forwards to inspect it. The hairs on my leg are coarse and black. I lap at the juice, the hairs tickling my nose. I tease a few into my mouth, clamp down with my teeth and rip my head back. The pain is short but sharp. There are three pinpricks of red welling up from the pores. I lick these up too.

I've never really been a people person.

It's Friday.

I forgot to put the bin out last night.

It's Saturday and I'm hitting rats with a spade. The rubbish in my bin is five weeks old. It's attracting them. I spotted four of them out in the garden this morning. They were scratching at the bin and trying to climb the sides. They scattered when I opened the door.

I should probably get a cat.

I mixed a tub of superglue with red food colouring and poured it around the bin. There were four rats stuck in it when I came to check. The red is so I don't step in it myself.

I have always been resourceful.

I raise the spade to my shoulder, taking aim and bringing it down, flat, onto a rat's head. The blow stuns it then it lets out a sickening scream. The second blow sends a satisfying crack from the head of the spade into my bones. The third blow decimates the rat's head, sending shards of bone across the patio. I can't tell what's glue and what's blood. The other rats are shrieking and thrashing their tails. I raise the spade and take aim on the next one.

I have always been resourceful.

It's Saturday.

I should probably get a cat.

It's Sunday and I'm wearing my beef shirt. The bottom half has been gnawed away, leaving a framework of threads. I've been keeping it in the bath, preserved in vodka. My mouth is buried inside the shirt and I'm eating a hole in the front. It's giving off some powerful fumes. I have an overwhelming urge to see how quickly it would go up in flames.

I find it hard to control these urges.

That blonde woman with the nipples is on my TV again but I don't know who she is. I've tried to glean some information, but everything sounds like rat screams. The patio is a mess. I thought about cleaning it but I'm hoping dead rats will attract cats. One of the rats is missing its back legs. I see this as a positive sign.

I hear a knock on the door but don't get up. I am far too busy with my beef shirt. I can make out a blonde shape through the frosted glass. It looks like my neighbour's blonde shape.

My neighbour's name can't be Sue.

A tiny part of me – something small, like a kidney – wants to talk to her, but I can't answer the door. I would have to remove the beef shirt. Clean myself. Find clothes. She wouldn't wait that long.

"Frank?"

I pull the beef shirt from my mouth. The hole in the front is big enough to get a fist through.

"Frank, are you home?"

My mouth feels dry. My hands twitch as if encouraging the rest of me to move.

I find it hard to control these urges.

It's Sunday.

My neighbour's name can't be Sue.

It's Monday and I'm in the town centre. There's a book out that I wanted to buy but I can't remember what it is. I'm standing next to a jacket potato cart, buffeted by its smells. Butter. Coleslaw. Chilli. My stomach is writhing, urging me to make contact with the potato lady. The potato lady is blonde.

I cannot look her in the eye.

I force my feet to move away from cart. My knees give way until I throw myself on a bench. I breathe through my nose to calm myself down. It's something I'm good at.

I get up and walk but I wish I was at home. I wish I was wearing my beef shirt. I find myself outside an adult store, the window frames black and flaky.

I was here last week.

I peel off a paint flake and head inside to the till. The same man is sitting behind it.

"Give me a dildo."

He raises an eyebrow.

"You . . . didn't like the other one?" he asks.

"That's none of your business," I say.

"If you explain what you didn't like, maybe I can . . ."

I make no response. We say nothing more as he fetches something and puts it in a bag. I place the paint flake on the counter and give him my card. The flake looks like a uterus.

I step out of the shop, the thinly-veiled phallus under my arm.

"Frank?"

I am face-to-face with my neighbour. Her eyes are wide.

"I thought it was a gift shop," I say, louder than is necessary. "I need a present for my mum's birthday. She wouldn't want any of that. Never been in before." I laugh as her eyes sweep the package under my arm.

I cannot look her in the eye.

It's Monday.

I was here last week.

It's Tuesday and I'm wearing my beef shirt. The front and main body have been gnawed away, so it's more of a beef bolero now. There's nothing but brunettes on the TV today.

My father's hair was brown. I don't like thinking about him, but I can remember every detail of his face. Bushy eyebrows. Square chin. One thick frown line across his forehead. He always had three hairs poking out of his left nostril.

My hands are trembling.

I switch off the TV and begin gnawing a hole in the shoulder of my beef shirt. I can feel my teeth grating against my skin. There is surprisingly little flesh between the skin and bone. If I shut my eyes it feels like I'm eating my own shoulder.

I don't know if I am happy.

There is a pounding at the door and I jump. The beef shirt slips to the floor. A cloud of dust rises around it.

"Frank! I know you're home."

"Fuck off, Sue!" I scream.

"Sue? Who's Sue? Frank, I'm worried about you."

I'm on my knees, rubbing my hands over the shirt.

"Frank, we're neighbours. We're meant to look after each other. Please open the door."

My eyes blur as I examine its delicious pink hues, peppered with dust and clumps of hair.

"Frank?"

I don't know what to do any more.

"Frank!"

I keep trying, but nothing makes sense.

"Frank, please let me –"

"I don't know your fucking name!" I shriek.

My heart is beating so loud I can almost see it. I wait for a reply, but nothing comes. Everything is silent.

A cluster of ants begins swarming over the beef shirt. There is no blonde shape behind the frosted glass.

My hands are trembling.

It's Tuesday.

I don't know if I am happy.

JONATHAN TAYLOR

SYNESTHETIC SCHMIDT

□ □ □ □ □

SINCE HE WAS A young man, Schmidt had listened in colours. Black was silence, brown was a Russian bass, blue was an Italian tenor, orange was his first Elisabeth Schwarzkopf concert, yellow was Herbert von Karajan's conducting, red was . . . well, red was something else.

For years, he'd told doctors and psychiatrists and neurologists that Bliss's *Colour Symphony* really was in glorious technicolour, that Gershwin's *Rhapsody in Blue* was actually more of a magenta-mauve hybrid, and that Scriabin's *Prometheus* didn't need the light organ, because it was already there, in front of his eyes. Best of all, Bach's *Art of Fugue* was a counterpoint of rainbows. That's how it had been since the '40s, when he had first heard the *Art of Fugue* arranged for a rather scratchy orchestra.

Of course, none of the doctors had believed him – they'd

been interested in other kinds of diagnoses and experiments back then. Fifty years later, though, the medics and scientists were fascinated, and wanted to put him through all sorts of neuro-imaging tests. Was it genetic or adventitious synesthesia, they wondered? Was it caused by undetected temporal lobe epilepsy in his youth? Was it narrow band or broadband synesthesia, or a mixture of both?

But it was too late for these questions and tests, and Schmidt knew it. The glory days of hearing Mozart as refracted light were gone. One day, he'd woken up to hear a screaming, whistling, in his left ear, as a progressive tinnitus started dyeing the world red.

"What are you hearing?" the GP asked.

"Red," Schmidt said.

"But how would you describe the sound?" the GP asked.

"Red," he said.

"But what kind of note is it?"

"Red," he said, looking around. Everything was red – the GP, the GP's notes, the sky outside the GP's window – everything. Everything was dyed red by a shrill C-sharp above the stave.

"We can't find anything, Herr Schmidt, in our tests. There are no apparent causes, no ear infections, no foreign objects in the canal, no related nose allergies. You do not seem to have a low level of serotonin, you do not regularly take aspirin or Quinidine – the sorts of things which sometimes cause ringing in the ears. Without a cause, there is nothing we can do . . . Unless . . . unless you can think of a cause, Herr Schmidt?"

But no, Schmidt couldn't think of a cause.

Schmidt couldn't think of a reason why he would spend

his last few years in a red world, under a red sun, with a red wife crying tears reddened by the never-ending dissonance of a C-sharp above the stave. He couldn't think of a reason for all this.

He couldn't think of a time when, as a young man, he'd first heard the colour red.

He couldn't think of a time when, as a young officer, he'd listened to a scratchy orchestra playing outside a huge factory; a factory in which he'd spent no more than a few days, before being drafted elsewhere; a factory where he'd tried not to be part of anything, tried to keep his distance, tried and for the most part succeeded – well, except for one minor incident, one long-forgotten moment, when a flautist from the orchestra had needed shooting, and he'd not been able to think of an excuse in time, and he'd heard her last C-sharp and then seen the earth and air dyed red round her, and he couldn't, wouldn't think about it any more.

No, he wouldn't, couldn't think of that time when Strauss tasted of raining ash, when ash smelt of Léhar, when shoes felt like dead waltzes, when barbed wire looked like a Wagernian prelude – and when symphonies were ash, shoes, barbed wire, tears, blood.

CONTRIBUTORS'
NOTES

□ □ □ □ □

Judith Allnatt is an acclaimed short story writer and novelist published by Random House. Her latest novel, *The Poet's Wife*, was shortlisted for the East Midlands Book Award. Judith's first novel, *A Mile of River*, was selected as Simon Mayo's Book of the Month on Radio 5 Live and was shortlisted for the Portico Prize for Literature. Short stories have featured in the *Bridport Prize Anthology*, the Commonwealth Short Story Awards, and on BBC Radio 4. Judith lectures on Creative Writing for various universities and freelance, and is currently working on her third novel. www.judithallnatt.co.uk

Jo Baker was born and grew up in the north west of England. She was educated at Oxford and the Queen's University of Belfast. She is the author of four novels: *Offcomer* (2002), *The Mermaid's Child* (2004), *The Telling* (2008) and *The Picture Book* (2011). She lives in Lancaster, with her husband, the playwright Daragh Carville, and their two children.

Claire Baldwin is a De Montfort University graduate with an MA in Creative Writing by Independent Study. She mostly writes prose fiction with a touch of dark humour, but also maintains a poetry blog, as well as working on various ongoing poetry projects. Her poetry has appeared in pamphlet form, and in *Hearing Voices Magazine*.
David Belbin's short stories have appeared in many magazines and anthologies. His most recent novels are *What You Don't Know* (Tindal Street Press) and *Student* (Five Leaves Publications).

Kathleen Bell is a poet, fiction writer and critic who has published and performed her work widely. She is also Principal Lecturer in English and Creative Writing at De Montfort University.

Will Buckingham writes fiction, philosophy and for children. He is the author of two novels, *Cargo Fever*, published by Tindal Street Press, and *The Descent of the Lyre*, published by Roman Books. He is also the author of several philosophy books, and a children's book, *The Snorgh and the Sailor*. He is currently Senior Lecturer in Creative Writing at De Montfort University, Leicester.

PJ Carnehan lives in London. His stories have been read by the Liars' League. He is writing a collection of stories and *Literary Shrew*, a short book about Brigid Brophy.

Ailsa Cox's fiction has appeared in various journals and anthologies, including *The Virago Book of Love and Loss*, *The London Magazine*, *Metropolitan*, *Katherine Mansfield Studies*, *Warwick Review* and *Paraxis*. Her collection, *The Real Louise*, is published by Headland. Other books include *Alice Munro* (Northcote House) and *Writing Short Stories* (Routledge). She is the editor of *Short Fiction in Theory and Practice*, and teaches at Edge Hill University near Liverpool, where she is based.

Katy Darby's work has been read on BBC Radio, won various prizes, and appeared in magazines including *Stand*, *The London Magazine* and *Mslexia*. She studied English at Oxford and Creative Writing at UEA, where she won the David Higham Award, and now teaches Novel and Short Story Writing at City University, London. By night she runs the live fiction event Liars' League: www.liarsleague.com. Her Oxford-set historical novel *The Whores' Asylum* is available in Penguin paperback as *The Unpierced Heart*. She lives in London and her website is www. katydarby.com.

Louis De Bernières, who lives in Norfolk, published his first novel in 1990 and was selected by *Granta* magazine as one of the twenty Best of Young British Novelists in 1993. Since then he has become well known internationally as a writer and his sixth novel, *Birds Without Wings*, came out in 2004. *Captain Corelli's Mandolin* (1994) won the Commonwealth Writers' Prize for Best Novel. *A Partisan's Daughter* (2008) was shortlisted for the Costa Novel Award, and *Notwithstanding: Stories from an English Village* was published in Autumn 2009. As well as writing, he plays the flute, mandolin, clarinet and guitar. He was born in London in 1954.

Vanessa Gebbie is a novelist, a prizewinning short story writer and a fledgling poet. She is author of a novel, *The Coward's Tale* (Bloomsbury), two short story collections, *Words from a Glass Bubble* and *Storm Warning – Echoes of Conflict* (Salt) and contributing editor of *Short Circuit: Guide to the Art of the Short Story* (Salt). Her poetry can be found in print in *The Ver Prize Anthology*, WordAid's *Did I Tell You?* and *Not Only the Dark* anthologies, *Envoi*, *Tears in the Fence*, and online at *Shadowtrain* and *Eclectica*, among others. She teaches widely.

Denise Hayes is a Senior Lecturer in English and Creative Writing at Newman University College, Birmingham. She has previously had a short piece of life-writing published in the *Family* section of the *Guardian*, and poems published in *New Poetry* and *Mslexia*. She enjoys working in a number of different genres and has just completed her first novel.

Tania Hershman's second collection, *My Mother Was An Upright Piano: Fictions* (Tangent Books), was published in Spring 2012. Her first book, *The White Road and Other Stories* (Salt), was commended in the 2009 Orange Award for New Writers, and her flash fiction and short stories have been widely published and broadcast on BBC Radio. She is founder and editor of *The Short Review*, an online journal reviewing short story collections, and writer-in-residence in the Science Faculty at Bristol University. www.taniahershman.com

Jane Holland has published five books of poetry, plus numerous novels, articles and critical literary reviews. She lives in Cornwall with her husband and four children, and writes historical fiction under the name Victoria Lamb.

Panos Karnezis was born in Greece in 1967 and came to England in 1992. He studied for an MA in Creative Writing at the University of East Anglia. He is the author of a collection of short stories, *Little Infamies*, and the novels *The Maze*, shortlisted for the 2004 Whitbread First Novel Award, *The Birthday Party* and *The Convent*. He lives in London.

Hanif Kureishi is the author of numerous novels, short story collections, screenplays and plays. In 1984 he wrote *My Beautiful Laundrette*, which received an Oscar nomination for Best Screenplay. His second film, *Sammy and Rosie Get Laid*, was followed by *London Kills Me*, which he also directed. *The Buddha of Suburbia* won the Whitbread Prize for Best First Novel in 1990 and was made into a four-part drama series by the BBC. *Intimacy*, his third novel, was published in 1998, and was adapted for film in 2001. His work has been translated into thirty-six languages. He has been awarded the *Chevalier de l'Ordre des Arts des Lettres* and a CBE for services to literature. In 2008 *The Times* listed him as one of 'The 50 Greatest British Writers since 1945' and in

2010 he was awarded the PEN/PINTER prize. Hanif Kureishi lives in London with his wife and children.

Joel Lane lives in Birmingham. His recent publications include a collection of short stories, *The Terrible Changes*; a novella, *The Witnesses are Gone*; a chapbook, *Black Country*; a collection of poems, *The Autumn Myth*; and a booklet of crime stories, *Do Not Pass Go*.

Emma J. Lannie was born in Manchester and now lives in Derby. Her short stories have been published in *100RPM*, *Jawbreakers*, *Dzanc Best of the Web 2010*, *Even More Tonto Short Stories*, *Six Sentences Volume One* and *Bugged*, as well as in various online publications. She has performed her stories at spoken word and live literature events, including Summer Sundae and Manchester Literature Festival. As a member of music/literature collectives Hello Hubmarine and Time Travel Opportunists, she has organised literature events, produced chapbooks, and delivered workshops. She can be found at www.garglingwithvimto. blogspot.com.

Ian McEwan was born on 21 June 1948 in Aldershot, England. He studied at the University of Sussex, where he received a BA degree in English Literature in 1970. While completing his MA degree in English Literature at the University of East Anglia, he took a Creative Writing course taught by the novelists Malcolm Bradbury and Angus Wilson. McEwan's works have earned him worldwide critical acclaim. Among them are the Somerset Maugham Award in 1976 for his first collection of short stories *First Love, Last Rites*; Whitbread Novel Award (1987) and Prix Fémina Etranger (1993) for *The Child in Time*; and Germany's Shakespeare Prize in 1999. He has been shortlisted for the Booker Prize for Fiction three times, winning the award for *Amsterdam* in 1998. His novel *Atonement* received the W.H. Smith Literary Award (2002), National Book Critics' Circle Fiction Award (2003), Los Angeles Times Prize for Fiction (2003), and the Santiago Prize for the European Novel (2004). In 2006, he won the James Tait Black Memorial Prize for his novel *Saturday*. His novel *On Chesil Beach* (2007) was shortlisted for the 2007 Man Booker Prize for Fiction, and was winner of the British Book Awards Book of the Year and Author of the Year Awards. *Solar* (2010) was the winner of the 2010 Bollinger Everyman Wodehouse Prize and his new novel *Sweet Tooth* will be published in 2012.

Blake Morrison was born in Skipton, Yorkshire. His books include two collections of poetry, *Dark Glasses* and *The Ballad of the Yorkshire Ripper*; two bestselling memoirs, *And When Did You Last See Your Father?* (made into a film starring Jim Broadbent and Colin Firth) and *Things My Mother Never Told Me*; a children's book, *The Yellow House*; several play adaptations and libretti; and three novels, including

South of the River (2007) and *The Last Weekend* (2010). He lives in south London and is Professor of Creative Writing at Goldsmiths College.

Adele Parks was born in Teesside. She published her first novel, *Playing Away*, in 2000 and was the debut best seller of that year. She has since published eleven more *Times* Top Ten bestsellers, including *Husbands* and *About Last Night*. Her latest novel, *Whatever it Takes*, was published in June 2012. Adele is translated into twenty-five different languages. She writes regularly for magazines and newspapers and works as an ambassador of the charity The Reading Agency, an organisation dedicated to improving adult literacy in Britain. To learn more about Adele visit www.adeleparks.com or follow her on Twitter @adeleparks.

Simon Perril is a poet, critic and collagist, and Programme Leader for Creative Writing at De Montfort University, Leicester, England. His poetry publications include *Nitrate* (Salt, 2010), *A Clutch of Odes* (Oystercatcher, 2009), and *Hearing is Itself Suddenly a Kind of Singing* (Salt, 2004). His poems have appeared in many magazines including *Jacket*, *Poetry Wales*, *Shearsman*, and *Angel Exhaust*. As a critic he has written widely on contemporary poetry, editing the books *The Salt Companion to John James*, and *Tending the Vortex: The Works of Brian Catling*, and contributing book chapters to *Removed for Further Study: The Poetry of Tom Raworth*, *A Man of Utterance: the Poetry of J.H. Prynne*, *The Salt Companion to John Tranter*, *The Poetry of Peter Riley*, and Blackwells' *A Companion to Twentieth Century Poetry*. He lives in Oakham, Rutland. Visit www.simonperril.com for collage work, video, and poetry recordings.

Alexandros Plasatis is an exophonic writer undertaking a Creative Writing Ph.D in the UK. He was co-editor of the third volume of the literary magazine, *Hearing Voices*, has performed his writing in various venues, and has a story forthcoming in *Coffee House Magazine*. He is currently working on his first novel.

Kate Pullinger writes fiction for both print and digital media. Her most recent books include her collected short stories *A Curious Dream*, and the novel *The Mistress of Nothing* which won the GG, Canada's Governor General's Literary Award for Fiction, 2009. Other novels include *A Little Stranger* (2006), and *Weird Sister* (1999). Pullinger's many digital fiction projects include her multiple award-winning collaboration with Chris Joseph on 'Inanimate Alice,' a multimedia episodic digital fiction – www.inanimatealice.com – and 'Flight Paths' – www.flightpaths.net – a networked novel. Kate Pullinger is Professor in Creative Writing and New Media at Bath Spa University. Find her at www.katepullinger.com.

Adam Roberts lives just west of London with his wife and two children. He has published twenty novels, the most recent being *New Model Army* (Gollancz, 2010), *By Light Alone* (Gollancz, 2011), and *Jack Glass* (Gollancz, 2012), as well as many short stories. He is Professor of Nineteenth-Century Literature at Royal Holloway, University of London.

Catherine Rogers loves stories in all their shapes and forms. Her love has taken her on a curious story trail working for Daunt Books in London, to dressing up in velvet trousers and sparkly eyeshadow telling stories to small and big children, supporting and developing writers as a Literature Development Officer and managing the education programme for Writing East Midlands. Somehow curious little stories seep into everything she does. Catherine lives in Belper, Derbyshire with her husband, two children and that oldest holder of tales, a tortoise.

Lee Rourke is the author of the novel *The Canal* (winner of *The Guardian*'s Not The Booker 2010), the short story collection *Everyday* and a work of non-fiction *A Brief History of Fables: From Aesop to Flash Fiction*. His debut poetry collection *Varroa Destructor* is forthcoming Autumn 2012.

Salman Rushdie is the author of eleven novels, one collection of short stories, and four works of non-fiction, and the co-editor of *Mirrorwork*, an anthology of contemporary Indian literature. *Midnight's Children* won the Booker Prize in 1981, the 'Booker of Bookers' in 1993, and, in 2008, the 'Best of the Booker.' *The Moor's Last Sigh* won the Whitbread Prize in 1995 and the European Union's Aristeion Prize for Literature in 1996. In 2007, Salman Rushdie was awarded a Knighthood for services to literature. He is a Fellow of the Royal Society of Literature and a *Commandeur dans l'Ordre des Arts et des Lettres*.

Gemma Seltzer writes fiction and has developed a series of digital writing projects including *5am London*, a collaboration with a photographer documenting the city during the early hours of the day, and *Look up at the Sky*, charting the quiet parts of London through walking and writing. She is the author of the daily fiction blog *Speak to Strangers*, 100 stories of a hundred words about random interactions with Londoners, subsequently published as a book (Penned in the Margins, 2011). She has presented her work on BBC radio, Resonance FM and at festivals including Latitude and the Venice Biennale. Gemma was writer in residence for the Olympic torch relay in Devon.

Robert Shearman has written three collections of short stories – *Tiny Deaths, Love Songs for the Shy and Cynical*, and *Everyone's Just So So Special*. Between them they have won the World Fantasy Award, the Shirley Jackson Award, the Edge Hill Reader's Prize and the British Fantasy Award. He's probably best known, though, for bringing the Daleks back to the screens in the first series of the revival of *Doctor Who*, in an episode shortlisted for a Hugo award. He regularly writes plays for BBC Radio, and his interactive project for them, *The Chain Gang*, has won two Sonys. As a playwright he was resident dramatist at the Northcott Theatre in Exeter, and regular writer for Alan Ayckbourn at the Stephen Joseph Theatre in Scarborough; he has won the World Drama Trust Award, the *Sunday Times* Playwriting Award, and the Guinness Award for Theatre Ingenuity in association with the Royal National Theatre. In 2012 he was resident writer at Edinburgh Napier university.

Felicity Skelton's publications include *Eating a Sandwich*, a collection of short stories, stories in *The North, Mslexia*, and *Sheaf*, and articles and chapters on the short story and the novel in *1000 Key Moments: Books* (Cassell 2007), *The Good Fiction Guide* (OUP 2001), and some academic books and journals. She performs both her prose and her poetry at festivals and readings in Sheffield and the surrounding area. She has been teaching Creative Writing and English Literature at Sheffield Hallam University since 1996, when she graduated with distinction from the Writing MA. From 1966 to 1984 she worked in professional theatre around the UK, including many years at the Octagon Theatre in Bolton, where she was Resident Director and wrote several plays and documentaries for performance by the company.

Karen Stevens is a Senior Lecturer at the University of Chichester, and has a special interest in the novel and short fiction. Her short stories have been published in *The Big Issue, Pulp Net, Panurge New Fiction, Mouth Ogres, Fish Publishing, Dreaming Beasts*, and *Riptide*, vol. 5. Her edited collection of essays, *Writing a First Novel*, is forthcoming with Palgrave Macmillan.

Maria Taylor is a writer and reviewer, whose work has been published in various literary magazines, including *Times Literary Supplement, Guardian Online, Under the Radar, The North, Staple, Tears in the Fence, Obsessed With Pipework* and others. Her poetry collection, *Melanchrini*, is published by Nine Arches Press. She regularly performs her work at festivals and live events. Maria blogs at miskinataylor. blogspot.co.uk

Sara-Mae Tuson has had short fiction, poetry and articles published in *Elbow Room, Pen Work Media's Mayday Stories, The Loose Muse*

Anthology 2012, Rising, Erotic Review, Jupiter, UK Theatre Network, Obsessed with Pipework, Trespass, The London Magazine and more. Recently she was a finalist in the erbacce press chapbook prize (chapbook forthcoming in 2013). Sara-Mae was the first female editor of *The London Magazine*, which is over 296 years old. Apart from her work as a freelance copywriter and editor for companies as diverse as The Scouting Association, *Opera Magazine* and online media company Gamaroff Digital, she is a consultant for InkTears, a short fiction promotion project. She has devised workshops and performed as a guest at Loose Muse, Paragram, Angel Poetry, The Hot House and Book Club Boutique and two of her stories have been performed live by White Rabbit. She works with film, creating interviews and music videos. Read her blogs: www.sara-maetuson.blogspot.com or www.zeitgeistschadenfreude.wordpress.com

Deborah Tyler-Bennett has had many short stories published in the UK and Ireland. She is author of four collections of poetry: *Clark Gable in Mansfield* (King's England, 2003), *Pavilion* (Smokestack, 2010), *Mytton...Dyer...Sweet Billy Gibson* (Nine Arches, 2011), and *Revudeville* (King's England, 2011). She reads at many venues, past ones including the tearooms at Brighton's Royal Pavilion, Keats House, Hampstead (where she was a Poetry Lives Here resident writer in 2010) and The Usher Gallery, Lincoln. Her work has been published in many countries, and was recently translated into Romanian.

Michelene Wandor is a poet, dramatist and short story writer. Her two collections of stories are *Guests in the Body* (Virago), and *False Relations* (Five Leaves). Her stories appear in many contemporary anthologies, and she is regularly commissioned to write short stories for Radios 3 and 4. She reads and performs her work at festivals and other venues, in the UK and abroad. Her poetry collection, *Musica Transalpina*, was a Poetry Book Society Recommendation, and she has completed a first novel, *Music and the Devil*.

Harbouring a long love affair with literature, **Aimee Wilkinson** writes short stories, radio scripts and is currently working on her debut novel. She is part of the Derby-based New Writing and Spoken Word collective, Hello Hubmarine, which aims to promote new writing in all its different shapes, forms and sizes and manifests itself through workshops, quality publications and live events. She works in literature development at Writing East Midlands and coordinates literature events and projects with a particular passion for supporting new writers and promoting writing to new audiences. She is also an experienced workshop leader and a great advocate of all things creative and the power art has to enrich lives.

ACKNOWLEDGEMENTS

▫ ▫ ▫ ▫ ▫